THE BROKEN BLUE LINE

THE
BROKEN
BLUE LINE

Connie Dial

THE PERMANENT PRESS
Sag Harbor, NY 11963

For information, address:
   The Permanent Press
   4170 Noyac Road
   Sag Harbor, NY 11963
   www.thepermanentpress.com

Library of Congress Cataloging-in-Publication Data

Dial, Connie–
   The broken blue line / Connie Dial.
      p. cm.
   ISBN 978-1-57962-200-8 (hardcover : alk. paper)
      1. Police corruption—Fiction. 2. Police internal investigation—
   Fiction. 3. Police—California—Los Angeles—Fiction. 4. Los Angeles
   (Calif.)—Fiction. I. Title.

PS3604.I126B76 2010
813'.6—dc22   2010010307

Printed in the United States of America.

to Sam Milazzo

PROLOGUE

*A*s a child in Juarez, Mexico, Ramona Sanchez saw her father
shot and killed by the police. Her mother was dragged from
their home into the dirt street where she was raped and strangled. Relatives hid Ramona and her older sister in an empty oil
tanker and drove them across the border to the United States.

She grew up hating the police and senseless violence, the
two things she believed were responsible for her miserable life.
She was twenty years old now and spent her days cleaning rich
women's toilets to help her sister keep a roof over their heads.
She was overweight, uneducated, and tired most of the time.

Tonight, like every night, she walked from the Hollywood
bus stop on Melrose, south to their cramped two-room apartment on Gower. She saw the black-and-white police car drive
slowly past her, but ignored it because they only bothered the
young men and the Latinas in tight jeans and low-cut blouses.

The patrol car turned around and came back. She looked up
and saw the two white men in dark blue uniforms, staring at her
as they drove by. She glanced around at the empty sidewalks
and moved a little faster. She hadn't done anything wrong but
she was frightened. She heard the car pull to the curb behind
her. She kept walking.

"Senora," one of them shouted.

She stopped and for a second was insulted. Senora? She
didn't look that old . . . ignorant Americans.

"You speak English?" the taller one asked. They were
standing in front of her now, blocking the sidewalk. That other
one looked familiar, but she couldn't remember where she had
seen him.

7

"Of course," she said. "What do you want?" Her voice was strong, but her hands were shaking.

"You know me?" the short one asked.

"Why do you bother me? I'm going home." She tried to move around them, but couldn't. "What d-do y-you want?" she asked with a stutter that surprised her. She stared at their shirt pockets. Where were their names? Her sister always said if they bother you look for the names, and you can complain at the station, make trouble for them.

"Just answer the question. Do you?"

What harm can it do, she thought. "No—may I go now?" she asked and hesitated before adding, "Maybe . . ." Suddenly, she did recognize him, and fear paralyzed her arms and legs. She wanted to scream for help but couldn't make any sound.

The officers exchanged looks. Without a word, the short one with the rodent eyes took a small gun out of his jacket pocket. He pointed it at her. It was so small she thought it was a toy, but the last thing Ramona Sanchez saw before she died was his twisted smile as he fired the pistol at her face.

ONE

The alley was a cesspool in the heart of downtown Los Angeles. Mike Turner hated Metcalf for ordering him to be here in the middle of the night, but mostly he hated this crappy case.

Turner looked at the six-story building across the street. Lieutenant Metcalf would be sitting on the roof of that apartment building, a safe distance from the ground pollution. From the comfort of his folding chair, with binoculars in one hand and a thermos of hot coffee in the other, Metcalf had been directing this worthless operation like an army general.

"Lieutenant, you awake?" Turner whispered into the microphone tucked under the collar of his bulky jacket.

Silence and then, "Yes, Detective Turner, I'm cold and hungry and awake."

"Just a radio check; you're loud and clear," Turner said, trying not to laugh. It was obvious from Metcalf's gravelly voice that he'd been napping, probably under a warm clean blanket.

"Forget the radio check, Turner. Watch the alley." It was Tom Weaver's voice. Turner usually respected the veteran police sergeant's instincts, but tonight his boss had six supervisors including himself sitting in the middle of L.A.'s skid row exposing themselves to who knew what diseases—for what, to catch one uniformed sergeant jerking off with the ugliest drag queen in the city. Turner almost envied Patty, the newest member of the squad. She had to babysit the lieutenant, but at least she wasn't down here freezing her ass off. It was Turner's suggestion she stay on the roof. Patty was a sergeant and nearly thirty, but she looked like a pretty teenager in her tight jeans

9

and long stringy brown hair. He would've spent all night swatting the derelicts off her.

Turner was miserable, but even at times like this he had to admit that for some weird and inexplicable reason he loved this job, and he kept hoping that some day they'd get a decent investigation again. The department brass formed the internal surveillance unit to catch bad guys who had sneaked into its ranks. He'd jumped at the opportunity to participate even if it meant working out of Internal Affairs again. He was willing to give up his job in Narcotics because the only thing he hated more than a drug dealer was a dirty cop. But when he signed on, it wasn't for this kind of stuff. This guy was just sick.

He glanced around the wall of a boarded-up warehouse at the corner of the alley and recognized the two large bodies warming their hands over a trashcan fire. Detectives Vogel and Miller wore shabby clothes and day-old beards, but they were still too clean and well fed for this neighborhood. Turner guessed they had chased away the local bums and confiscated the makeshift furnace. Miller waved at him and made a jerking motion with his right hand. He wasn't fond of Lieutenant Metcalf either, but that wasn't surprising. Miller didn't like anyone. He was an overweight, thirty-year detective with a stubby grey beard, carrying twenty extra pounds in his belly and a chip on his shoulder.

A man sitting on the ground and leaning against a street sign across the alley gave him a lazy wave. Like all of them tonight, he was bundled in several layers of clothes covered by a shabby wool coat and a scarf wrapped around his head and neck. His face was hidden, but Turner knew it was his partner Reggie, hunched over, scribbling in his notebook. Reggie kept a diary and wrote incessantly, but Turner didn't worry about him anymore. Somehow he could write and stay alert. It was peculiar that Reggie wrote the way some guys munched on sunflower seeds, a nervous habit. Turner squatted near him under the faint glow of a street light. He wrapped his scarf around his neck and leaned against his partner for support.

"How do you keep your food down sitting this close to the asphalt shiter?" Turner asked, blowing a puff of cold air with every word. He put his knee down and felt something damp soak through his Levi's. He didn't look at the ground. Sometimes it was best not to know.

"It's warmer." Reggie put his notepad inside his coat and glanced up. The watery grey eyes were vacant, not a hint of what he was thinking. He rarely smiled and his icy stare made most men look away. He still had his Marine Corps haircut and military mannerisms even though he had left the service twenty years ago to join the LAPD. The only person he occasionally talked to was Turner, but Reggie could follow anyone, anywhere. He became something of a legend by tracking a drug-dealing detective to Miami and then the Cayman Islands. He came back and gave Sergeant Weaver the detective's bank account number and a list of his criminal associates including the highest-ranking Asian in the police department.

"Is this sorry excuse for a cop gonna show?" It was a stupid question, but Turner was cold and annoyed; his pant leg was wet, and he needed to talk.

"Black and white eastbound through the alley, lone occupant," Reggie said, getting up on his knees.

Turner heard him and then again in his earpiece. He scrambled to the other side of the alley. He saw Weaver's tan Chrysler parked half a block away with the drag-queen snitch crawling out of the backseat.

The black and white police cruiser slowed. Turner recognized the accused sergeant who cautiously scanned the walls of the alley with a handheld spotlight as he drove. When the powerful beam finally located the drag queen, standing at the mouth of the alley where Weaver had deposited him, the cruiser stopped.

The little dragon was decked out in red platform shoes, a short leather miniskirt, black fishnet nylons and a leather bra top stuffed with damp kitchen sponges and a transmitter. His lice-infested head was topped with a bright orange, shoulder-length

11

wig. Turner was downwind and got a whiff of the drugstore perfume that conquered all the other gross odors.

The powerful light gave the little Mexican queen an otherworldly look for just a second, and then he smiled. His stained, crooked teeth framed by purple lipstick ruined the illusion. He hugged his bare arms trying to stay warm. The sergeant turned off the light and inched the patrol car closer. He'd been on vacation for several weeks, and was probably eager to reunite with his lover.

Secretly, Turner hoped the sergeant would get a hot call or change his mind and drive away. Screw this stupid case. At first, like the rest of the squad, Turner had dismissed the drag queen's allegations as too incredible to be true, but other witnesses had come forward confirming that this sergeant regularly visited drag queens during his graveyard shift. He always trolled a few blocks from the Central Division police station near this alley at Fifth and Ceres.

Turner shook his head. How does a guy get so screwed up? The only thing he could imagine sicker than this sergeant was a bunch of highly trained cops waiting to pounce on him at the height of his perverted ecstasy.

The drag queen wobbled to the driver's side of the patrol car.

"What's happening?" the lieutenant asked from his rooftop perch. Turner heard the question in his earpiece, but the break in radio silence surprised him, and he instinctively lowered the radio's volume.

"Shut up!"

Turner immediately recognized Miller's angry voice and knew Miller's partner would panic. Vogel had both the look and temperament of an accountant. He was nervous and timid, and Miller's behavior frightened or embarrassed him most of the time.

The interior light went on in the cruiser as the drag queen approached the open driver's window. He'd been told to give a verbal signal when the sergeant exposed himself.

Turner had also directed the drag queen not to touch the sergeant, but at the moment, the queen's torso was so far into the patrol car that his cheap leather skirt was sticking straight up, exposing the fishnet stockings, black garters and his naked ass.

"Take him," Weaver ordered finally.

Now, Turner was in charge. He jumped up and grabbed the drag queen by his bra strap and waistband and threw him away from the car's window. Turner was a big man, over six feet tall, but he didn't realize his own strength until he heard the crash of crates and bottles behind him. There was no time to look back. He was staring at the face of Sergeant Alex Gomez who sat frozen with his hands on the steering wheel, exhibiting a full erection salute. Gomez was sitting on his service weapon and backup revolver and seemed almost relieved when Turner identified himself.

Gomez looked around the car at the faces outside watching him. He awkwardly pulled up his pants and tucked in his uniform shirt. He started to secure his Sam Browne, but Turner took hold of his hand and yanked the gun belt from under him.

"Get out of the car," Turner ordered and stepped back to open the door.

"Am I going to jail?" Sergeant Gomez could barely ask the question.

"Not my call," Turner said, knowing that jail wouldn't fix what was wrong with him. He escorted the humbled sergeant to a waiting car where a team of IA investigators stood ready to take him back to their office. Turner tried not to show his disgust. It was enough for him that the guy would probably lose his job. There was no need for further humiliation.

The captain from Central Division was waiting near the IA car. He approached Gomez and put his arm around the sergeant's shoulder. Turner saw Miller, standing behind the car, put his finger in his mouth and pretend to vomit. He knew Miller was right, but it was all a bullshit command performance. It was the captain's job to act as if he cared.

"The prick is treating that pervert like he just got the Medal of Valor or something," Miller said.

13

"That's why he makes the big bucks, and you and I will probably never promote," Turner said, leading Miller away from the car. He was certain Lieutenant Metcalf had narrowed down the possible radio culprits by now, and Miller had to be at the top of his list. Turner often wondered how the outspoken Miller got into this elite unit. He was a good surveillance officer, but his sarcasm was irritating.

He also worried that Weaver was tired of cleaning up after Miller's big mouth and might transfer him. Turner knew that he and Reggie were the core of Weaver's squad, but Miller and Vogel were good, too. Patty was still learning; Tony and Earl were part of the squad but mostly window dressing. Turner trusted and relied on Reggie, but he knew they needed Miller's expertise. The squad looked to Turner to take the lead when Weaver wasn't around. Miller wasn't afraid of Weaver or Metcalf, but he knew better than to challenge Turner. He'd only tried it one time and found himself on the ground nursing a bruised lip.

Weaver told them the debriefing would be held in the parking lot behind the Staples Center arena. That was what Turner loved about this job. His squad had all the fun, and after they made a case, the suits at Internal Affairs did all the paperwork and cleaned up the loose ends while the surveillance detail disappeared into the night like a band of Lone Rangers.

It was nearly sunrise. Turner was looking forward to a long shower and sleeping all day, but the debriefing wasn't as quick or congenial as he'd expected. Lieutenant Metcalf immediately put a damper on the meeting. He understood the need for maintaining radio silence but insisted his minor mistake hadn't warranted such disrespect. He promised to deal with it later. Everyone except Miller and Turner pretended to look repentant and mumbled something that sounded like an apology to keep the lieutenant off their backs.

Weaver wasn't happy either. He didn't think it was necessary for Turner to toss the drag queen into a pile of garbage. Turner didn't know what else he could've done and didn't care enough to ask. He did what he had to do. Patty was standing behind Weaver and the lieutenant. She gave Turner a shy thumbs up approval.

"When you break an informant's arm, Turner, it costs us plenty to get the turd to testify," Weaver said in his best self-righteous tone. Metcalf stood beside him nodding in agreement.

"We must've done something right, Lieutenant. The guy's sitting in your office by now, pissing his pants and perusing retirement brochures," Miller said, matter-of-factly.

Metcalf took a step back, getting some space between himself and Miller. He coughed and mumbled something about "of course, in spite of everything, you did the job." His hand trembled as he fumbled in his jacket pocket for his car keys.

Weaver waited patiently until Lieutenant Metcalf drove out of the parking lot.

"Watch yourself, Miller. He knows it was you," Weaver said, attempting to make it sound like a friendly warning.

Not one for backing down, Miller said, "He's an asshole, and you know it. He's only been here six months. He's always in the way and doesn't know shit. Does he?" Before Weaver could answer, Miller interrupted. "What the fuck are we doing on a case like this? My mother could've made this bust. Since he's been here we haven't worked one decent case."

Turner wasn't expecting a satisfactory response from Weaver, the company man, and he didn't get one.

"He's in charge. We do what he says," Weaver said. "You never know what these guys are gonna do when they get caught. Somebody could've gotten hurt," he added, trying to put a different face on what they all knew was a giveaway case.

"Metcalf's afraid we're going to make a mistake and fuck up his career." Reggie said what most of them including Weaver believed to be true.

"What we do scares him," Turner said and caught Earl and Tony in his peripheral vision. They exchanged a smirk confirming his suspicions that they were a pipeline back to Metcalf. They were ambitious but lazy and saw this high-profile assignment as a stepping stone to their next promotion. They were satisfied with safe, insignificant cases. If they didn't do anything, they couldn't get in trouble. Turner suspected their snitching would eventually pay off, and Metcalf would reward them, but he didn't care. He'd be glad to get rid of them.

"So, what's next, Sarge?" Turner asked, trying to change the subject before Reggie or Miller said too much. Bitching wouldn't help. He wanted to work, and if they kept handling cases, something good was bound to come up in spite of Metcalf.

Weaver was short and stocky with a drill sergeant personality, but he seemed embarrassed. He stared at the ground as the morning sunlight bounced off his bald spot. "Hollywood cop," he mumbled without looking up.

The pause was too long. Turner figured it had to be another disappointment. "IA catch him driving without his seatbelt?" he asked, glancing at Miller who laughed.

"What're you eyeballing me for, Turner? I didn't tell you to say that," Miller protested and shrugged innocently at Sergeant Weaver.

"We got an anonymous tip that the guy might have some illegal weapons," Weaver continued, ignoring both of them.

"That's real unusual for a cop to have illegal weapons. You know one guy on this job that doesn't have an unregistered piece or switchblade in his locker? How many Uzis you got, Reggie?" Miller folded his arms and fell back against his car.

Turner was disappointed. Miller was right. Metcalf had assigned them another dead end case. How could they prove what a guy had hidden in his basement safe?

"Any of you crybabies want to go back to your office jobs let me know. There's plenty of coppers out there dying to get out of their polyester suits and have a take-home city car." Weaver was smug. He'd played his trump card. As frustrating as it got, this job was better than anything they had waiting for them.

"Where's the worksheet?" Vogel asked. His wife had become accustomed to the surveillance squad's big overtime checks. She scared Vogel a lot more than Miller or Metcalf could.

Patty took a stack of papers from the trunk of Weaver's car and passed them around. Turner studied the worksheet with the police academy graduation picture of a good-looking redhead. Ian Conner was a six-year police officer, living at home with his mother and milking an on-duty back injury allegedly sustained when he fell off a stool behind the front desk at the Hollywood station. He worked the graveyard shift, and nobody saw him get hurt, but he hadn't been back to work for seven months. Conner had filed for a pension, but according to the informant, he was faking his injury, stealing guns and committing felonies with a gang of white boys and Mexicans in the Valley.

"This has possibilities," Turner said as soon as he finished reading. "What's the catch?" He couldn't imagine Metcalf allowing them to work this investigation.

Weaver hesitated before answering. "Conner might suspect he's being watched." Nobody said anything, and after a lengthy pause he added, "Metcalf let it slip we might be keeping an eye on him, but he was talking about Conner faking his back injury." He held up the worksheet. "It was before we got this information."

Turner groaned, and Miller crumpled up his worksheet and threw it on the ground.

"Pick that up," Weaver ordered. Before Miller could argue, Patty retrieved the worksheet and gave it back to Miller. "Most of these assholes think they're being followed anyway," Weaver said.

"When did Metcalf tell him?" Turner asked. He knew Weaver was right. Conner probably watched his rearview mirror for days and took circuitous routes until he got tired of looking and decided Metcalf was lying.

"A couple of weeks ago. He's had time to look over his shoulder and under the bed, and we weren't there. Unless you guys do something stupid to make him suspicious again, this could work," Weaver said, slamming down the car trunk.

Weaver left, but the squad hung around. Turner figured Weaver knew they always talked about the real problems after he'd gone. The sergeant was smart enough to let them bitch and work stuff out among themselves. Weaver was a good supervisor, but he wouldn't buck the system, so what he didn't know he wouldn't have to deal with.

When Miller finished ranting about Lieutenant Metcalf, he started on Earl and Tony.

"You ever get out of your car this morning?" Miller asked Earl. "You and Tony give yourselves a pass on this one?"

The big black man looked down at Miller. "Like you said, John, your mama could've made this bust. So Tony and me figured you and Vogel might handle it," Earl said, laughing and motioning for Tony to follow him back to their cars. Unlike the rest of the squad they were dressed in clean khaki pants and sport shirts. Tony was a shorter, brown-skinned version of Earl. No one said anything as the two men drove out of the lot.

"This could be a good case," Miller said when the cars were out of sight. "I'm not gonna let those guys or Metcalf fuck it up."

"We'll do what we've got to do and let them try to figure out what's going on," Reggie said. He showed them a low band, encrypted radio frequency that the lieutenant, Tony and Earl wouldn't know about and wouldn't monitor. They could do ordinary business on the surveillance frequency and then switch over for the important information.

"Do we tell Weaver?" Vogel asked. "What if he finds out? I'm not sure we should be doing this without letting him know."

"We don't tell Weaver. If he knows, he's got to do something," Turner said. He would never put Weaver in that position. If Metcalf found out, Turner was more than willing to take the heat, and Weaver could honestly say he was clueless.

"Metcalf will say we're doing something wrong. That's why we're hiding the frequency," Vogel insisted.

"If it bothers you, don't do it," Miller said, glaring at his partner. "Me, Reg and Turner can do this without you."

"What about me?" Patty asked. "I want in."

"That's four. What about you, Vogel? Taking down sexual deviants challenging enough for you?" Miller asked. "Because that's all you're gonna work if Metcalf gets his way."

"I'm in," Vogel said, reluctantly.

Turner programmed the new frequency and realized he wasn't tired anymore.

18

TWO

Most people can't remember their dreams. It was easy for Turner. He only had one. It didn't happen every night, but when he dreamed it was always the same. He'd be in a gunfight, and his backup gun would jam. He'd pull the trigger, but nothing happened. While he struggled to fire his weapon, some helpless victim from his past died again and again. His own death was usually imminent when he woke up frightened and confused. It seemed so real, and he wondered why that particular nightmare plagued him so often. He'd toyed with the idea of asking the department's shrink to interpret the dream, but thought better of it when he saw how little good the guy had done for Reggie.

Last night, he had the dream again. His gun jammed as a crazed teenager on the psychedelic drug PCP unloaded a shotgun at his partner. However, it wasn't really a dream. He was recalling something he tried not to remember during the day. The nightmare woke him in a cold sweat at 3 A.M. this time, and he couldn't get back to sleep. He rolled over, turned on the light, and examined his hands, half expecting to find the blood that had drenched them that night so many years ago. He needed to find another woman. The nightmares had nearly disappeared when Paula slept with him, but she'd been gone for over a year. After he bought this house he met Miriam, but a few months ago she left, and the nightmares returned. He had a little grey in his curly black hair but he was still a young guy in his forties, reasonably fit, and should've been able to find the right woman. Paula had been ambitious, independent, smart and confident but really didn't have time for him. Miriam was just the opposite . . .

needy, unsure, unpredictable, sometimes a little crazy but fun and a great lover. Some combination of the two would be his ideal woman.

Daryl watched him with one eye open, pretending he was still asleep. The dog wasn't stupid. Turner always ordered him outside as soon as he looked awake. Turner stepped over the Basset hound's flabby body and tossed a shirt on the bed. He dressed, secured his leg holster and checked the action on his backup semi-auto. It was working fine.

"Go outside, Daryl," he ordered.

The hound struggled to its feet, lumbered into the living room and out the doggie door. Turner worried that Daryl was moving a little slower these days and might not live much longer. They'd been together a year but the dog was nearly nine years old. He smelled bad, farted, drooled, and dragged dirt into the house, but Turner had a real fondness for the animal because despite the negatives, he knew unconditional, non-judgmental love was a rare thing.

The house was warm and clean for a change. After Miriam left, Turner lost interest, and housekeeping chores seemed to pile up. She was a slob, but he'd kept after her and the house always looked nice. He'd spent all weekend dusting, scrubbing and doing yard work. This small two-bedroom home in Redondo Beach had taken nearly every penny he had for a down payment. Now it was his sanctuary. He enjoyed being here and was almost used to being alone with Daryl again, except at night.

Turner filled the dog's dish. He had to drive out to Harbor City and pick up Reggie who wanted to ride with him today. He pulled on his coat. It had the lingering smell of the downtown alley, and the transmitter was still in the pocket.

He turned on the garage light and inventoried the equipment in his car, a daily routine. He threw away yesterday's smelly food containers and made room for his partner. This car was his second home. He ate most of his meals over the steering wheel and occasionally slept in the backseat.

"You got insomnia or somethin'?" the thin voice of Eddie Jones asked. His neighbor stood outside the garage in his plaid flannel bathrobe, holding a flashlight, his black skin fading into the darkness.

"Sorry, did I wake you? Starting early, Reg and me."

"Bet that strange boy never sleeps anyhow. I'll take care a things 'round here, better if I do," he mumbled and shuffled across the driveway to his house. "Be careful," he shouted as his frail body disappeared inside the house next door.

Later Eddie would bring in Turner's mail, walk Daryl, prune his rosebushes, and wash off his driveway, and Turner let him do all those things because it was good for both of them. Eddie had been a street cop for thirty years and served with Turner's father. They talked about the good old days and complained about the new LAPD. Eddie, one of the first black cops, lamented that he was a black man who never got a break, but he had loved being a cop. They agreed Eddie's son, who was an LAPD commander, got all the breaks, but didn't give a shit about police work.

It was getting late, but Turner knew at this hour he could drive from Redondo Beach to Reggie's place in about fifteen minutes. He'd never been inside his partner's bungalow because he'd never been invited. Reggie ate dinner at his house and slept over whenever he passed out on Turner's couch from too much beer or old-fashioned fatigue. During those times, Daryl wouldn't leave Reggie's side. The dog had fleas and peed on the carpet, but Turner trusted the animal's instincts, so he decided that Reggie, despite his strange behavior, was probably a decent man.

Turner parked the silver Taurus at the curb in front of Reggie's manicured lawn. Not surprisingly, Reggie was waiting on the front porch. He got in the car, looking on the floor and behind his seat.

"Smells like French fries in here. You have breakfast without me?"

"That's yesterday's smell . . . I hope, but if you can find any, they're yours."

Reggie almost smiled. He took a map from his inside jacket pocket, and unfolded it over the console. Using a small flashlight, he traced the route to Conner's place.

21

"Thanks for driving," he said, putting his seat back.

"No problem." That was more conversation than Turner usually got. As it turned out, that was it until they arrived in Santa Clarita. Reggie wrote in his notebook occasionally, but slept for most of the trip. After an hour or so, he was talking in his sleep. Turner watched and wondered if Reggie had the gun dream but knew better. His partner had his own special demons. After a few minutes, he felt like an eavesdropper and was glad he couldn't make sense of the mumbling.

He pulled off the freeway a few miles before they reached their destination and found a twenty-four-hour drive-through. He needed caffeine.

"Hamburger, fries, large coke," Reggie said, without opening his eyes.

Turner's stomach tightened at the thought of eating that meal this early, but he ordered it and an egg sandwich for himself. The egg tasted like rubber, but he ate it and drank two large cups of stale coffee. He ate whatever was available now because he might not get another opportunity later.

"Keep both radios on," Reggie said, wiping catsup off his chin. "I'll want to use our other frequency."

Turner nodded and pulled another radio from his black bag in the backseat.

"Weaver's too smart. He's gonna figure this out," he said.

"Not unless Vogel tells him," Reggie said, and opened the map again studying the area around Conner's house. "Drive here," he said pointing at a street that was several blocks away.

"That's too far. Get closer."

"It's as close as we're gonna get," Reggie said. "These lots are a couple of acres."

"You've been here." Turner wasn't surprised. Reggie didn't want to drive because he'd been up all night finding the best observation point to watch the house. He always wanted the perfect one.

"Drop me off and I'll take the point before it gets light."

Turner drove until the road curved at the bottom of a hill. He watched Reggie work his way through the heavy brush until he was out of sight. There were no houses here, no nosey neighbors to call the police about strange men climbing the hill. Reggie hadn't wasted a night's sleep. This was the perfect place.

Turner returned to the fast-food parking lot and directed the rest of the surveillance squad to his location. Reggie tested both frequencies and told Turner the lights were on in the Conner house. Ian Conner was already moving around, going from the house to what looked like a barn or storage shed.

Weaver was the first to arrive. Turner switched off the second radio feeling a little guilty about hiding it from his boss. The squad trickled into the lot as the sun came up, and Turner showed them the map and the place where they would relieve Reggie. He could feel some tension this morning. This case might actually turn into something. Even Tony and Earl carefully studied the map.

In ten minutes, they were set up surrounding the house. Turner parked between two abandoned shacks off a dirt road, lowered the car windows and reclined his seat. He didn't want to fall asleep, just get comfortable. It looked as if it might be an overcast day. He was grateful because this area north of downtown L.A. was practically rural and even in the winter could get very hot.

Watching the sun come up in this peaceful, deserted field was a pleasant change from busy streets and city noises. He always thought someday it might be nice to own a few acres, let Daryl run around on the dirt chasing jackrabbits he'd never catch. Turner laughed picturing the dog's stubby legs and long ears that kept getting under his feet as he walked. Maybe he should let Reggie take the dog. Reggie was alone too much, and Daryl was good company, almost human. Every day his partner seemed to sink deeper into his own thoughts. Turner knew that cops who didn't have anything outside the job eventually fell apart . . . drank too much . . . blew their brains out. He wouldn't allow that to happen to his friend.

He wondered what Reggie wrote in those diaries and if any of it was about him. Partners talked. Turner had confided in him, said some personal things he wouldn't want anyone else to know. Reggie wouldn't discuss his writing, but claimed it was all lies. Lately, Turner realized he'd been cautious about telling his friend any private thoughts he wouldn't want to see in print some day.

He stretched and closed his eyes. A cool breeze, smelling like cut grass and cow manure, drifted into the car. As badly as he wanted a real case, he hoped Ian Conner planned to spend the morning at home. A few more hours of country therapy would be nice. He got his wish until 10 A.M. when Reggie's calm voice announced Ian's mother Beverly was out of the house. She was dressed in what appeared to be a skimpy waitress uniform. She was a little overweight but attractive, with short red hair. She drove away from the house in a 1968 red Impala.

Turner could almost hear Reggie drooling as he described the vintage car. He put his seat up and checked the worksheet. A 1999 Jeep Cherokee was the only car registered to Ian Conner. Weaver then called the office for the Impala's registration and found it belonged to the fifty-six-year-old Beverly Conner. Vogel followed her away from the house and would find out where she worked. Patty immediately took his place. Turner liked Patty and not just because she was better looking and younger than most of the female detectives who usually got assigned here; but she smelled better than the guys and was a natural team player who was always the first one to volunteer for the dirty work.

Minutes after Beverly's departure, Conner's property suddenly came alive with activity. Half a dozen off-road vehicles spewed clouds of red dust and gravel as they raced from the dirt road over an acre of barren land to an asphalt parking area between the garage and barn. Turner jotted down the car descriptions and the license plate numbers that his squad shouted over the radio. Reggie described each of the drivers and took particular care in describing the assault rifles some of them carried. The tiny hairs at the base of Turner's skull felt like electric wires, as Reggie recited a litany of killer weaponry—AR-15, HK-93, AK-47 and some Israeli armament Turner had never heard of. He tried not to think about his puny Beretta handgun and department shotgun in a shootout with Conner's well-armed buddies.

When Ian Conner walked out of the barn, he was carrying a FN FAL, a beautiful .308-caliber, gas-operated rifle. It was a masterpiece that Turner dreamed of owning but couldn't easily afford, and he wondered how a disabled policeman on limited income could.

Conner took a long look over the flat landscape before ushering the deadly little group inside the barn. Turner waited for Reggie to say something, but the radio was silent for several seconds. He had to wait. As their observation point, Reggie was the squad's eyes, and the forward gears in their brains froze until Reggie gave them enough information to see what he was seeing.

"Point, you wanna tell the rest of us what the fuck is going on?" Weaver asked. He didn't have a lot of patience.

"Sorry," Reggie said, finally, but he didn't sound sorry. "They're inside the barn. There's a camera on the barn and one on the house. The kind of crappy equipment you see on Korean markets."

"Can I get close on foot?" Miller asked.

Turner wasn't surprised when Miller asked that question, but it would be dangerous prowling outside the barn, trying to peek in a window with all that firepower inside, so he was taken aback when Earl quickly volunteered to go too. Reggie directed Miller to the north side of the barn where there weren't any cameras and plenty of shrubbery for cover.

"Is this a good idea?" Weaver asked. "You could burn this thing on the first day if you're seen."

"Guess I'd better not get seen," Miller said. He sounded annoyed. "If we don't know what's happening in there, we might as well go home now and read about it in the newspaper."

"Don't get seen," Turner said, ending the discussion.

Turner hated to admit Weaver might be right. He didn't know if Weaver was worried about the case or his own skin should something go wrong, but surveillance was all about weighing the risks against the gains. After seeing all those weapons, Turner

25

didn't like his squad going anywhere near that barn until they carried a lot more firepower; and he wasn't certain how much valuable information Miller could get standing outside the barn, but it was worth a try.

After a few minutes of silence, Reggie broadcast that Miller and Earl had worked their way across the property and were near the barn. Miller crawled the last twenty-five yards by himself, leaving Earl behind a pile of dead brush. When he reached the barn, Miller stood and flattened his body against the wall. He remained in that position for over an hour. Finally, he knelt and waved in Reggie's direction. He crawled back to Earl, and they ran across the property to the dirt road, barely reaching the safety of a deteriorating stone wall before Reggie reported the barn's front door was opening.

The heavily-armed men departed the way they'd come. Conner came out of the barn without his rifle and went to the house where he remained for the rest of the day. When Beverly Conner returned that night, Weaver called off the surveillance until the next morning.

Turner had taken the best notes all day, so he became the case agent—meaning he became the primary detective on the case and would be stuck doing the daily logs and all the legwork. Vogel gave him Beverly's work address. He'd followed her to The Tavern on Washington Boulevard in Venice. It was a dingy bar and restaurant with two pool tables and cheap liquor. Turner knew the place. It was a notorious cop hangout for LAPD's Pacific and Wilshire divisions.

"She usually works the late shift, but she switched with another girl today," Vogel said, smiling. "She's pretty good looking up close."

Turner took Vogel's notes and put them on top of his messy stack of papers. He was eager to hear Miller's information. Weaver hadn't stopped smiling since Miller briefed him on what he'd overheard.

"I couldn't get all of it," Miller said, after he had everyone's attention.

"Just tell them what you told me, so we can get the fuck out of here," Weaver said.

"They think they're some kind of Jesse James' gang with automatic weapons. They got some plan to rob businesses in the Valley. What we saw today was a weapons' check."

"Is this their first time," Patty asked, timidly.

Miller shook his head. "Don't think so. They were bragging like they've done other stuff, some kinda initiation for the new guy. Tattooed gangbanger type with a shaved head talked like he might've ripped off a car or two."

"When are they planning to do these robberies?" Tony asked, looking at Earl.

"Don't know," Miller answered. "Sounds like they're ready now, but for some reason they're waiting. I couldn't hear all of it."

"Any more cops?" Turner asked, but somehow he knew the answer. Bad cops very seldom went sideways by themselves. They felt obligated to drag as many of their buddies as they could into the mud with them.

Miller glanced at Weaver who nodded. "Maybe two more," he said.

"I had IA run all the license plates," Weaver said. "Two of the plates came back to guys who worked with Conner. One of them is still assigned in Hollywood."

It would be Turner's job to pick up all the paperwork from the IA office and put the casebook together. He didn't mind. It was a good way to keep the investigation moving in the right direction. This could be complicated. He trusted himself more than anyone else not to screw it up.

On the tedious drive back to Redondo Beach, Reggie stared out the window or leaned against the headrest and closed his eyes. He didn't sleep. Turner had a feeling he wanted to talk about something, but knew it was futile to ask. Reggie would nod or shrug or generally ignore him unless it was one of those rare moments when he actually wanted to hear what Turner had to say. About half an hour from downtown, Reggie opened his eyes.

"Mind if I spend the night at your place?" Reggie asked.

Actually, he figured Reggie knew the answer. Since Turner was living alone again, he didn't have a reason to say no. It wasn't that he wanted or even enjoyed company. Sharing his home with other cops was an intrusion, except with someone like Reggie whose presence amounted to no more than a human slipcover. Eddie and Daryl were his only companions these days. Daryl didn't talk and neither of them expected anything from him.

For months, he'd hoped Miriam would make that first call, but her silence told him she'd moved on and was doing fine without him. He couldn't explain why, but he missed her even more than Paula, or maybe it was just the closeness of a woman he wanted. They hadn't argued or said terrible things to each other when she left. She just decided it was better if they didn't live together. He could remember that conversation as if it happened today. They were at his favorite Italian restaurant, and she waited until he'd nearly finished a bottle of wine before letting him in on her decision. It didn't make sense, a jumble of words . . . she was restless, wanted change but was crazy about him. She said they were a bad match, didn't know if she could live without him, but needed to try. It was teenage breakup language from a grown woman, but not really a surprise considering Miriam's eccentric personality. Sometimes she behaved like a child in a woman's body. Turner loved her simplicity and amorous nature. He hated her impulsiveness, but didn't realize how much he wanted her in his life until she was gone.

She crept back into his thoughts at times like this or at night when he was lonely. He needed Miller in the car. Miller never stopped talking, and if the subject of Miriam came up, he'd make Turner feel foolish for wasting his life thinking about a woman who didn't want him. Miller told him on numerous occasions to find another woman, any woman. But Turner knew that kind of sex never satisfied him. He needed the closeness. Sometimes, he had that with Miriam.

They made better time on the return trip and were back in Turner's garage before midnight. As soon as Turner switched on the living room lights, Eddie was on the front porch with Daryl.

"He's ready to settle in for the night, been walked and fed," Eddie said, and gave Turner the leash. He stood quietly for a moment, looking around Turner to see who was in the house. "Company?" he asked.

"Reggie," Turner said. Eddie didn't leave. "Want a drink, Eddie?" he asked. He was exhausted but knew that look. His neighbor wasn't going to leave until he got a beer and cop talk. The old man tightened his bathrobe and pushed past Turner into the living room. He sat on the couch near the recliner where Reggie was sitting. Turner couldn't imagine two more unlikely companions. Reggie never talked, and Eddie wouldn't shut up. But this time it was Reggie who started the conversation.

"You ever work IA, Mr. Jones?" Reggie asked, his grey eyes fixed on the black man's craggy unshaven face.

A guttural noise came from the old man and then, "Wouldn't catch me bein' no headhunter. Don't get me wrong. I hate crooked cops worse 'n shitbirds, but that business ain't for me."

"Ever known one, a bad cop?" Reggie asked, and Turner wondered what had inspired his partner's burst of conversation.

Eddie laughed. "You're jokin', right? I walked a beat in the forties and fifties. Hard part then was findin' a good one." He shook his head. "Lotta them got too close to the fire in those days. Not me. Couldn't put a man in jail and then be doin' the same thing he done. There was some that come on the job to steal. That's different."

"How'd you mean?"

"Them that used the uniform and badge to get what they want. Some others was like Jimmy, just weak."

"Jimmy?"

"Poor old Jimmy Jefferson." Eddie stared past Reggie as if he were remembering something he thought had been long forgotten.

"Don't know that name," Reggie said, and put his empty beer bottle on the coffee table. He went to the kitchen and came back with three more. Turner didn't want another one, but took it because he hadn't seen his friend this interested in anything in a long time.

"Why would you?" Eddie asked, a little edginess in his voice now. "He weren't Rodney King kind of famous. He come on the job with good intentions, convinced his self it weren't so bad to take a bit now and again . . . got caught stealin' a paperback book and got fired."

"He should've been fired, right?" Reggie asked, as if there wasn't any other possible answer.

"Maybe, but he liked bein' a cop. Took nickel 'n' dime stuff without thinkin', never figured that little stuff mattered. Wasn't takin' no bribes or stealin' to get rich. He was fair with folks, tried to help." Eddie cleared his throat. "Never understood how he could get fired for such a little thing."

"What happened to him?" Turner asked. He didn't know where Reggie was going with this discussion, but knew it wouldn't take much more to ignite Eddie's short fuse.

"Killed his self. Wasn't a bad man, just weak." Eddie put the nearly full bottle on the coffee table. He slowly pushed off the couch, waved away Reggie's helping hand. "See you folks later. I'm tired."

When Eddie was gone, Turner collected the bottles and threw a blanket and pillow on the couch.

"He's wrong," Reggie said as soon as Turner switched off the lights.

"About what?" Turner asked, flipping the toggle up again. He never thought much about what Eddie said.

"It's not a weakness; it's a choice. If one of us slips, it all falls apart." He wrapped the blanket around his shoulders and lay facing the back of the couch. Daryl crawled under the coffee table near him. Turner shut off the lights and went to bed. He didn't think it was possible for a man like Reggie to understand a man like Eddie.

THREE

The aroma of strong coffee woke Turner at 7 A.M. He jumped from the bed and swore at the alarm clock he'd forgotten to set. The bedroom door opened, and Reggie stood in the hallway with two steaming cups.

"You need to take me home, so I can get my car," Reggie said, handing him one of the cups.

Turner had slept in his clothes again. He pulled off his sweater and grabbed a clean shirt from the closet. A shower would have to wait until tonight. He sipped the coffee in between brushing his teeth. Toothpaste and caffeine were a bad combination.

"Don't worry about the dog. I fed him," Reggie said as he walked back toward the living room.

"Thanks. Eddie usually comes over around noon and does it if I forget. Sorry, I meant to make us breakfast." Miriam was right. He wasn't good at taking care of other people.

"No problem, I'll get something on the road. Patty called. She's already out at the Conner place. It's quiet." Reggie hesitated and then added, "Weaver's going downtown to brief Metcalf and wants to meet you at the office."

"Shit," Turner said. He was hoping for a relaxing day without the moody, uptight lieutenant standing over his shoulder. "If Metcalf figures out this is a decent case, he'll either give it to the suits to screw up or want to control everything we do." He took one last look around the house. Reggie had put away the blankets and straightened up the living room.

"We'll see," Reggie said, lifting his backpack. They left and that was the end of that discussion. Turner didn't ask Reggie what he meant. He doubted Reggie would tell him anyway, but he would welcome anything that kept Metcalf from interfering.

Turner dropped off Reggie at his bungalow and drove to Parker Center, the LAPD headquarters in downtown Los Angeles. The surveillance squad generally avoided police buildings, but Turner had to stop here for a few minutes to pick up Weaver's paperwork from yesterday. The department had rented office space in Chinatown to keep the surveillance officers and their cars out of sight as much as possible. They needed to follow dirty cops on the street, in bars or stores without being recognized as cops.

The Internal Affairs office at Parker Center was a floor down from Press Relations where Miriam worked. She was a civilian who had been with the department less than a year when Turner met her. She was a management analyst, but with her good looks and writing ability, she quickly became the media spokesperson for the chief of police. Sometime during the night, Turner had made the decision to talk to her today. The idea made more sense when he was alone in his bedroom at 3 A.M.

He would use the freight elevator or the stairs to avoid being seen by too many people. Normally, he'd be annoyed skulking around the police building to do an errand for his boss, but today he was happy to have a legitimate reason to be here.

Before he could see Miriam, he'd have to take care of business. Senior clerk typist Jenny Furcal had deposited Weaver's information in a manila envelope at the IA front counter. As Turner retrieved the envelope, Jenny waved and shouted for him to come to her desk. Turner almost pretended not to hear her, but he knew Jenny could make life intolerable for a cop if she didn't like him. She was a loud, overweight, bisexual Mexican with the personality of an inbred poodle. She wore too much makeup, and her hairstyle was a bleached explosion of curls under half a dozen layers of hairspray. She'd been at IA so long she thought she knew more than any of her bosses. Every new captain wanted to transfer her, but when they tried, she'd claim to have dirt on everyone including the chief of police. No one believed she really had anything, but they weren't willing to go through the ordeal of accusations and the inevitably messy misconduct complaint. So, Jenny stayed at IA in virtual perpetuity. Turner tried to avoid her whenever possible, but Jenny liked him and took every opportunity to flirt. She wasn't stupid, and her lengthy tenure at IA had given her some valuable institutional knowledge, so Turner flattered her at strategic moments. It was tricky to get what he wanted, but not let the poodle get too close.

"I pulled complaint histories on both those cops," she said loud enough to be heard down the hall. "Let me know if you need anything else." From her wink and grin, Turner wasn't certain she was still talking about paperwork.

She moved closer and gripped his arm. He stepped back. "Wait," she whispered. "I'm not gonna bite you. I found out something you guys might wanna know."

He relaxed a little. It was still business. "What is it, Jenny? I'm running really late," he lied.

"Just thought you oughta know Metcalf's talking about dumping Miller and Vogel and leaving just one surveillance squad."

"Weaver would never agree to that . . . especially now."

Jenny laughed. He hated that squeaky noise she made. "So what," she said, snorting and very pleased with herself. "Weaver doesn't matter anymore. Metcalf's in charge and he doesn't trust you guys."

Turner started to use a derogatory term about Metcalf but stopped himself. If Jenny ever got mad at him or believed Turner had slighted her in any way, she'd tell the lieutenant everything he said, with her embellishments to make it sound worse.

"Did he say when this was supposed to happen?" Turner asked, forcing a smile.

She grinned and scratched under her mattress spring hair.

"They both got a year left on their tour. Metcalf's gotta find a reason to dump them early, and then the rest of you can sit at a desk doing investigations."

Turner knew, at least with Miller, that wouldn't take long. Miller had no use for Metcalf and routinely found ways to let the lieutenant know. Warning Miller would be a waste of time. The man didn't understand pretense, and the idea of being transferred out of IA didn't bother him as much as the others. He'd be sent back to Narcotics Division, not some boring detective table.

Turner wanted to leave, but Jenny seemed to have more on her mind. The poodle suddenly became the Cheshire cat watching him squirm in front of her desk like a trapped mouse.

"Thanks for the heads up, Jenny," he said, attempting a good exit line.

"You can show your appreciation by taking me for a drink." She wasn't smiling.

"Great idea," he said, hoping his expression and the tightness in his throat wouldn't betray him. "When this case is over, we'll do that." He didn't move for a few seconds. She stared at him as he backed away.

As soon as he passed the front counter, Turner tucked the manila envelope under his arm and quickened his pace. He tried to imagine himself and Jenny naked on his bed. She might've just triggered a new nightmare. He wondered how she slept on that hairy helmet and how many hours it took to remove all her makeup. Miriam had soft silky brown hair and didn't wear much makeup. He envisioned his fingers stuck knuckle deep in Jenny's sticky hairspray, and knew his decision to talk to Miriam was the right one.

The door to Press Relations was open, and Miriam in a black tailored pantsuit sat at her desk, hunched over a computer. She was about five feet six inches tall and looked too big for the swivel chair. She was chewing on the remains of a pencil and absentmindedly playing with the switch on a desk lamp.

He watched for a few seconds, but she didn't look up.

"Hi kiddo," he said, trying to sound casual.

She glanced in his direction, spit out the pencil and beamed, a big, really happy-to-see-you smile that made Turner shiver. Swinging the chair around she jumped up, gave him a bear hug, then stepped back quickly. "Sorry, did I scare you? It's been so long," she said.

"That's what I was thinking. So, I figured I'd come by and see how you were doing and if you missed me." He bit the inside of his lip. What was he doing? He sounded feeble and hadn't intended to say all that.

She stopped smiling and looked down at the floor. "As a matter of fact, I do miss you."

It was too easy. "Can we go someplace and talk?" he asked.

"No," she said, grinning at what must have been his pained expression. She pointed at the office to her right where a female lieutenant in uniform was watching television and ignoring them. "Gotta work. Can I come by tonight?"

"Sure, I'll call when we're done." He felt a jolt of energy surge through his limbs, excitement and anticipation. His body was alive again. "We've got a good case so it might be a little late."

"That's fine. I hardly sleep anyway," she said.

"Are you okay?" he asked. He noticed that she'd lost a lot of weight. "You look kind of pale and thinner."

"Thanks, you look shitty too," she said laughing, and interrupted his attempt to apologize. "I've had to eat my own cooking, and I'm working too many hours, as usual."

It wasn't true, he thought. There's something else. He could see it in her eyes. She was never a good liar.

The female lieutenant in the other room had turned off the television and began shuffling through a stack of papers. Miriam's big brown eyes glanced up at the ceiling and she shrugged.

"I've got to go to work," she said, backing away from him. "Call me as soon as you're done." The office door closed, and she was gone before he could say anything. He stood there wondering if she had said what he thought he heard. It would be cruel if this were another version of the daydream he'd concocted to combat his loneliness, but he could still smell the faint odor of her sweet perfume on his shirt.

He had nearly reached the fifth floor stairwell door when Weaver called out to him. Weaver was leaving the IA captain's office with Lieutenant Metcalf. A few more steps and Turner could have escaped down the stairwell. So much for his plan to get inside the building, snatch the paperwork and get away through the back door before anyone saw him. He had to remind himself that seeing Miriam was worth having to deal with Metcalf.

The lieutenant shook his hand, which surprised Turner. Metcalf usually just nodded at him. He did, however, have a strong urge to wipe his palm on his shirt after releasing Metcalf's moist doughy grip. Metcalf was a boyish man who had very little time in any field assignment. The reason was obvious to Turner. The man was delicate and nervous with thinning black hair and an ink line mustache. He was the sort of guy that Turner instinctively left as far from the action as possible. Metcalf's smile was forced and always made Turner feel as if he harbored some inside joke at Turner's expense. Everyone kept telling him the lieutenant was intelligent and well educated, but it was difficult for him to respect a guy who was so out of place, albeit successful, in a profession Turner loved. Working cops seemed to scare Metcalf. Turner could see it in his body language and in his eyes whenever Miller or any of them challenged him. He thought it was peculiar how guys like Metcalf always got themselves into special operations where they were the least suited.

Weaver had finished talking about his meeting with the IA captain and seemed pleased. Turner didn't know why; he hadn't heard a word Weaver said.

"You ready to go?" Weaver asked, staring at Turner as if he knew he'd been talking to himself. "The lieutenant will be riding with me today."

Thanks for the warning, boss, Turner thought as he nodded politely at Metcalf. His first order of business would be telling the rest of the squad. Reggie's secret radio frequency was already proving to be a good idea.

Turner left them at the elevator and walked down the five flights of stairs, relieved to be alone again. He wanted to drive out to Santa Clarita before Metcalf got there and tell Reggie what Jenny had told him. In his own self interest, Weaver should fight Miller's and Vogel's transfer at least until this Conner investigation was finished, provided Miller didn't do anything too outrageous.

He debated whether or not he should tell Vogel. The tense detective was liable to have a nervous breakdown if he believed his transfer was imminent. He'd come from the elite Robbery Homicide Division, but didn't seem eager to return to dead bodies and endless paperwork. He was an excellent detective, good at surveillance and a loyal friend to Miller. Turner didn't want to lose either one of them and didn't want the squad to break apart. If the squad was disbanded he'd go back to Narcotics because he'd refuse to go inside as an IA investigator.

During the long drive to Conner's house, Turner kept thinking about his conversation with Miriam. Something was different; she was different. Maybe if the surveillance squad did fall apart, he'd take the lieutenant's test again and try to get promoted. He'd been on the list a couple of years ago, but got ranked too low to make it. Turner still loved police work in the trenches, but he was getting older and had to get off the streets sometime. As a lieutenant, he would have more time to spend with Miriam. She never understood his crazy work schedule. He knew several television stations had tried to hire her away from the police department, but she was holding out for a cable network and a bigger salary. If it worked out, she might be home less than him.

He missed her and believed that in her way she cared for him. The real question was how much either one of them was willing to sacrifice to stay together. It was a familiar problem for him. This job always had a way of messing up his personal life.

FOUR

It was late afternoon before Turner reached the Conner neighborhood. The point person had changed several times, but no one had seen anything resembling yesterday's scary gathering. Reggie finished his turn on the hill and was relocating near the highway when Turner asked to meet with him. They found an abandoned gas station about a quarter mile from the house.

"Where's Metcalf?" Reggie asked, climbing into the passenger seat.

"He's riding with Weaver, so you know Weaver's gonna take his time getting here."

"Too bad. I was hoping Metcalf was alone."

"I'll make a couple of jokes about his driving ability. He'll take his own car tomorrow," Turner said, knowing arrogance was so predictable. He hoped Reggie's plan, whatever it was, embarrassed the lieutenant enough to keep him in his office, but didn't do any permanent damage. "We need to talk about Miller and Vogel," he said.

Reggie's expression never changed as Turner repeated Jenny's information. He liked using Reggie as a sounding board. His partner was clever and usually offered some options.

"I guess we'll need to make sure it doesn't happen," Reggie said, after a long pause.

"Should we tell them?" What Turner meant to ask was, should they tell Vogel and give him another ulcer.

"Why? Miller won't do anything different, and Vogel will shit all over himself trying to do everything different," Reggie said. His cold eyes studied Turner as if he were a lab experiment gone bad.

"What's wrong with you?" Turner asked, defensively.

"Miller volunteered to watch Beverly Conner at The Tavern for a couple of nights. You've gotta go with him," he said in his unique way that didn't leave much room for discussion or refusal.

"What about Vogel. They're partners," Turner protested. He really didn't want to babysit the unruly Miller.

"Vogel can't keep Miller out of trouble."

"Nobody can keep him out of trouble. Fuck, what am I worried about? Weaver's never gonna let him work undercover in a bar."

"He's already approved it," Reggie said with a rare grin.

Turner leaned forward and gently tapped his forehead several times against the steering wheel. It didn't take a genius to recognize true evil. Metcalf was giving Miller all the rope he needed to hang himself. "I can't believe Weaver would cave like that. He knows putting Miller undercover in a cop bar by himself is a recipe for disaster. He might as well sign the guy's transfer now." Turner was probably the only one who had a chance of keeping Miller out of trouble, and both he and Reggie knew it.

"If you tell Weaver you want to work the bar with Miller, he won't say no. You're the case agent." That was it, end of conversation. Reggie had made his case and was out of the car. "He starts tomorrow night," Reggie said, closing the door.

Turner sat quietly for a few minutes. He was uneasy and not certain if it was because of Metcalf or Weaver or maybe even Reggie. Maybe it was all of them, but he knew better. It was Miriam. It was always Miriam. She somehow kept him off balance, out of sync with the rest of his world. He didn't like that feeling, but it was the price he always paid to be with her, and he wanted to be with her. When they were together, he was happy, but they were so different he never understood why. He saw himself as confident and stable, and Miriam wasn't the sort of woman that should attract him, but she did and that made him uncomfortable.

THE SQUAD watched Conner's house until the lights went out around midnight. Weaver summoned them to the fast food parking lot, but his remarks were uncharacteristically brief. Metcalf stayed in the car but kept the window open.

"It's the prick's way of looking interested," Miller whispered loud enough for Turner to hear. He leaned closer. "If Metcalf closes the car window, then he really doesn't give a shit." Nobody laughed, so Turner hoped he was the only one who heard it. The best way to keep Miller out of trouble might be to tape his mouth shut.

The day had been long and boring. There wasn't the usual banter that night, partly because Metcalf was still there, but mostly because the inactivity had drained their energy. No one came onto the property. Beverly Conner had walked to the road once to pick up the mail, but Ian never left the house.

Turner felt sorry for Weaver, who had to sit in a car with Metcalf for ten hours with no distractions. The way he hurried through his remarks and gave them their start time for the following day said that Weaver couldn't wait to unload the lieutenant.

It was easy to put Metcalf on the defensive. Turner made a few good-natured remarks about how much safer it was having the lieutenant ride in Weaver's car. Metcalf's nervous lip-biting told Turner the lieutenant would be driving his own car tomorrow, and Reggie's plan, whatever it was, could go forward.

He wanted to get out of there, but Turner knew his mission wasn't complete.

"I want to work with Miller at the bar tomorrow night," he said, trying to make it sound as if it were his idea.

"No, I need you here," Weaver said.

Sometimes, Turner thought, he might be too clever for his own good.

"If the lieutenant drives, you'll have more than enough cars, especially if this guy sits home again," he said, looking directly at Metcalf.

Weaver shrugged. The idea probably sounded better when it took Metcalf out of his car.

"Alright, but two nights, and if you don't see anything, the two of you are back here with the squad," Weaver said. He avoided Metcalf's stare and told them to sign off and go home.

Turner was the first to leave. He wanted to call Miriam even though it was very late. If he didn't talk to her tonight, he was afraid he would change his mind, or she'd realize nothing was different. He was still the same stubborn, work-consumed cop she'd left several months ago. As soon as he pulled out of the parking lot, he punched in her number and waited until her answering machine picked up. Her whispery voice asked the caller to leave a message. Disappointed, he hung up. He drove a couple of miles, pressed the recall button. Four rings . . . the message played again.

"Hi Miriam, it's me. I'm glad I didn't wake you." He took a deep breath. "No, I'm not. I really wanted to talk to you tonight. It's almost 1 A.M., but we just finished. Guess I could have called in the morning, but you said you'd be awake and I . . ." A loud dial tone interrupted. He slumped in the seat, energy draining from his body. Redondo Beach might as well be San Francisco; it seemed that far away. Fortunately, the roads were nearly empty. He drove fast and hoped the Highway Patrol was too bogged down with drunk drivers to notice him.

As Turner pulled into his driveway, he saw the lights were on in his living room. Usually, knowing that Eddie was waiting in his favorite chair watching his television didn't bother him, but he wanted to be alone. Making small talk with an old man about things they couldn't change would be an annoying exercise tonight. Turner thought about being rude and asking Eddie to leave, but knew he wouldn't hurt the old man's feelings. Instead, he opened the door and forced a smile as Daryl lumbered across the room to greet him.

When he finished petting the dog and stood up, Turner realized Eddie and Daryl weren't alone. Miriam was sitting on the arm of his overstuffed chair, her long legs crossed, as she leaned on Eddie's shoulder. She made a bulky pink sweater and worn jeans look as sexy as an evening gown.

41

"Mind some company?" she asked, exchanging a look with Eddie. They laughed a little. Obviously, they had spent some time together talking about him. Turner knew Eddie had been disappointed when she moved out. The old man talked about her every day until finally Turner insisted he stop mentioning her name or not come to the house anymore. Eddie still managed to work Miriam's name into their conversations once or twice a week, and at the moment, he was grinning like someone put vodka in his Metamucil.

Miriam slid her arm from around Eddie's shoulder and touched his hand. He struggled to pull himself out of the chair.

"Dog's fed. I'm goin' home. Unless you two want some old fart hangin' 'round."

She rolled onto his place in the chair and said, sweetly, "Goodnight, Eddie."

Turner opened the door but didn't pay much attention to his neighbor's departure. It was 2:30 in the morning, and Miriam was in his living room. She was still the same quirky, unpredictable woman.

"Are you ready for this again?" she asked when he hadn't moved.

"Are you?" He bounced the question back because he wasn't certain he had an answer.

"I was stupid," she said.

"Maybe not."

"I don't want somebody who thinks too much like me. It's tedious."

"What happened?" he asked.

"Does it matter?"

It did, but he wasn't going to push her.

"I'm not going to change," he said. He was sorry he admitted that as soon as he said it. Looking at her smooth skin and soft pink lips, he might consider changing just a little bit.

He still hadn't moved, so she went to him. "I don't care," she whispered, her sweet warm breath on his cheek. She kissed him like a long, thirsty drink of water. He pulled her closer. She was so thin. He worried she might be sick until they were undressed, and he saw she was lovely, pale and delicate but still beautiful.

Their lovemaking wasn't as physical as it had been in the past. He was afraid he might hurt her. He wanted her more than ever, but was gentle and fell asleep with her in his arms. He woke several times during the night, reaching out for her. She was still there, and he was content, but he couldn't shake the nagging feeling that something was wrong.

FIVE

Sometime after the sun came up, Turner finally fell into a deep sleep. A persistent leaf blower finally woke him about 10 A.M., and she was gone. He found her trail of damp towels and his robe on the floor of the bathroom. A second toothbrush was lying on the sink near a half-filled cup of cold coffee. She's still a slob, he thought with a bit of frustration as he picked up his robe and threw the towels in the tub. The robe was cold and wet, but he slipped it on anyway. The dog was nowhere in sight, so he had been fed. Eddie must have been here because Miriam never remembered to feed him.

It was as if she'd never been gone. He hadn't missed the clutter of her things in the bathroom and in his closet, but he did miss the smell of her long auburn hair on his pillow every morning. The nagging uneasiness of last night was ebbing, or he was choosing not to let it affect what was happening. He wasn't certain that he was happier or that his life was even better with her, but this morning he couldn't imagine it any other way.

He was hungry and had plenty of time for a leisurely breakfast. Miller had agreed to meet him at The Tavern around seven that night. They would go separately and pretend not to know each other. Hopefully, one of them would see or hear something. If they got lucky, Beverly Conner would be a blabbermouth. He even had enough time to go to the Chinatown office for a few hours and arrange his case file. He still needed to review the DMV printouts Jenny had given him and do some background on the other two cops.

He made scrambled eggs and bacon. Miriam left the loaf of bread open on the counter and a fresh pot of coffee. She probably had her routine breakfast of black coffee and a slice of toast. At least when they got up at the same time, he knew she ate a lot better because he made her eat a real breakfast. In a few months, he would have her healthy again. He pulled a stool over to the kitchen phone and started to dial her work number, but hung up. No, he would call her as soon as he got to the office. The fear of pushing too hard made him hesitant to do the things he had done so naturally before she left.

He showered, dressed, and was greeted by Eddie and Daryl relaxing in his living room.

"Come to get the beast," Eddie said, laughing. "Glad to see she didn't kill you or nothin'. Started to worry when you didn't move all mornin'."

"What were you two talking about when I got home last night?" Turner asked, hoping to keep the old man from asking too many nosy questions.

"You—what'd you think?"

"Does she seem okay to you, Eddie?"

"No, she seems better than okay, little skinny is all."

"She can't cook and eats like a teenager."

"Who cares? She's a sassy woman." Eddie had a way of getting to what was really important. "And I like her, besides which she cares about you. You finally goin' to work?"

"Late shift tonight. You keep Daryl?" He didn't need an answer, and Eddie didn't give one. They both knew Eddie would be in Turner's living room around six with a couple of tacos, drinking Turner's beer, watching Turner's television and feeding Daryl a bag of nachos that would make the dog fart all night.

When he locked the rear kitchen door, he saw the blinking message light on the phone near the refrigerator. Miriam must have called while he was in the shower. She left a message to call her at the office. That was it, no reference to last night, no playful innuendos, no mention of the word love. She was the same perplexing woman.

45

"Don't worry. I'll take care of everythin' and everybody 'til you get home," Eddie said, and winked as Turner closed the front door.

On the ride downtown, Turner was anxious to find out if Conner had done anything that morning. He called Reggie on his car phone and was disappointed that Conner hadn't left his house yet. But they both knew it was early and the probability of another gang get-together would be better as soon as Beverly left for work. Metcalf hadn't arrived either, a fact that seemed to annoy Reggie.

"Be grateful. The prospect of actually having to do police work might've scared him away for good."

"Maybe," Reggie said, "but I'm not counting on it."

Turner didn't pursue the subject of Lieutenant Metcalf. He knew Reggie had something planned to make the lieutenant miserable, but he wanted to stay out of it. He hung up as he reached Chinatown and pulled into the underground parking lot.

The surveillance detail's clandestine office was on the third floor of a rundown building occupied primarily by Chinese lawyers and accountants. A psychiatrist had the only other space on their floor. Dr. Tom was an older man with an unruly beard who seemed to wear the same brown suit every day. Turner heard from the other tenants that he had an excellent, prosperous practice until his nervous breakdown a couple of years ago. Now, his wife acted as his secretary, staring at phones that never rang; and he didn't seem to have much to do all day except wander the halls and play with the elevator buttons. Other tenants complained about his habit of leaving fresh chicken bones in the sandy ashtrays by the elevators, but Turner and Miller liked him and always bought an extra bucket of KFC parts for him whenever they got the fried chicken urge.

Dr. Tom had become the surveillance squad's coal mine canary. He warned them when anyone other than another tenant was on their floor. Two quick knocks followed by three knocks was his signal. When they opened the door, he would be gone. No one knew why Dr. Tom had started guarding the hallway, but

Turner suspected Miller in a moment of boredom had made the doctor a secret agent just to give the man something to do.

The hallway was deserted, and Turner made it inside the office before Dr. Tom could corner him. The room was cold and smelled unused. For security reasons, the building's janitors didn't have the key to their office, so it was filthy as usual. Cops weren't good at picking up after themselves. It was that civil service "it's not my job" mentality. When he was working uniformed patrol, Turner hated taking a patrol car from the previous shift. The backseat was always full of empty food containers and Styrofoam cups. If he were really unlucky, one of the officers would chew tobacco and leave a half-full spit cup under his seat. The surveillance guys weren't any better, and Patty was the worst. Her desk was covered with stale food, piles of debris and too many pictures of her boyfriend and her dogs. A coffee mug was balanced precariously on her computer monitor. All the other desks strategically placed around the crowded room were in similar stages of ruin except his and Reggie's. Reggie had nothing on his desk except a telephone and his computer—not a single piece of paper—and every drawer was locked. Turner kept his space organized, but wasn't concerned about leaving non-sensitive materials neatly stacked on top.

He walked around the cramped space with just a few feet between every desk and picked up old newspapers and food containers. He emptied the trashcans in one large container and placed it outside the door for the janitor. When the room was reasonably clean, he could sit down and work. He spread the materials from his case folder on his desk.

Notes from Miller and Vogel, the DMV printouts, the worksheet and a driver's license photo of Beverly Conner, he put in separate piles. He picked up her picture. She reminded him of some actress with an Irish name he'd seen in an old John Wayne movie. She had a determined almost angry look, but it didn't alter the fact that she was a very handsome, appealing woman. It wasn't a big surprise that Miller would've volunteered to work The Tavern.

Turner thumbed through the DMV's and found the two officers that Jenny had highlighted with fluorescent pink. Andy Cullen and Pete Goodman were both in their late twenties and former police academy classmates. They lived together in the Valley. Turner pulled a street guide from his desk drawer and discovered they were only a few miles from the Conner house. He moved to the department's internal computer system and didn't find any assault weapons registered in their names. Several cars were registered to them, including the four-wheel-drive truck Reggie had seen at the Conner house.

Goodman was working Pacific division where The Tavern bar was located. He was assigned to the prostitution enforcement detail, and Cullen worked Hollywood division patrol. Somehow, Jenny had made copies of the two officers' personnel packages. The woman was a pain in the ass, but she knew how to work the system. Both Goodman and Cullen had numerous "neglect of duty" misconduct complaints. They frequently missed court appearances, failed monthly qualifications with their service weapons, and had several traffic accidents. He wondered how Goodman had talked his way into the coveted prostitution detail. It was usually reserved for the better officers. Turner called someone he knew at Scientific Investigation Division and ordered pictures of both officers for the new worksheets.

By the time he had finished computer runs on all the names from the DMV's, he had identified a couple of gangbanger, high school dropouts. None of them had been to prison or even county jail, not exactly what he expected to find in the gun-toting Valley boy mob. He couldn't identify any of the older Mexicans including the big tattooed one with the shaved head. They gave nonexistent addresses, and Turner suspected their birthdates were phony too.

A dull pain started to spread above his eyes, and Turner realized he'd been sitting at the computer for several hours. He sat up straight and rubbed the back of his neck. It was nearly four, and he still hadn't called Miriam. She'd sounded so distant on her message. Maybe she was having second thoughts. He was stalling, afraid to hear bad news. What the hell did she want from him? He never lied to her, never pretended to be something he wasn't. In a way, he found himself wishing he'd never started this again. Perhaps it was just his premonition that it was probably going to end badly for him.

She answered the phone on the first ring. He felt himself cringe inside at the sound of her voice.

"Hi, it's Mike," he said quickly before he could hang up.

"I can't talk right now. Are you at a phone where I can call you?"

She's going to dump me, he thought, and was beginning to feel annoyed. "Are you okay? Is anything wrong?" he asked, not wanting to wait for the inevitable second blow.

"Everything's great. You worry too much. Life is great. I'm crazy about you. Sorry my message was so bland. The boss was standing over my shoulder. So, should I move my stuff back? Or would you rather we wait a little while?" She sounded happy.

"Don't wait. It's okay as soon as you want. Eddie's got a key if I'm not there." He thought this was what he wanted, but there was that nervous twinge in his stomach again.

"I really can't talk now. The boss is about to start a staff meeting. Love you. Call me later. Okay?" she said and hung up.

"I love you," he said as the phone clicked. He should've felt better.

"You're regressing, the sappy teenager syndrome," he whispered. "Think about something else." The phone rang. It was Miller who offered to bring Chinese food to the office so they could eat before making the trip to the bar.

"Did Reggie call you?" Miller asked, trying not to laugh.

"Not lately, why?"

"Metcalf finally got there this afternoon, but it seems his tires picked up a nail or two or four. I wasn't there, so he doesn't know who to blame."

"He'll still blame you."

"Maybe, but I don't think so. Weaver convinced him he parked on an old construction site." Miller laughed and said, "I got this hunch Metcalf's run of bad luck is just beginning."

"Where was Reggie?"

"That's the beauty of it. Reggie was on the point."

The man's a genius, Turner thought. "Did Conner do anything interesting?"

"Reggie said the guy finally moved and was all over the Valley this afternoon. He started traveling as soon as Beverly left for work. Reg has a bunch of notes for you. You find anything?"

Turner described the information he had on the two officers and the other men who had met at Conner's house.

"Not exactly hard-core types," Miller said after a lengthy pause.

"I did find a couple of robberies in Devonshire and West Valley that have the same MO with assault-type weapons and a mix of white and Mexican male suspects, plus two stolen vehicle reports with cars similar to the ones you heard them talking about, but it's all computer guesswork. Where's the lieutenant?"

"Still out there. He refused to leave his car. The garage had to find four new tires. I love this job," Miller said.

Turner started to repeat what Jenny had told him, but decided against it. Miller was feeling good about Reggie's expensive prank. He wouldn't spoil the moment. Miller had arrived at the restaurant and hung up after getting Turner's order.

Turner browsed through the casebook. It was in chronological order with plenty of room for daily logs and added information. Organizing this investigation was easier than getting his personal life together. Anyway, it made a lot more sense to him.

"You THINK too much," Miller said with a mouth full of eggplant and tofu dripping garlic sauce. He had barely laid out their lunch before Turner began worrying out loud about his renewed relationship with Miriam. "She's a great lady, but if she dumps you what's the big tragedy. You didn't die the first time, did you?"

"Did you get a chance to talk with Reggie again?" Turner asked. Sharing your feelings with Miller was an invitation for ridicule.

"I'm good for one conversation a day with him. The guy's major league surveillance, but he's got some serious life issues."

"He's quiet."

"Like a dormant volcano. You know why he keeps that journal, don't you? Department shrink told him to do it after he nearly had a nervous breakdown."

"That was a long time ago. He keeps it now because he likes to write."

"We all see things we'd rather not remember. I seen my share of some pretty gross-out stuff. You lost a partner. You block it out and go on, or you quit and become a banker or a truck driver or something."

"Some guys can't forget, and they don't know how to do anything else."

"I understand all that, Turner. I just don't want to spend a lotta time with the guy."

Turner was aching to tell Miller what Metcalf was planning and how Reggie was keeping the lieutenant preoccupied and away from him, but he didn't. Reggie was right. It would make things worse. Reggie might be strange, but at least his was a controlled madness. Miller was mayhem with zero containment.

They waited until dusk, then drove separately to The Tavern bar in Venice. The building looked exactly like Vogel had described it. Chipped green stucco and an ugly red wooden door sandwiched between a laundromat and a real estate office. The door was cracked open with music drifting out. As Turner pushed open the door, cigarette smoke covered him like a nasty fog bank. It took a minute to adjust to the lack of light and oxygen. So much for the "no smoking" ordinance in L.A. bars, at least in cop bars. He didn't look for Miller. It would be a waste of time in this crowded room crammed with a hundred cops and police groupies. The music, whatever it might be, was drowned out by too many loud voices. Only the monotonous drumbeat kept pounding in his head. He hated these places. They were designed to keep your thinking muddled and your inhibitions buried. It meant losing control, a condition that scared him worse than being shot.

Metropolitan Division must have worked around the Venice area that day. Turner recognized familiar faces in several elite groupings that sported the Metro tuxedo; the white t-shirts with uniform pants stood out even in this crowd. He slowly worked his way toward the bar and tried to decipher faces in the shadows hoping to spot the two cops, Cullen and Goodman. It was hopeless. He found several empty stools near the end of the bar. Apparently most of the barflies preferred to stand. He straddled the stool and leaned against the bar. The light was better here, and he wasn't surprised to see Miller at the other end of the polished oak and black marble, laughing and joking with the pretty Beverly Conner. She was flushed, but relaxed and friendly, and moved deftly to dispatch drinks and gather empty glasses as they found their way back. She was prettier than her picture and looked much younger, or maybe it was the magic of saloon lighting.

She saw Turner and nodded to acknowledge him, patted Miller's hand and abandoned him. The lady was all business.

"What can I get you?" she asked Turner while pouring another beer for an overweight detective sitting next to him.

"Club soda with lime," he said and smiled. She smiled back in a way that was very disarming.

"Should've come after work," she said. "You could've had an adult drink."

"Not unless I want alcohol for breakfast."

"Graveyard shift?"

"Not by choice." He liked the sound of her voice. It was strong, but friendly. She had a tone that made him feel as if he'd known her a long time, as if they were friends.

"I haven't seen you before. Do you work Pacific?" she asked.

An older woman with pink hair and dressed in the bar uniform tapped him on the shoulder and lifted the gate near his elbow. She slipped behind the bar touching Beverly's arm as she walked behind her and started serving drinks.

"Are you done for the night?" he asked.

She laughed. "I wish. No, Joyce comes in for a few hours to help me when it gets busy. I'm Beverly." She extended her hand, and he quickly did the same. It surprised him. Most women didn't seem to like shaking hands, but she did it easily with a firm grip.

"Mike," he said, and looked past her at Miller who was staring in their direction. Suddenly, he had become the primary operator on this little mission, and Miller didn't look too happy about it.

Beverly rested her hip against the bar. She studied his face. "So, where did you say you work?"

He hadn't, but used his standard response when anyone asked. "I work a downtown narcotics task force." He glanced at Miller and wondered if Beverly had asked him that question and what Miller's answer might've been. Probably something like, "I work an internal surveillance detail, and I'm following your asshole son."

"What are you smiling at?" she asked.

"I'm happy I came in here tonight," he said, putting Miller out of his thoughts.

"A cop bar isn't the best place for an undercover guy."

"I'm not undercover. We do surveillance on heroin dealers." A lie should be as close to the truth as possible. "You married?"

She laughed and stood away from the bar. "No, divorced. And you?"

"No, too busy. Kids?"

"I have a son. He's a cop."

"L.A.?"

She nodded. "I'm a size ten, and my hair is really red, and my eyes are greenish blue. You ask a lot of personal questions."

"Sorry, I guess I just want to know you in a hurry. You're a very attractive woman even if you are related to a cop."

"Well, he's not exactly a cop. I mean he's hurt and hasn't worked for a long time."

"Too bad. What happened?"

"I don't really know," she said with a faint smile. "Ian's kind of a flake. I mean he's my kid, and I love him, but he's a flake." Her demeanor changed when she talked about her son. She nervously twisted the bar towel, and she wouldn't look at him.

"What do you mean?" It was so easy to talk to her. Turner almost forgot why he was there. He genuinely liked her and

53

wasn't comfortable pretending to be something he wasn't. "Sorry, I didn't intend to pry, but you seem upset." He forced himself to get back in the game.

"It's okay. Ian's lazy, and he's a scammer, always trying to work an angle." She shook her head. "Just like his father. I'm afraid he might be using his injury to get a pension."

"Maybe he's really hurt."

"No, his back is fine." She hesitated and looked up at the ceiling. "I shouldn't have said that."

"Beverly, I'm not an Internal Affairs spy," he said, touching her arm. "Nothing you tell me will get him in trouble. Maybe I can help." He sensed she was on the edge of really opening up to him.

She looked away for a few seconds before saying, "I'm scared he might be doing something . . ." She moved closer to him. "He's got some really weird friends. He thinks I don't know, but I've seen them."

"What do you think he's doing?"

She stared at him and stepped back from the bar. "I don't know, probably just a case of motherly jitters."

He could feel the protective shield drop around her. Something made her uncomfortable, and she stopped confiding in him. Maybe he'd asked too many questions, too soon. He wasn't very good at this. Maybe Miller would have better luck. She brought him another club soda and handed him a piece of folded paper.

"That's my home phone number. I like talking to you, Mike. If you want, give me a call sometime, and maybe we can go for coffee or something."

He opened the paper. It was her number. He remembered it from the worksheet. "I'd like that," he said, trying not to sound too anxious. "I don't know this area code. Where is this?"

"Santa Clarita. I live with my son. Too far for you?"

"He won't mind another cop dating his mother?"

"Actually, he lives with me," she said, moving away from him and then without turning around added, "I'm off tomorrow; call

54

early." She was pouring drinks at the other end of the bar before he could answer.

Miller was staring at him with a frozen smirk. Turner didn't need to ask him what he was thinking. His partner wanted this woman, but she'd made her choice. Miller finished his drink and dropped a tip on the bar. Beverly Conner grabbed it and thanked him, then quickly shifted her attention to a drinking customer. Miller worked his way to the pool tables, and Turner joined him as soon as Beverly Conner was busy at the bar.

Several younger cops were playing for quarters. They were noisy and drunk. Turner recognized Pete Goodman from the picture in his personnel package. Andy Cullen arrived a few minutes later carrying a tray full of tequila shooters. They had lost the last game and bought drinks. Like a number of the younger officers, the two men in t-shirts and tight jeans spent many hours on the weight machines and enjoyed showing off their bulging biceps. Turner figured they were over-compensating like the guys who had monster wheels on trucks. These baby cops were hoping their size would scare off the bad guys, but it didn't work that way. Sixteen-year-old punks with stolen guns didn't care how strong you were. The plan was to wait until a cop got careless and then shoot him in the back. If the cowards didn't fear you, they would try to kill you. Turner knew that. The street lice feared him because he'd look them in the eye and dare them to try. He wanted them to try. He'd bet money that Goodman and Cullen didn't.

"Hey, old man, want to try your luck?" Goodman was talking to Miller who was chalking a pool cue. Miller looked like a dope cop. He was out of shape and had a day-old beard. The last weight-lifting he did was the heroin addict he threw out of a two-story window at the Paradise Hotel on Sunset Boulevard. Drinking and playing pool were his favorite competitive events.

"You and me for what?" Miller asked and turned away, a quick wink at Turner.

"Quarter and a round of shooters," Goodman said. He slapped a quarter on the corner of the pool table and stared at Miller.

Miller set another quarter on top of Goodman's. Andy Cullen grabbed the coin and flipped it in the air. Miller called heads and got the break. He managed to clear the table in about thirty seconds. Goodman's puffy eyes narrowed as he put another quarter on the table. Miller won the toss again and cleared the table.

"Grandpa's cleaning your clock, Pete," Cullen said. "Where you work?" he asked Miller.

"Narcotics and I'm thirsty. Where's my drinks, partner?"

"You ain't my partner," Goodman mumbled.

"I'm grateful for that if you don't shoot any better than you play pool."

"He can shoot just fine," Andy Cullen said, defending his partner.

"So, how many paper targets you killed during your extensive career of what two . . . three years?" Miller was starting to push the buttons. Turner leaned against the wall and watched. Miller could get under a man's skin faster than the worst case of poison ivy.

"You learn to shoot with a musket, old man?" Cullen laughed at his own joke, and turned to Goodman who was glassy-eyed staring at the floor and didn't seem to hear his friend. He staggered and hung on to the edge of the pool table to keep from falling.

Miller grabbed the younger man's arm and kept him on his feet. "Hope he walks better than he drinks."

"Fuck you," Goodman said to the ceiling.

"You're fucking with the wrong people, old man," Cullen said and pushed Miller's hand away from Goodman.

Turner slowly moved a few feet closer, but knew Miller was a long way from needing help.

Miller turned his back on the two younger men. He leaned over and hit the eight ball cleanly into the corner pocket. "The department's been screwing with me for twenty years, sonny, and they don't scare me. Why should I break a sweat over two kiddie cops?" Miller asked.

Cullen leaned a shaky Goodman against the table and picked up a pool cue. Turner wanted to warn Miller, but something told him to wait.

"Put a quarter or that stick on this table," Miller said, "or you'll be farting chalk dust for breakfast."

Miller never looked up at Cullen, but kept shooting balls. Cullen nervously twisted the pool stick in his hands. Turner almost laughed. The young cop was frozen in place. He glanced at Miller and then at the pool stick in his hands as if some careless stranger had left it there. In frustration, he broke the stick in half over his knee and threw it on the floor.

Cullen helped Goodman navigate to the door, and the two men left without another word. Activity continued in the bar as if nothing had happened. Miller hit another ball but quickly motioned with his thumb toward the door. Turner saw it and immediately stepped behind a group of Metro cops, slipped out the back door into the cool dark night air.

Two years of working surveillance had taught Turner to park across the boulevard away from the streetlight where he had a clear view of The Tavern's parking lot. He opened the passenger door and slid in across the seat and behind the wheel. He slouched down and waited. He was watching the lot's exit in his rearview mirror, but didn't worry about the car getting away from him. He expected Miller to be in place before the two young cops turned on the headlights.

"Sitting east," Miller said, as if on cue. Turner turned down the volume on the radio and clicked the microphone twice to acknowledge Miller's transmission.

Headlights popped on in the parking lot. A Chevy truck moved slowly around parked cars and sat in the driveway. Turner recognized Cullen's vehicle from the notes he'd taken at Ian Conner's house. The green truck came equipped with four-wheel drive and an AR-15 assault rifle.

Turner described the truck for Miller and then, "Two occupants . . . turning eastbound to you, Miller."

"Relax, I got him," Miller said. Turner didn't move and watched the truck drive east on Washington. It suddenly made a quick turn south. "Don't move, Turner. He's cleaning up."

Miller was right. Turner saw the truck come back onto Washington from the south. It had gone around the block and was now in front of him driving back in his direction. He slid down further until it passed.

"Is he going around again?" Turner asked when he sat up and didn't see them.

"No, he turned off the headlights. We're eastbound Washington," Miller said. "He's so shitfaced he can hardly find his lane with the lights on. He's gonna get stopped before he goes a mile."

Turner started his engine and made a U-turn to follow Miller. He couldn't see either car, but he knew they would be about a mile in front of him. He turned and drove south to a street that ran parallel to Washington. Listening to Miller's directions, he drove faster until he was only a block or two behind them. Cullen turned north on Sepulveda and Turner was in perfect position to take the point. He stayed back several blocks, but the traffic was heavier here and he had plenty of cars for cover. This was a part of the job he loved, hiding behind three or four cars, a lane over and catching just a glimpse of the truck's taillights. A blink at the wrong time and Cullen would disappear into traffic. Turner broadcast their direction and felt like he was in complete control. He could do this all night long, and Cullen would never know he was there.

The truck made a quick eastbound turn north of Venice Boulevard and parked near the curb. Turner went west and watched in his rearview mirror as he drove in the opposite direction.

"Don't turn, Miller. He's sitting at the curb waiting with the lights off."

"I'm down the street," Miller said. "He should come right to me."

"You've got it. I'm off," Turner said as he turned at the next corner, went around the block and waited to see what Cullen would do next. He could feel his heart beating faster. The chase had started. In every surveillance, the prey always thought he could hide, outsmart the hunter, but he couldn't. Turner was confident that he and Miller were too good at this. They would slip and dodge until they followed Cullen and his partner to whatever it was Cullen was trying so hard to hide.

"We're moving again eastbound on Cherry, south on Bentley and into a driveway three buildings from the corner. Stand by. I'm out on foot."

Turner wouldn't drive past the building, but parked near the corner behind Miller's abandoned car where he could watch the street. He didn't see any movement, but knew Miller was lurking somewhere in the shadows. He pulled the folder with his case notes from his bag and looked for the personal information on Cullen and Goodman. Neither of them gave this location as a home address.

After nearly forty-five minutes, Turner's passenger door opened, and Miller climbed inside. He handed Turner a piece of paper with an address and apartment number.

"I heard at least two other voices in the apartment," Miller said. "I think one of them was the Mexican asshole from Conner's place that steals cars."

Turner put the note in his case folder. "What now?"

"We wait. There were a lot of cars in the underground. The only ones I recognized were the truck and Goodman's black Montero."

"How will we know if one of the other guys leaves?" Turner asked, but was starting to think they should get the whole squad involved before these guys took off in different directions.

"We got a list of license numbers from Conner's place. Check every car that comes out of there."

"I'm giving Weaver a heads up . . . see if they're done at Conner's place," Turner said, and scrolled to the sergeant's number on his cell phone.

"He'll tell Metcalf," Miller whined.

"I don't care. He needs to know about this."

"Suit yourself, but Metcalf will find a way to fuck this up."

Turner shrugged. He wasn't going to argue. Miller was stubborn and probably right, but if Weaver heard about this afterwards, he would be pissed at him, not Miller. Weaver expected Miller to be flaky, but Turner was supposed to be the levelheaded, reliable one.

"Weaver's the boss. He should be calling the shots."

Miller twisted in the seat. Even in the dark, Turner could see his partner's face flush, the slow burn before the explosion.

"How long you been making cases?" Miller asked. He didn't try to hide his displeasure. "You still need someone to hold your hand?"

"I still need to do it right." Turner knew he was doing the one thing you should never do with Miller—try to reason with him.

"We're big boys. We don't need a fucking babysitter," Miller said and hit the passenger window with the back of his hand.

Turner looked away to talk with Weaver, trying to ignore Miller's outburst. Weaver had just gotten home from Conner's place a short time before and was falling asleep when Turner called. He was groggy, so Turner repeated the night's events. Miller groaned, mumbling something inaudible. Turner told Weaver to hold on a minute and put his hand over the phone.

"I'm real close to grabbing you around the neck and dragging you out of this car," Turner said, as calmly as he could.

It wouldn't be the first time Turner had knocked him on his ass when he pushed too hard, so Miller sat back and waited quietly until Turner and Weaver finished their conversation.

"Sorry," Miller said, as soon as Turner put the cell phone in the glove compartment.

"You're an asshole."

"It's not Weaver," Miller said. "Metcalf makes me nuts."

"Actually, you're nuts most of the time. If you don't put a lid on it, you're gonna lose this job." Turner was tired of trying to keep him out of trouble. "Metcalf's looking for a way to dump you before your tour is over, and you're making it easy for him."

"So, what's new?"

"No, this time he's gonna do it. Jenny told me you and Vogel are on the official hit list."

Miller studied his face for signs that this was just another empty threat. "He's got to have a reason."

"You give him ten reasons every day. All he needs is to keep good books. And don't think Earl and Tony aren't taking notes for him."

"Shitheads."

"I'm not saying pretend to be something you're not. Just be smarter."

Miller smiled. "Okay, mom, I get the message. Call Reg, too. I'm gonna try to sneak another look in that apartment." He was out the door and back on the street. The morning's grey light didn't offer much cover as he walked briskly toward a two-story white building. In a few seconds, he disappeared behind the driveway hedges.

Turner shook his head. It was the reasonable, balanced Miller again. He knew the transformation wouldn't last.

Less than thirty minutes after being called, Reggie was parked around the corner from the apartment building. The others arrived within the hour. They had barely settled in with their first cup of coffee when Miller walked down the driveway and back to Turner's car. He climbed in the passenger seat and exhaled.

"Let me see those DMV pictures," Miller said and added, "we're too late."

Turner opened his casebook to the section with the driver license photos and handed them to Miller. The pictures weren't clear, but good enough.

"Too late for what?"

"This guy and him." Miller pointed to two of the photos, a young-looking dark-skinned boy with a shaved head and a tattooed older dark-skinned guy who was six feet three and weighed 250 pounds.

"They're in the apartment with Cullen and Goodman?" Turner asked, still wondering who was too late for what.

"They are now, but I think they killed somebody last night while we were chasing the lightweight drunks."

Turner asked Patty to take the point and told everyone else to meet in the parking lot behind the Albertson's market on Sepulveda. Weaver was waiting when Turner pulled into the lot. He didn't look pleased. Getting out of bed in the middle of the night to drive from Pasadena to West L.A. for half an hour of surveillance didn't sit well with him. Turner had taken charge and was calling the shots. That wasn't making Weaver happy either because he didn't like anyone usurping his authority or worse, acting as if he could do the supervisor's job. The final straw was when Miller laughed at Weaver's pillow hair.

"You and Turner better have something fucking phenomenal, or I'm sending the both of you to bunco-forgery for the rest of your careers."

"I heard these guys talking about a killing last night," Miller said quickly and held up the two DMV photos. He paused but already had everyone's attention. "Some kind of initiation for the younger one . . . random violence . . . prove you can do it."

"Where, who?" Weaver asked. He was looking at Turner, but Turner shrugged. Miller hadn't shared this with him.

"Best I could tell, West Hollywood. Some poor fag walking his dog," Miller continued.

"Did you check with the Sheriffs? Does any of it fit?"

"I checked," Miller said. He avoided eye contact with Turner. He hadn't revealed any of this information, and Turner knew why. Miller would show all of them they couldn't afford to dump him. "Sheriffs had a homicide on Melrose about nine last night. The guy was shot in the face. No wits, no prints, no motive, nothing taken, stolen gun left at the scene . . . the perfect senseless crime."

"Do we go in and drag them out of there?" Turner asked Weaver.

"No," Reggie answered before Weaver could. "We can't prove anything, and we let them know we're watching."

"Get a warrant. There's always some evidence." Turner didn't like the idea of letting killers run free.

"And what if they didn't do it, and there's nothing there? They'll find a hole and hide or be a lot more careful," Reggie said.

"This isn't an IA case anymore. We're talking Robbery Homicide and SIS surveillance." Turner knew he was saying what Weaver was thinking. Special Investigation Section working with RHD was supposed to handle high profile cases.

"Fuck SIS," Miller said. "We take down bad cops, not SIS. We've got experience here. This is our case."

"We would need to use both our squads," Weaver said.

Turner stared at Weaver. Was his boss saying he wanted to keep this case when it would be so easy to pass it on to RHD? It would be smart and safe to give this can of worms to anybody else. Was don't-rock-the-boat Weaver actually going to let them keep it?

"We'll see what Metcalf says," Weaver said.

Turner figured his question had been answered.

SOMEHOW, WEAVER convinced Metcalf to go along with IA keeping the investigation. Turner didn't push him for the details, but suspected the prospect of several cops being involved in criminal activity, despite any reservations Metcalf might've had, made the case fit the internal surveillance profile better than that of Robbery Homicide and SIS. It probably helped that the guys at SIS hated working any investigation that targeted fellow police officers. Most officers despised bad cops, but got all queasy when it came to putting on the handcuffs and booking a brother in blue. Turner didn't share their reticence. As far as he was concerned, bad cops were fair game.

Metcalf showed up at the Chinatown office and appeared to be more jittery than usual. He clearly craved the glory of making arrests in this case, but feared the fallout if something went wrong. He ordered Weaver to report to him twice a day until all the renegade officers were in custody.

SIX

Miller was devastated when he found out Beverly Conner preferred to date Turner. He was convinced that another night in the bar was all he needed to win her over. She had agreed to meet Turner for lunch at a little coffee shop in Van Nuys.

Over Turner's strong protests, Weaver ordered him to wear a wire. Turner argued that lunch with a middle-aged, female bartender shouldn't require such extreme precautions. It was unnecessary. One-on-one conversation with a woman, Weaver countered, was a formula for disaster.

Of course, the boss was right, but there was a reason Turner rarely worked undercover. He didn't like lying to people, pretending to be someone he wasn't, and having the whole squad listen to his performance. He'd hoped Miller would've been the one to hook up with Conner's mother. Instead, he found himself in a position he'd always avoided—the center of attention.

He went home for breakfast and a few hours sleep before his meeting with Beverly Conner. Miriam seemed interested when he told her what he was doing. She wanted to know all the details and listened intently. She usually didn't care about his work unless it was something that might end up on the six o'clock news or involved her in some way.

"Just be yourself," she said. "Let her do the talking and don't do anything you can't tell me about."

"I feel stupid doing this," he said, "but don't worry. She's too old for me. I don't know why I let Reggie talk me into that bar."

"Better you than Miller," Miriam said, taking a gulp of coffee. "From what you said, her son's a bad guy. She's gotta know

64

what's going on, so buck up, lover. You're doing the right thing."
Then in the same breath added, "If you don't want to do it, don't
do it," wiped her mouth with a dishtowel, and kissed him while
he was still chewing his toast. "Gotta run. You'll be great," she
said with her back to him, disappearing out the kitchen door.

He sat at the breakfast table for a few more minutes thinking
about Conner's mother. Maybe it wasn't the wire that was bothering him. Maybe it was pretending to be something he wasn't
with that particular woman. He couldn't deny that he liked
Beverly Conner. Maybe that's why he'd told Miriam every detail
about this case. He was feeling guilty. Beverly was older than
him, but he'd felt comfortable and relaxed with her.

"I really like you, Mrs. Conner. You don't mind if I put your
kid in prison or maybe shoot him before we start a serious
relationship, do you?" He figured saying it out loud would
make this foolish idea go away. It didn't. She was fogging up
his brain and doing what no other woman had done for a long
time . . . pushing Miriam out of his head.

TONY'S WAS a favorite diner for many of the officers who worked
the Valley. Beverly Conner had embraced the lifestyle of a
working cop better than her son. She liked being around the
men and women in blue and seemed to know all their hangouts,
even suggesting this location when Turner drew a blank looking
for a place to meet.

After a nap, Turner made a quick stop downtown to pick up
the transmitter. It looked like an ordinary pen that sat unob-
trusively in his jacket pocket. The squad would be set up outside the restaurant half an hour before he got there. Weaver's
second squad would watch the apartment on Bentley waiting for
Goodman, Cullen and their buddies to do something.

Beverly was waiting outside Tony's smoking a cigarette as
Turner parked in the red zone across the street. He'd borrowed
a car from his old narcotics squad just in case she was more

involved than he wanted to believe and managed to jot down his license number.

As he waited for the traffic to clear, a trickle of sweat ran along the side of his face, and he could smell the aftershave that Miriam had given him last Christmas. He'd never worn it and worried it might be too much. With new Levi's, polished boots and that unfamiliar odor all over his face, he flashed back to his first high school date. It wasn't just another case. She smiled at him and threw her cigarette on the sidewalk.

Her frizzy red hair was almost orange in the sunlight. She wore a sage green, off-the-shoulder sweater with tight black spandex pants that flaunted her full, womanly figure. He thought her pale smooth skin made her look much younger than her age. It was a graveyard-shift pallor that suited her. Despite her slender figure, Miriam was athletic. If Beverly liked sports, they must have been the indoor variety.

"They saved me a table," she said, taking hold of his arm and leading him toward the front door. This close to her, Turner could smell her perfume. It was strong, but not unpleasant. Her arm rubbed against his. "I like your boots, cowboy," she said. He smiled. Miriam hated his boots. She complained that they made him look like a bumpkin and a redneck.

"Sorry, I'm late," he said. He was on time but couldn't think of anything else to say.

They sat at a corner table in front of a bay window facing the sidewalk. Turner thought the seating arrangement, at least, should make it easy for the surveillance guys. The waitress knew Beverly and took their order while joking about a mutual friend, a married captain that the young girl was dating.

"Are you nervous?" Beverly asked when they were alone again.

"No," he answered, truthfully.

"I am. I don't usually give my number to strangers or meet with them after a ten-minute conversation. You're gonna think I'm just saying that, but it's true."

If Miller was listening to the wire, Turner could imagine him saying something stupid at that point.

"I believe you. You're a nice woman."

She smiled a nervous, timid smile that took him by surprise. She might've even blushed a little. She wasn't that bold woman he'd met at the bar.

"So, are you married?" she asked in between sips of water.

He laughed at her bluntness. "No, but I have a dependent, an eight-year-old Basset hound."

"I've got a twenty-eight-year-old baby at home." It was meant to be funny but neither of them laughed.

"What's the story with him?" Turner figured he might as well get down to business.

"I don't wanna talk about Ian."

"Maybe I can help."

She studied his face. "Maybe," she said.

Their food arrived before he could pursue the subject. They ate and talked about the police department and officers she'd met at The Tavern. He managed not to tell her too much about himself and tried to think of a way to turn the conversation back to Ian Conner. She liked talking about her property and her plan to eventually board horses. After a barrage of questions and his insistence on not talking about anything else, she finally invited him out to see her house and land.

"I'd like to. It sounds great," he said, trying to sound surprised at the offer, but he'd never worked so hard to get an invitation.

"We can go after lunch if you want to follow me out there."

He agreed and excused himself to go to the men's room. His cell phone rang before he'd taken half a dozen steps away from the table.

"Hi Grandpa," he said, thinking it was Weaver.

"Hi Asshole," Miller responded. "I can't believe you're hitting on that old woman."

"Get over it," Turner said, as he entered the empty restroom. "It's a job." He hoped that sounded more convincing to Miller than it did to him.

"Reggie's set up at her house. Ian's home. Weaver says get a look in that barn . . . cowboy," Miller said, but added, "you okay with this?"

"I gotta get back. Just wanted to make sure you heard I was going out there." Turner put the cell phone in his pocket and was tempted to turn off his pen. Weaver would kill him if he did, but he might do it anyway before he got to her house. What if Ian was smart enough to search him? A close inspection would reveal that it wasn't a real pen, not exactly what a guy wears on a first date.

About half an hour later, he was parking on her dirt driveway. As he got out of his car, he tried not to look up at the hill where Reggie would be watching him. In a few seconds, Weaver should realize the transmitter wasn't working. Almost on cue, his cell phone rang.

"I left it in the car," Turner said before Weaver could ask. He waited until his boss had finished the long list of his mental deficiencies. When there was silence on the other end of the phone, Turner said, "Reggie will know if things go sideways. Besides, I've got my phone." He ended the conversation as Beverly got close enough to hear.

"Everything okay?" she asked.

"Work . . . we're starting early today, but I've still got plenty of time," he said. The lies were coming easier.

She took his hand and pulled him toward the ranch-style house with a wraparound front porch.

"Good."

Ian Conner was sprawled on the couch in the living room watching a big screen television when Beverly opened the door. He glanced toward them, but immediately went back to staring at the screen. Turner looked around at the comfortable well-furnished room with a mixed décor of country and early fifties. It was a woman's space, with spindly oak furniture, colorful pillows, afghans, and a collection of dolls and porcelain figurines, the sort of place Daryl could destroy in an afternoon.

She introduced her son who put out his hand without moving from his position on the couch. Turner leaned over and shook hands. Although he had a strong grip, Ian's arms looked soft and flabby, and his tight-fitting t-shirt revealed a substantial belly. The big redhead was obviously out of condition. He had his mother's fair skin and carrot-colored hair, but none of her personality. After a mumbled hello, he clicked off the television and left the room without another word.

"Sorry," she said, after a few seconds of awkward silence.

"What does he do all day?" Turner asked. He knew about some of the young man's activities, but saw his rudeness as an opportunity to get more information.

She moved closer and started to whisper until she noticed her son walking outside past the bay window, going toward the barn.

"I wish I knew. I know people have been here while I'm at work. More food and beer than even Ian could eat is missing, and dirt's tracked everywhere. When I ask, he's real secretive, says a couple of friends."

"Maybe that's all it is."

"I don't think so," she said, nervously looking out the window. She studied Turner's face, still not certain how much she should confide in him. "I found something on my property . . . like a militia thing."

"What kind of militia thing?" Turner asked, attempting to sound only mildly interested. He wanted her to keep talking, but he was afraid to push too hard. She was protective of her loutish son.

"Those training camps with targets and stuffed dummies you pretend to kill . . . bullets everywhere. They're shooting a lot. I don't hear it, but I don't know why the neighbors haven't called the cops."

"You've seen empty casings?"

"Tons."

Great, he thought, these assholes probably have silencers, too. "Where's the camp?"

She stared at him, but didn't answer. He knew he'd made a mistake by asking too much, too soon.

"Why?" she asked.

"Figured I'd take a look. Lots of guys have setups to practice tactics and shooting, especially when they've been off a while," he said, and saw her shoulders relax a little. "Maybe it's nothing, and I can put your mind at ease."

"Okay, but not while he's home. I don't want him to know I've seen it."

"Are you afraid of him?" Turner asked, thinking out loud. It wouldn't be the first time a mother had been bullied and abused by her son.

She laughed without smiling. "He's my kid. I don't want him to think I'm spying. He's bitter enough already."

Turner was prepared to drop the subject. He decided he'd pried out all the useful information he was going to get from her. He asked to see the rest of the house, and she readily agreed. She seemed relieved to talk about something else. As he expected, the house was clean and well kept. The only room he didn't have access to was Ian's. The door was locked, but he knew when the time came Reggie could find a way to get inside.

"How about the barn and storage shed?" he asked, as soon as she finished the house tour.

"I'd show you, but there's really not much to see out there, yet," she said, looking out the window. After a few seconds, she turned back to him and said, "The truth is I hate to bother him. He goes there to be alone."

"Maybe I can help, get him to talk to me."

She thought about it for a moment and then touched his arm. "You're a good man," she said, and led the way out the kitchen door toward the barn. He felt like a heel. She trusted him, and just like her no-good son, he was lying to her.

The musty smelling barn was almost as big as the house. It had eight stalls and a loft, but there weren't any horses or hay. From the look of the place, there hadn't been any for a very long time. It was empty except for a covered car parked against the back wall. Ian was gone.

Turner wandered through the stalls pretending to examine the workmanship. He was hoping to find a hidden automatic weapon or two.

"You don't have horses?" he asked.

"Not yet, but I will." She followed him into the last stall and seemed nervous, as if she expected Ian to jump out at her.

"Appears your son's gone," Turner said, peeking in the corner. He casually lifted the car cover for a quick look. The front license plate was gone, but it looked like a new yellow Corvette. "Nice ride—yours?" he asked.

She stared at the car and shook her head. "He must be keeping it for one of his friends." She took another long look around the barn. "Ian?" she called.

There was no answer. She smiled weakly at Turner, but her thoughts were obviously somewhere else, and the gesture faded quickly.

"Want me to go?" he asked. He guessed Ian had removed anything of interest while they were in the house.

"I'm sorry," she said, still preoccupied. "I wish he hadn't been here. Today wasn't supposed to be about my son. I just wanted to spend some time with you." She turned and slid her arms around his waist, hugging him before he realized what was happening.

Turner wrapped his arms around her and held her close for a few seconds. She was warm and smelled like gardenias. He imagined she would be an easy woman to love and wished they had met at another time, in some other way.

"Gotta get to work," he said, not loosening his embrace. "Maybe we can get together tomorrow."

"Come to the bar," she whispered, arching her head back and stretching to kiss him before he could answer. Her breath was an unpleasant mix of stale cigarettes and beer, but her moist lips rubbed softly against his mouth, and her breasts touched his chest in a way that made him wish they really were alone. He'd be surprised if Miller wasn't leaning against the outside wall,

71

peering through the same gap in the wood where he'd spied on Ian and his friends.

She walked with him to his car and continued to wave as he retreated in a cloud of red dust down her long driveway to the county road. He watched her standing in front of the barn until she gradually disappeared from his rearview mirror. He felt guilty again about his feelings toward her. She was an uncomplicated, attractive woman with a dipshit kid. At some point, Turner would probably arrest her son or worse. Beverly was most likely only a bit player in an investigation that might include murder, but Turner wouldn't allow himself to get involved with her. He was going to use her and lie to her. She would hate him when this was over, regardless of how it ended, but he knew the rules. As much as he might think he liked her and wanted her, he wanted this job a lot more.

SEVEN

The squad met with Turner behind an abandoned gas station several miles from the Conner house. He told them about the training camp, but was surprised to learn they not only knew about the camp, but had seen it. Reggie had the point on the hill when Ian left the house. He saw Ian enter the barn and immediately go out the back door. Patty followed him; she hid behind trees and heavy brush until he reached a small clearing. The camp was just as Beverly had described it to Turner.

Patty had hidden and watched as Ian stored the targets and dummies in a large wooden box that he dropped into a trench covered by a piece of plywood. He shoveled dirt on the plywood and then threw leaves and dead shrubs on the dirt. Ian carefully collected the empty bullet casings from the ground, tossing them into a large canvas bag that he took with him. When he walked away, there was no sign of the camp. He finished his cleanup just minutes after Turner drove off the property.

"I must've made him nervous," Turner said, leaning against his car as the rest of the squad gathered around him. "Maybe mom doesn't usually bring cops to the house."

Miller was quiet. If he'd seen the kiss, he wasn't going to say anything. Either he hadn't been peeking through the gap in the barn wall, or he saw it but didn't want Weaver to cut off Turner's head. Turner figured if he owed Miller for keeping his mouth shut, at some point, Miller would make him pay.

"Conner's probably being careful," Reggie said. "He doesn't know you, and he doesn't know how much of the property his mother's going to show you."

"I don't think so," Patty said. She was sitting on the hood of Weaver's Toyota and looked like a teenager in her low cut jeans and short leather coat. Her mousy brown hair was tucked into a baseball cap. She rarely spoke up at these debriefings, so everyone turned to listen. "It looked permanent, like he was shutting down for good." She spoke softly, still intimidated by her lack of tenure, but the fact that she was the only one who had seen the camp gave her some courage.

"Does he know we're watching him?" Turner asked, thinking out loud. Nobody answered. They looked at each other and then at Weaver, wondering what he would do next.

The boss didn't hesitate. "Set up on the house again. Whatever he's doing, we need to be there. I'll keep the other squad on Goodman and Cullen."

"Thanks," Turner said to Miller as they walked back to their cars.

"For what?"

"For not saying anything about what happened in the barn."

Miller smiled, and Turner figured payback was imminent. Instead Miller said, "I wasn't watching the barn; Earl was." He stopped and folded his arms. "Is there something I should know? Did you molest that poor old woman?"

"Shit," Turner whispered. He watched Earl drive out of the parking lot without so much as a glance at him. His mind quickly devised a defense for the questions Metcalf would certainly ask. Kissing and hugging her were part of the deception, the role he was forced to play. The lieutenant might be persuaded that was the truth, but Turner wasn't convinced.

In a few minutes, they were back in their cars and set up around the Conner property. Turner took the point on the hill, feeling uneasy as he scanned the grounds for Ian's jeep. He had Miller move closer on foot to search for the car, but it wasn't there.

The squad stayed, but Conner and the jeep never returned. At midnight, Weaver called the other squad and had them verify that Goodman and Cullen were still in the West L.A. apartment. He sent Earl and Tony to the house listed in personnel records as the residence of Goodman and Cullen. The jeep wasn't there or at any of the other addresses Turner had taken from the DMV's. None of the cars they'd seen at Ian's house were at any of the known locations.

The other squad hadn't seen any of the players leave the West L.A. apartment, but they were gone. Weaver went to Pacific and Hollywood divisions to check the timebooks. Shortly before their watches were scheduled to begin, both Cullen and Goodman had called in and taken the night off.

As the reports came back, Turner had a sick feeling. He was afraid something was going to happen that night or had already happened, and they just hadn't heard about it. He monitored the desk at Detective Services. All major events were reported to that group so the night watch commander could dispatch the chief's duty officer to the scene of homicides or unusual occurrences. The detective on duty said it was a quiet night. He hadn't had one call all evening.

Weaver kept the squad in Santa Clarita until daybreak. Ian Conner never returned. Cullen and Goodman never came back and none of Ian's buddies could be found. The squad managed to get back to their Chinatown office shortly before the rush hour traffic inundated the downtown streets.

They could have gone home, but no one wanted to leave. Even Earl and Tony stayed. Turner kept calling the detective desk, but nothing was happening. He worried that today might be the gang's big score, the one Miller had heard them talking about. He wanted to warn someone, but didn't know who, where or when.

A couple of times, Weaver ordered them to go home, but they couldn't seem to break away from each other. He threatened to leave, but sat at his desk and drank coffee. They discussed possible scenarios—Ian moved the training camp to a more isolated location. Ian spotted the surveillance and went underground; or the least palatable explanation, Ian and his Valley boys were in the middle of a bank robbery, and any minute something like the North Hollywood shootout would begin.

75

Turner felt as if he had failed. He knew Metcalf would see it that way, too, unless they could find one of these guys and pick up the surveillance again. His embrace with Ian's mother wouldn't help his case either. He hadn't talked to Ian long enough to make him suspicious. Beverly must have seen or heard something. He was such an idiot. She was playing him.

About 11 A.M., the crazy psychiatrist knocked twice and then three times on the office door. Vogel and Miller stood near the door and yanked it open as the knob started to turn. The uncoordinated Lieutenant Metcalf lost his balance and nearly fell into the room, while the office exploded in laughter until they realized who had performed for them. It got quiet just as quickly.

"I'm surprised you're so cheerful considering that fiasco last night," Metcalf said. He tucked his shirt back into his pants and looked around the room. No one argued. Miller turned his back and filled his coffee mug. "We have a shooting victim in West Hollywood and five missing suspects including three police officers." Metcalf, gaining courage, glared at Patty. "I don't get what's so damn funny."

"Actually," Miller started to respond, but Turner cut him off.

"Nobody thinks it's funny, Lieutenant. We've been up all night," Turner said. "I must've blown it. Somehow his mother must have figured it out."

Metcalf sat on Weaver's desk. "When is that moron roaming the hallway going to recognize me? I've been here half a dozen times."

Miller grinned. Turner knew why. Miller had instructed Dr. Tom that Metcalf didn't belong in the building, and told the psychiatrist to warn them whenever the lieutenant arrived.

"It's not your fault, Turner," Weaver said, trying to change the subject. "Something spooked him, or this disappearing act was all planned. You didn't have enough time to make anyone suspicious."

"It's somebody's fault. Three heavily armed cops are missing. What am I supposed to tell the chief of police?" Metcalf asked, looking around at a room full of blank expressions. "We fucked up, Chief, but it's nobody's fault," he said, sarcastically.

Weaver's face flushed, but he didn't say anything. Turner wasn't thinking clearly, or he would've shut up too. Instead, he stepped in front of the lieutenant.

"We don't know what's going on, yet," Turner said. "Don't tell him anything until we figure this out."

Metcalf's expression twisted into a painful smirk. His pencil-thin mustache arched like a black inchworm.

"Who brought you people into this unit? Are you all that stupid? This isn't something I can keep from the chief of police."

Now, Turner was pissed. He couldn't believe this misfit was calling him names. He started to say something, but Reggie interrupted.

"We're end of watch. Let's get out of here," Reggie said, putting his arm around Turner's shoulder and leading him away.

"You're leaving?" Metcalf asked, looking at the faces standing in a circle around him. "You can't. You've got to find them."

"You got any ideas where we might start looking, because we've been everywhere we know about," Miller said. "They ain't there."

"Then we've got to do a press release or something, let the public know they're out there."

"The chief's gonna love that one," Miller said, snorting. "Three renegade cops lost in the city with automatic weapons. They're maybe gonna do something bad, but we don't know what or where or when." Miller leaned back in his chair and scratched his head. "We know this is your baby, Lieutenant. Me and the guys, we hate to see you look bad, so why not give us a day or two to find these assholes, take away their guns, and then we'll all look like LAPD's finest."

Metcalf's brain seemed to freeze. He stared at Miller and then Weaver. The prospect of looking incompetent in the eyes of the chief of police was more terrifying to him than listening to Miller. The fear forced a nervous twitch in the corner of his mouth. The right thing would be to tell the chief and the public about this potentially dangerous situation, but, as Miller suspected, Metcalf wouldn't jeopardize his career.

"You have two days," Metcalf said. "After that I can't protect you any longer."

Turner almost laughed out loud. In two days, Metcalf would find a way to blame the squad and extricate himself from any responsibility. He would deny any knowledge and have a convenient memory lapse about approving any decisions in this case. Weaver would most likely take the fall, and the squad would be disbanded. Turner knew shit rolled down the chain of command, and he was certain Weaver knew that too, but the boss would accept Metcalf's offer of two days because there wasn't any other real choice.

"Let me talk to you outside," Weaver said. He didn't wait for an answer and walked into the hallway. The lieutenant followed quietly, not venturing a glance around the room before pulling the door closed behind him. Everyone inside the room was quiet for a few seconds, maybe hoping to hear the boss shouting at Metcalf. It didn't happen. Turner figured Weaver got the lieutenant out before Miller had a chance to say something that would make matters worse.

"He's one stand-up guy, our lieutenant," Miller said.

Turner grabbed Miller in a playful choke hold. "You're a psycho," Turner said, letting him break loose.

"Maybe, but I'm a psycho with a good job to go back to when asshole pulls the plug on this one."

"We've got two days," Patty said. "All we've got to do is find one of them and let him lead us to the others."

Vogel was at his desk concentrating on a computer screen. He didn't seem to hear or understand what was happening. The prospect of leaving the detail would be hardest for him, Turner thought. Vogel's wife was a witch. She got pregnant so he would marry her, and she constantly badgered him for more money. The overtime he earned working the surveillance squad had temporarily satisfied her. He was away from home a lot because of their crazy hours, but seemed to be happier when he was working. It was no secret Mrs. Vogel wore the pants in that family, and their daughter was a chubby, annoying little replica of mommy.

After ten minutes, Weaver returned. Everyone stopped talking and waited for him to say something, but he walked across the room and sat at his desk without any explanation of what had occurred in the hallway. Turner had hoped he'd convinced Metcalf to give them a few more days, but from the dour expression on Weaver's face, he guessed that hadn't happened.

"Go home," Weaver finally said. "Get some rest. Come back at 1800 hours. I can't think. I'm too tired." He looked around the office. "Where the hell's Tony and Earl?"

For the first time, Turner realized they weren't there. The two men had slipped out sometime during the morning. No one ever paid much attention to them, so it wasn't a surprise that their departure went unnoticed. Reggie and Miller were talking in muffled whispers near the coffeepot. They were looking at the empty desks where Tony and Earl should've been. Turner wasn't surprised they'd deserted. That's what rats do when you start taking on water. He was more concerned as he watched Miller and wondered what he was discussing with Reggie. The only thing worse than either one of them planning something was the two of them plotting together. They were his friends, but Turner felt a lot more comfortable when they ignored each other.

Reggie noticed him staring and ended the conversation. He picked up his utility bag and moved closer to Turner.

"Okay if I stay at your place?" Reggie asked. "Can't sleep at mine during the day, too many kids around."

Turner thought about Miriam but figured she'd be at work until 7 or 8 P.M. "No problem," he said, thinking this might be an opportunity to find out what Reggie and Miller were concocting. Reggie said he had some errands and would meet Turner at the house in about an hour.

Turner needed sleep. Too much energy had been expended figuring out how they had screwed up. What should they do now? That was their real problem. He wondered if Beverly was aware of his lies yet. Why did it bother him that she might think badly of him?

79

EIGHT

The drive home was a blur. Daryl greeted Turner at the door by rubbing against his pant leg and drooling on his shoe. The dog always made him smile, and this morning that was good. Eddie's absence was an unexpected but pleasant circumstance. Turner wouldn't have to explain the night's events again. Miriam had slept here and left her usual trail of debris in the kitchen and bathroom. He was relieved she wasn't home to ask all the questions he didn't want to or couldn't answer.

He was aching to sleep but couldn't stop thinking about the case, and how they could've handled it differently. It was a mess and would probably get worse. They should let the world know these maniacs were out there with havoc on their minds. How stupid would that make the surveillance squad? They'd lost three cops and an assortment of wannabe gangsters with an arsenal of assault rifles, let them loose to prey on innocents. It was only when he convinced himself that in a couple of days he and Reggie could find them that he finally drifted into an uneasy sleep.

Three hours later, he was awake, not completely refreshed, but at least able to think clearly again. Reggie wasn't there. Apparently, he decided to sleep at home. Turner checked the answering machine for messages. It was empty. Miriam hadn't called. Why wasn't she curious about his absence last night? He would have been frantic if he hadn't heard from her for two days. But the mystery of Miriam's feelings was too much to throw into the mix of other worries today.

There was some time before the start of watch. He fed Daryl and ate a couple pieces of leftover pizza that he found in the living room. Eddie hadn't appeared yet. The old man never stayed away this long. Turner pulled back the curtains in the kitchen window and looked at the house next door. It was quiet.

He threw his gear into the backseat of the car and walked across the lawn to the white, craftsman-style home. The front porch was clean with the exception of a few maple leaves scattered around the teak bench and wicker chairs. He knocked and waited, no answer. The front door was locked. Eddie's grey Malibu was parked in the driveway in front of the garage where it had been sitting for at least a year.

Turner unlatched the side gate and entered the backyard. A spare key was hidden under a loose brick on the patio. He unlocked the rear door and stepped inside the musty-smelling utility room. The house was quiet and cold. He called Eddie's name and felt a chill when there wasn't any answer.

Eddie was there in the living room, sitting in front of a dead fire. Wrapped in his favorite flannel bathrobe, he held an empty whiskey glass. A half-empty bottle of Jim Beam sat on the small table beside him.

"You alright, partner?" Turner whispered. Eddie nodded, but wouldn't look at him. "Bad night?"

"Don't never have no ingrate children," the old man said, and slammed the glass on the table.

"What happened?" Turner didn't want to do this. He hated getting involved in other people's lives. For twenty years, he'd solved strangers' problems, but this was Eddie.

"Nothin'"

"Must've been about a half bottle's worth of something," Turner said, trying not to smile, relieved his friend wasn't dead but just drunk.

Eddie looked up at him. "Don't you be laughin' at my misery, punk."

"Sorry, I was worried you were hurt or something." Turner pulled over a footstool and rubbed the old man's leg. "Tell me what happened. Maybe I can help."

"Wish I'd fall down and break my neck, so I don't have to look at his sneaky face no more."

"Who?"

"Danny, who you think."

"Your son?"

"'Course my son. How many Danny's I know? He wants to sell my place and put me on the street. Thinks I need some a that . . . what'd he call it . . . assisted livin' shit. I don't need assisted. I need to be let alone." Eddie was trying not to cry, but the tears came, and he couldn't keep them from spilling. He rubbed his eyes with the bathrobe sleeve. "My grave is where he's gonna put me."

"Don't let him. He can't sell unless you agree," Turner said. He knew he should stay out of this. It was family business, but Eddie didn't deserve to be warehoused.

Eddie stared at his hands and was quiet for a few seconds. "Yes, he can," he whispered. "I put the house in his name, case somethin' happen to me." He straightened up. "He promised I could stay here long as I lived," he said in a strong voice. "I'll die before I go live in a old folks home."

"The house is in his name, not both of you?" Turner asked, and Eddie shook his head. "Fight him."

"I ain't got no money, and I'm eighty-three years old. How'm I gonna fight him with all his money and his drinkin' buddies sittin' in the courthouse?"

Turner knew what he shouldn't say, but it was on the tip of his tongue. Move in with me. He couldn't speak the words. It was a significant commitment, not to mention how much it would piss off the young Commander Jones. When this Conner fiasco was over, he might still have a career. Eddie's son was in a position to make Turner's job as miserable as he was about to make his father's life.

"You want me to talk to Danny?" he asked instead.

"Won't do no good," Eddie said, leaning back in the leather recliner, taking a deep breath, and exhaling as if he'd been climbing a mountain. "Got a head like your cement driveway."

Turner picked up the empty glass and screwed the top on the bottle.

82

"I'm gonna put these away. You try to get some sleep and let me see what I can do," he said, straightening the collar of Eddie's bathrobe. He patted the old man on the shoulder, and put the whiskey on a bookshelf near the kitchen where Eddie kept his brandy and two bottles of expensive wine Turner had given him last Christmas. He rinsed out the glass in the kitchen sink and took a quick look in the refrigerator. The top shelf was full of beer. There was a bag of beef jerky and a half-eaten sandwich, but nothing else. Two open bags of Doritos and a jar of peanuts on the kitchen counter were the only other edible things he saw.

The pantry contained a few cans of tomato soup, a jar of peanut butter, and a box of graham crackers. This was how Turner envisioned Miriam living in about fifty years. The only difference was Eddie was compulsively clean, and Miriam didn't believe in picking up after herself. He sometimes worried that the messiness around her reflected her state of mind, and when she was Eddie's age she'd be that crazy old lady living with stacks of newspapers, nine cats, and tin foil wrapped around her head to keep the alien radio signals out. He closed the cupboard and took a peek into the living room before he left. He heard gravelly, uneven snoring coming from the frail shape on the chair. He and Danny Jones needed to talk, but they might have a lot more to discuss than where Eddie should live.

THE SQUAD met at the office shortly before 6 P.M. Turner tried to call Miriam to ask her to check on Eddie. She wasn't at her office or at home. So he left a message on her cell phone voicemail asking her to pick up a healthy dinner for herself and their neighbor. Turner was certain Miriam would do it. She couldn't remember to lock the front door, but retrieved her messages religiously, and she cared about Eddie.

He didn't have long to worry about his neighbor. Weaver was stomping around the room demanding a game plan.

"Give me something, anything. We have two days to get this case back on track. I need some fucking place to start," Weaver shouted. "Where the hell are Earl and Tony?" he asked without taking a breath.

"MIA," Miller said. "I left a message on their answering machines telling them our start time."

"Metcalf took them out of the field to work inside with him," Vogel said.

"Who told you that?" Weaver's face was flushed. He was angry and embarrassed. The lieutenant was working around him.

"Tony called me this morning," Vogel said, trying not to look at Miller. "Earl and him asked to leave the squad, and Metcalf's going to let them go back to investigations."

"How about you, Vogel? You ask to leave, too?" Miller asked, staring at his partner.

Beads of sweat were forming above Vogel's upper lip. He ignored Miller. "We don't need them. We still got six cars," he said.

Turner figured he wasn't the only one who realized that Vogel had avoided answering Miller's question.

"Hey, Turner, you got a call," Patty hollered from across the room. It was Jenny from IA.

"Tell her I just left," he said. He wasn't in the mood to deal with Jenny this morning.

"She says it's important," Patty said, grinning.

"What's up, Jenny?" he asked, snatching the phone from Patty.

"Bad morning, Turner?" Jenny asked with a snort.

"I'm busy, Jenny."

"You had a call from a Sergeant Alex Gomez. He wants you to call him."

Turner closed his eyes and gently tapped the receiver against his head before saying anything. "Why would I want to talk to him? We just caught him playing doctor with a drag queen. Tell him to call the Protective League."

"He says he knows about a cop that's going to kill somebody, and he'll only talk to you."

A warning light came on in Turner's brain. It was telling him to hang up and stay away from this screwed-up sergeant, but this wasn't the kind of offer he could ignore, and Gomez knew it. "Why me?" he asked.

"He says you treated him with respect, and he wants to do you a favor. Call him; don't call him. Do what you want," she said, and gave him the number before hanging up.

"You ready to do some work, Turner?" Weaver asked, standing over his desk.

"Hold on, boss. Let me take care of this."

"When you get done with your personal stuff, get me on the air. We're gonna check all the locations again."

Turner repeated what Jenny had told him. He and Weaver both knew he couldn't ignore the sergeant's call.

"I don't need this now," Turner said as he dialed the number Jenny had given him.

Gomez wouldn't talk to him on the phone, but gave him an address in Hollywood where they could meet. He wanted Turner to come alone, but relented after Turner refused to go without Reggie and gave Gomez all the reasons why that was a really bad idea.

The surveillance squad had worked several cases during the past year. With Turner's help, some dirty cops got fired or resigned. A couple of them went to jail. Others were cleared of any wrongdoing. It was a great feeling when he proved a cop wasn't doing anything wrong, but this was the first time he had to talk to one of them after he'd helped take the guy's job away. He wasn't sorry Gomez couldn't be a cop anymore, but it was a strange sensation to come back and face the consequences of his work. He didn't want to see Gomez or talk to him, but this wasn't the kind of information he could dismiss without at least checking it out.

The address was a shabby two-story motel on Gower. The aroma of disinfectant mixed with the sweet smell of burning incense hung like a cloud in front of the manager's door. An older Armenian woman carrying a baby unlocked the security screen after Turner pressed his badge against the dense black mesh. She directed them to room number nine on the second floor. Turner could see every door from the courtyard. The building looked deserted. Shades were drawn in all the windows that weren't covered with aluminum foil. Weeds grew like bushes between the blocks of broken concrete. Pieces of a cheap Japanese fountain had been piled against the building. The place gave him a bad feeling, and he noticed Reggie slide his hand over his Glock semi-auto as they climbed the stairs.

Before they reached the room, Gomez stepped outside. He didn't offer to shake hands, and Turner was grateful. Gomez was gaunt; his pale skin had blotches of red that came and went like a blinking neon light when he was nervous. His thinning black hair was combed to one side, and for the first time, Turner noticed that the guy's left eye was slightly crossed. He hadn't realized how much he had focused on the uniform that night. He saw a bad cop and never really noticed this damaged man.

Reggie continued to scan the area, watching for anything that might signal danger, and never bothered to acknowledge Gomez who ignored him as well.

"What's this all about, Gomez?" Turner asked, impatiently.

"This is my cousin's place," Gomez said. He sounded hoarse and coughed a few times. "She's not legal, so she wants to stay away from the police. I convinced her to talk to you."

"What about the fact that I'm a cop?"

"I told her you don't care about her status. She's really upset. I think she'd talk to you anyway," Gomez said, ignoring Turner's question and opening the apartment door.

Helen Sanchez was a pretty, dark-skinned Mexican woman who looked to be in her early thirties. She was nearly five feet tall and probably weighed less than ninety pounds, but she stared straight into Turner's eyes when he talked to her. If she was afraid of the police, she wasn't going to let him know it. Her place was cluttered but clean. Boxes were stacked in the hallway leading to the bedroom. She explained that she and her sister had finally saved enough money to move to a nicer place. When she talked about her sister, tears streamed down the sides of her face. She didn't wipe them and kept talking.

"Ramona was killed three nights ago, one block from this terrible place," she said. Helen took a picture from one of the boxes and showed Turner an unsmiling, overweight woman who barely resembled her sister.

"You think a police officer killed her?" Turner asked.

"Yes, I think that's so," she said and hesitated. She glanced at Gomez, and he nodded at her to continue. "She cleans a house in the hills for a very rich man. A policeman, he comes to the house when the man is robbed."

"Somebody broke into the house?" Reggie asked. He sat on the couch near Turner and was beginning to get interested.

"Yes," she said. "The man he doesn't care about the stolen things, but complains about his business partner to the policeman. He would like his partner to go away forever. My Ramona is cleaning in the next room. She hears this. The policeman he says he can fix the rich man's problem for maybe fifty thousand dollars." Helen stopped talking and put both hands over her mouth as if she had remembered something awful. She composed herself and continued. "The policeman he sees my sister when he goes out. She pretends she doesn't hear or understand, but the policeman, he knows. She tells me she's very frightened and never will go back to that house, but then she's dead, murdered. That policeman, he killed her."

"Do you know where she was working?" Turner asked.

Helen gave him the address in the Hollywood Hills and all the information on her sister. Reggie called Hollywood division detectives, and they read him the homicide report on Ramona Sanchez . . . unknown suspect(s), no witnesses, a stolen gun left at the scene, another senseless, seemingly unsolvable killing like the one in West Hollywood two nights ago. The detectives also located the burglary report from the house in the Hollywood Hills. The routine report had been taken four days ago at 1500 hours by Officer Andy Cullen.

NINE

With the only witness dead, Turner hoped Officer Cullen would feel comfortable keeping in touch with Ramona's former employer. Fifty thousand dollars should be enough incentive to keep him interested. The only hitch would be if the contract killing had already been carried out. One way to know for certain was to confront the homeowner.

Weaver was desperate for a link back to the renegade cops. As soon as Turner called him, he had the squad watching the house in the Hollywood Hills. When Turner arrived, the point advised him that an older man and woman were the only two occupants. There had been no sign of Cullen.

James Sheffield opened the door cautiously. He had to be in his eighties, but still had thick white hair and was dressed in a sharp, three-piece business suit in the middle of the day. After Turner identified himself and Reggie, the elderly man's cheeks turned a shade of splotchy pink.

"Are you with him?" Sheffield asked in a shaky whisper.

"Who?" Reggie asked, looking over his shoulder.

"The other one . . . I want this to end." Sheffield rubbed his hands together. Turner thought he was about to cry.

Turner talked him into letting them come inside the house where they found Sheffield's fragile wife hiding behind the door. With some coaxing, Sheffield agreed to talk to them. It was obvious the man was terrified, but he decided to trust them. Cullen had come to his house initially to take a burglary report. Sheffield said he foolishly complained about his business partner and might have wished out loud that he were dead. Cullen immediately offered to eliminate the partner for a price.

"James didn't mean anything by it," Mrs. Sheffield said. "He's so passionate about everything," she smiled, sheepishly, as if she'd spoken out of turn.

"Did he say eliminate or kill?" Turner asked.

"Make him disappear permanently is what he said. My wife is sick. She can't endure this. He keeps coming back. Last night, he climbed over the garden wall. My God, we found him in the kitchen." Sheffield was walking in circles around the coffee table. "He's coming again tonight for my answer. Can't you do something?"

"Did he say what time?" Reggie asked.

"I don't want him here," Sheffield pleaded.

"What time?" Turner repeated.

"Eight o'clock. He wants to see the money. I don't have fifty thousand dollars."

"Do you think you could meet with him one more time?" Turner asked, checking his watch. He would have five hours to find the money.

"Look at me. I can't stop my hands from shaking. I'm afraid of him."

"You won't be alone. We'll protect you. If he takes the money and offers to kill your partner, we can arrest him and put him away for a long time."

"Aren't you listening to me? I don't have the money." The old man's throat was dry with fear. He was choking on his words.

"We've got the money," Turner lied.

"He'll do it," Mrs. Sheffield said, calmly. She winked at her husband who sighed and went to sit quietly beside her.

Turner explained that someone would be watching the house in case Cullen came back early, and he told the couple not to leave or call anyone. He promised to be back in less than two hours with the money and additional officers.

Sheffield seemed to relax a little. He followed them down the driveway thanking them, until Turner advised him to go back inside the house in case Cullen drove by.

It wasn't difficult to convince Weaver that putting a case on Cullen was a good idea. Cullen probably killed Ramona Sanchez or had her killed, but they couldn't prove it. Conspiracy to commit murder or attempted murder of Sheffield's partner was a charge that might give them the leverage they needed to make Cullen give up Conner, Goodman and the rest of the Valley boys for some kind of deal. Cullen could become a valuable witness.

If Sheffield kept his nerves intact, they might be able to pull this off. The only glaring problem was finding the money. Turner had two hours to do it, but trying to convince Lieutenant Metcalf to help them wasted nearly the first hour. Metcalf claimed that trusting the surveillance squad with fifty thousand dollars would be stupid. He suggested that Weaver abandon the sting operation and watch Sheffield's house. Cullen would eventually return, and they could arrest him without risking any of the city's cash.

"It's bad enough already," Metcalf said, "you people lost three heavily-armed rogue cops. I'm not about to give you the opportunity to lose fifty thousand dollars."

Miller waited quietly until Metcalf left their office, then immediately contacted a narcotics lieutenant he knew at Asset Forfeiture to borrow the fifty thousand dollars kept for flash money on narcotic buys. The money was delivered personally by the lieutenant who owed Miller a big favor because he'd testified at the man's divorce hearing and saved his pension, but the lieutenant wasn't too comfortable letting that much cash out of his sight. No one, except Weaver, seemed bothered by the fact that they were blatantly ignoring Metcalf's wishes.

"Metcalf's wrong, boss," Turner argued when Weaver was about to shut down the operation and return the money and the lieutenant to Narcotics Division. "Cullen is the only way we'll find the others. If you stop this, Ramona Sanchez and that guy in West Hollywood won't be the last victims."

"Go home, boss," Miller added. "You don't have to know about this. Me and Reg and Turner can take the heat. The squad's toast anyway, so we'll do what we gotta do."

Weaver looked as if he'd been slapped. Turner recognized the expression. He'd seen it before when a guy had been cajoled by Miller to do something really stupid. The squad leader fell into the trap and took charge again as if the whole operation were his idea.

In just a little over two hours, Turner and the rest of the surveillance squad except Patty, who'd been stationed outside the Hollywood Hills home, were sitting in the living room watching an electronics expert from Narcotics Division put a tiny transmitter on Sheffield's watch. It became an ordeal as the old man had a massive jangled-nerve attack, wiggling and squirming while the technician attempted to test his sound equipment. Just as the technician was about to give up, Sheffield's wife called her husband into their bedroom, and a few minutes later, he emerged mellow and composed.

"What did you do to him?" Turner asked Mrs. Sheffield.

"I told him to take his Valium."

Turner looked at the subdued man. "How many did he take?"

"I don't know, dear . . . a few."

Sheffield didn't remember how many he'd taken, but his speech while still excessive and annoying was beginning to slur. The drug inhibited his fears, but made it difficult for him to concentrate. Turner worried he wouldn't remember the explicit instructions he'd been given. It was important that Cullen admit, while he was being recorded, that he was taking the money to kill Sheffield's partner. Sheffield had to ask the right questions to illicit incriminating answers. The old man seemed anything but clever at this moment. Turner told him to sit on the couch.

"We have to leave. It's almost time," Turner said, scrutinizing Sheffield's glassy eyes for some sign of intelligence. "Tell me exactly what you're going to say before you show him the money."

"Do you think I should wear this suit, or a sweater and pants? Does a person dress for a . . . what do you call it . . . a payoff?"

"Concentrate, Sheffield, what will you say?"

"About what?"

Turner held Sheffield's face between his hands to keep him from turning away. "What will you say before you show Cullen our money?"

91

Sheffield pushed Turner's hands away. "Please, detective, I'm not a child. I'll simply say that before I produce the money, I want to know exactly what he's going to do for my fifty thousand dollars and how he's going to do it," he said in a steady, coherent voice.

Turner sat back on the couch and saw Reggie grinning at him. He rested his arm on the back of the couch behind Sheffield and held up his middle finger at his partner.

They were gathering their equipment and double-checking the house to be certain there wasn't any evidence that they'd been there, when the phone rang. Cullen was calling to ask Sheffield if he had the money. There were ten people in the living room, but it was as quiet as a cloistered monastery.

"Yes, I have it," Sheffield said. "You want to meet somewhere else?" he said, mimicking Cullen's half of the conversation. He looked at Turner, who nodded thinking it might be better if they met away from the house. Mrs. Sheffield wouldn't be exposed to Cullen. "Where?" Sheffield asked. "I'm sorry my hearing isn't very good. Did you say the parking lot on the southwest corner of Sunset and Western?" Turner mouthed the word, when. "When?" Sheffield asked. "You want to leave it at eight o'clock?" Turner nodded again. "Okay, I'll meet you there in a couple of hours."

Sheffield hung up and exhaled loudly. "Whew, I was so frightened. Did I sound alright? Do you think he knows I wasn't alone? He didn't seem suspicious."

"All he's thinking about is money," Reggie said.

"You did fine," Turner said. He started making plans for the new meet location. He asked Weaver to take what was left of the squad and set up early. The technician had a van that he could park in the lot. Turner would be in the van to hear all the conversation and be certain they had enough to make the arrest. He designated Reggie and Miller to take Cullen into custody and retrieve the money. The narcotics lieutenant volunteered some of his detectives and a helicopter to cover the perimeter to make certain Cullen couldn't escape once he picked up the money. Turner was grateful. His surveillance squad was reduced to only five cars with him sitting in the truck.

At exactly 8 P.M., Sheffield drove into the nearly deserted, well-lighted parking lot on the corner of Sunset and Western. The technician had backed his van into a stall directly across from the spot Turner had told Sheffield to park his black Lexus. The money was in a briefcase in the trunk of the Lexus. Turner monitored Sheffield talking to himself on the short trip from his house to the meet location. The transmitter picked up his rambling monologue on how he was feeling, how the traffic was moving, what he wanted for a late dinner, and an endless litany of complaints. Sheffield had been parked for ten minutes and was singing some obscure show tune when Cullen drove the black and white police cruiser onto the lot.

Turner broadcast the arrival. He knew Cullen hadn't been to work for days and had been carried on the books as AWOL. What he couldn't figure out was how Cullen managed to get the city police car. He was in uniform and wearing the full utility belt including his service weapon. This would complicate the arrest. Witnesses would see a uniformed police officer being surrounded by a bunch of scruffy-looking civilians with guns. Turner hoped none of the well-meaning bystanders would try to be a hero by attempting to rescue Cullen. He radioed the narcotics lieutenant to move in and clear the parking lot as soon as Reggie and Miller engaged Cullen.

Miller responded quickly, "Don't worry Turner, I won't shoot any taxpayers."

"You're the one I'm worried about. You look like a serial killer."

Cullen parked in the stall behind Sheffield and wasted no time sliding into the passenger seat of the Lexus. His sudden movement startled Sheffield who gasped but recovered quickly.

It wasn't warm in the van, but Turner felt the sweat on his face and the dampness under his shirt. He had no confidence that Sheffield could pull off this charade. At some point the old man's drug-soaked brain would falter.

"Did you bring it?" Cullen asked, immediately.

"I said I would," Sheffield said. His speech was slurring again.

"Let's see it."

"It's in the trunk," Sheffield said and opened the driver's door.

Turner's heart sank. It had gone to pieces faster than he'd expected. They were out of the car, and the trunk was open before Cullen had said anything about the killing. "Fuck," Turner said to no one in particular. He wasn't broadcasting what he was hearing or seeing because he was afraid of giving Weaver a stroke. He watched in disbelief as Sheffield opened the briefcase and moved aside so Cullen could lean halfway into the trunk to examine the stacks of currency. After a few seconds, Cullen backed out of the trunk. Sheffield secured the briefcase and slammed the trunk closed with the briefcase and their money locked safely inside.

They sat in the car again, and Turner took a deep, relieved breath.

"So, when's this going to happen?" Sheffield asked.

"You shouldn't know too much. That way if they give you a poly you'll seem truthful because you really don't know shit." Cullen's voice made Turner's skin crawl. He was cocky and condescending. Turner was certain Sheffield could easily be manipulated by this scum.

"I've got to know," Sheffield insisted. "That's a lot of money. I want to know exactly what you plan to do and when you're going to do it." Half his words ran together, and he repeated himself several times, but Sheffield was firm.

"What do you care, man, as long as the dude's dead?" Cullen asked. He was beginning to sound annoyed.

"So, you'll kill him?"

"Yeah, I said I'd kill him, and I'll kill him."

Turner heard the shuffling of papers and then Sheffield said, "Here's all the information, his home address, the office, the gym where he works out. When will you do it?"

"What the fuck's the difference. I'll do it next week. I'll do it fucking tomorrow if you want. Okay?"

"Yes," Turner said, and broadcast to Weaver and the others that he had heard and recorded the offer to kill.

"Next week will be fine. Does that conclude our business? I'm feeling a little fatigued," Sheffield said, and his voice sounded tired. Turner saw the trunk of the Lexus pop open again.

"You look like shit. Better cut back on the hard liquor and drugs, old man. Wouldn't want to OD or nothing, would you?" Cullen asked as he got out of the car. He was laughing as he lifted the briefcase out of the trunk. As soon as the trunk closed, Sheffield drove quickly out of the lot, over the curb, nearly side-swiping a retaining wall.

Cullen took half a dozen steps toward the cruiser before Reggie and Miller confronted him. From a distance of about twenty yards, Miller down on one knee held a shotgun, and Reggie pointed his handgun at the surprised officer. Miller identified himself as the police and shouted at Cullen to drop the briefcase and raise his hands in the air, but the man seemed frozen in place. After several seconds, he let the briefcase fall to the ground, but his hands remained down.

From the van, Turner saw Cullen looking around the parking lot. He's thinking about running, Turner thought. His second thought was, maybe this guy's not alone, but the perimeter was secure. He saw narcotics detectives surrounding the parking lot. There was no escape. Miller shouted at him again to raise his hands, but Cullen didn't move.

Using his binoculars, Turner saw Cullen's strange smirk before he took two small steps toward his cruiser. His right hand was on the gun's grip before Miller could react, but Reggie fell into a prone position and fired his .45 as Cullen dove toward the cruiser while firing two rounds in Miller's direction. Turner jumped out the back doors of the van and took cover behind the bed of a truck parked beside the van. Reggie used the ramp of a loading dock for protection, but Miller wasn't moving. He was on his stomach with the shotgun under him. Turner called out to him with no response. Reggie fired a barrage of shots at Cullen as Turner crawled as fast as he could toward Miller. He felt the asphalt tearing the skin on his elbows and arms. When he reached Miller, he pulled the shotgun out from under him and fired four rounds at Cullen. Seconds later, a spray of bullets hit the ground in front of him, and he realized Cullen had retrieved an automatic weapon from the cruiser and was firing back. Turner grabbed the collar of Miller's raid jacket and pulled him toward the truck. He felt a stinging pain in his right shoulder and let go. The pain was gone as quickly as it came. His immediate thought was he had ruptured a tendon, but it didn't matter. He had to get his friend to a safe place. He wouldn't survive the nightmares if another partner bled to death in front of him. He took hold of the jacket with his left hand and tugged until Miller's limp body was behind the truck. For the first time he saw Miller's face, bathed in blood and dirt, but he was breathing. The bullet had sliced a clean, superficial trench through his hairline producing a gush of blood, and Turner guessed it would eventually cause one super-sized headache.

Turner reloaded the shotgun and fired at the cruiser. Most of the narcotics detectives stationed around the perimeter were out of his sight now. He heard a brief report from handguns and automatic weapons and worried about crossfire, but the shots weren't directed at Cullen or him.

Reggie had somehow maneuvered around the lot and was crouched on the other side of the cruiser. When Cullen raised his torso for a better shot at Turner, Reggie leaned over the hood of the black and white and fired one round between the surprised man's eyes. The fight was over almost as quickly as it began. Turner was relieved and disappointed at the same time. They were safe, but their only known link to Ian Conner was silenced forever, sprawled on the ground as Reggie kicked the AR-15 automatic weapon away from his hands. Turner watched as Reggie straddled Cullen's body for a few seconds, and then leaned over and ripped the badge from the dead man's uniform.

The shooting on the perimeter had stopped, too. It was eerily quiet except for the wail of a siren in the distance. Turner was told by the narcotics lieutenant that his detectives had exchanged gunfire with unknown shooters outside the parking lot. So, Cullen wasn't alone. Conner and Goodman might've been there hiding among the storefronts on Sunset. Apparently, they weren't committed to dying with their friend and disappeared as soon as Cullen fell. None of the detectives were injured, and the lieutenant was clutching his briefcase full of money as he talked to Turner.

Before the ambulance arrived, Miller was conscious and angry that he'd missed all the action. He was sitting with his back against the truck's rear tire, holding a bunch of clean paper towels against his head wound, complaining to anyone who would listen.

Turner knelt down beside him and lifted the towels a little. The nasty cut was still bleeding and would require stitches.

"You're going to be even uglier than usual," Turner said, standing.

"Is that my blood or yours?" Miller asked, pointing to Turner's right shoulder.

There had been so much confusion that Turner hadn't noticed his raid jacket was stained with blood. His jacket and arms were scraped and dirty from crawling on the asphalt. He lifted his shirt away from his shoulder and saw a bloody jagged cut but didn't feel any pain.

"Mine, I guess."

"Sorry."

"Why? You didn't shoot at me."

"You saved my fat ass and got hurt. That's why."

"It can't be that bad. I didn't even feel it. Next time you save me," Turner said, trying to make him feel better.

"I don't think so," Miller said. "I don't really like you that much."

Turner walked away. Someday he'd learn not to be serious or sensitive around Miller.

The paramedic figured that a round fired from Cullen's weapon had most likely hit the ground or a concrete parking block and ricocheted off Turner's shoulder. It entered and exited cleanly, missing the collarbone. It was a flesh wound. The bruises from the asphalt felt worse. Turner got first aid from the paramedic who washed off the scrapes with antiseptic and bandaged the cut on his shoulder, but he refused to go to the emergency room for an MRI. The shoulder felt fine, and he could move it without pain. Miller, on the other hand, needed stitches and had to be transported to Cedars-Sinai despite his protests.

Turner wanted to stay on the scene until the shooting team and the command officers arrived. There would be questions, and he didn't want to abandon Reggie and have him face them alone.

As soon as the ambulance drove away, Reggie called Turner aside and showed him a motel key he had taken out of Cullen's pocket.

"That's all he had on him," Reggie said.

"Rummaging through the asshole's pockets isn't exactly shooting scene protocol, Reg," Turner said, taking the key. "As soon as they're done with you, I'll offer to take you back to the office, and we'll go visit this . . . Sunset Oasis," he added, holding up the key to read the badly faded name.

"We'll go to the motel first, then I'll come back and finish up here. It'll take them a couple of hours to get organized. They won't even know I'm gone."

Turner knew it was a bad idea to leave, but Reggie was right. Whatever was in that room wasn't going to stay there. He saw Lieutenant Metcalf's Buick pulling into the north end of the lot, and Weaver jogging around the parked police cars to meet him. Turner pulled Reggie behind the technician's van, and they waited until Weaver stood in front of the driver's window blocking the lieutenant's view. Reggie's car was parked across Sunset near the gas station pumps. They jumped in and drove westbound toward the motel. It was actually in West Hollywood, on the other side of La Brea Boulevard. By the time they arrived, Weaver was trying to contact them on the radio, and he didn't sound pleased. After a few seconds, Lieutenant Metcalf came on the frequency and threatened them with serious repercussions if they didn't answer.

Reggie turned off the radio.

"You know we're screwed," Turner said, wondering why he wasn't more disturbed by Metcalf's threats. Maybe because he trusted Reggie's instincts and knew the prospect of not finding

Cullen's buddies had worse repercussions than delaying a shooting investigation. They needed to get in that room before the bad guys did. There wasn't much choice. Explaining the situation and getting Metcalf's approval, if they could get it, would take too long. He wanted to play by the rules, but guys like Metcalf made it really difficult; plus he felt responsible for letting Cullen, Conner and Goodman loose to prey on the public. Cullen wasn't going to hurt anyone again, but the other two were still out there, and he needed to find them.

It was almost midnight, and the motel office was dark. The "no vacancy" light was flashing above the Sunset Oasis sign on the building. The key belonged to room fifteen where Turner noted steel bars on every window. The only way in or out was the front door.

They crept under the windows and listened at the door. The sound from either a television or radio was turned up and Turner couldn't make out any other voices. He carefully slid the key into the lock and turned it, opening the door a crack. He nodded at Reggie who then kicked the door hard, crashing it against the inside wall. They drew their guns and entered the cramped room yelling, "Police." Turner came in low behind a bed with a torn bare mattress, and Reggie quickly reached the bathroom.

"It's clear," Turner shouted, after searching under the bed and in a small alcove that served as a makeshift kitchen. He turned off the television.

"Come in here," Reggie called from the bathroom.

Turner stood in the doorway of a filthy, closet-sized room with a brown-stained porcelain toilet, and a stopped-up sink that smelled like an open sewer mixed with the unmistakable odor of decaying human flesh. Hanging from the shower curtain rod, with a belt pulled tightly around his neck, was the late Officer Pete Goodman.

TEN

It was late morning before Turner arrived home exhausted, but unable to stop the overflow of adrenaline. He'd been interviewed by the shooting team and Internal Affairs investigators about the hastily prepared and—according to Lieutenant Metcalf—the "ill-conceived" sting operation that culminated in the demise of Andy Cullen. He was interrogated by Robbery Homicide detectives concerning his discovery of the decomposing body of Pete Goodman, and questioned several times on how he came to have knowledge of Goodman's whereabouts. Apparently, none of his answers were satisfactory. No one believed the motel room key had fallen out of Cullen's pocket, but then again they couldn't prove it didn't. He and Reggie stuck to their stories, and Lieutenant Metcalf assigned them to the office until the investigations were finished. The squad was officially disbanded. Patty and a despondent Vogel were transferred back to their divisions. Miller was sent home to recover from his head wound, but would probably go back to Narcotics when he was able to work again.

Fortunately, Turner was too tired to sleep because he wasn't home twenty minutes before Reggie arrived. Miller got there ten minutes later, looking pale and wearing a heavily taped gauze turban. Miriam had left half a dozen messages on Turner's cell phone before she went to work that morning, but he wasn't in the mood to repeat yesterday's events or try to explain why the perfect plan fell apart.

Although Turner couldn't think straight, he intended to drink until the edge was taken off his strained nerves. Before he could finish his first beer, Eddie returned from walking Daryl. He waved at his neighbor, but the old man didn't look at him or say anything as he gently pulled the dog into the kitchen. Eddie appeared sober and fully recovered from his last binge, but didn't say a word as he quietly removed the dog's leash. He wasn't bashful about sharing Turner's food or alcohol or friends, but this morning he seemed reluctant to join them.

"You okay?" Turner asked, offering him a beer.

Eddie nodded at Reggie and Miller, then moved closer to Turner, pushing the bottle away. "Becuz' a you, I'm fine," he said, sheepishly.

Turner hesitated. He'd been so busy he didn't have a chance to do what he'd promised.

"I'm sorry, Eddie. I never spoke with Danny."

"Don't matter no more. He can have that drafty old house. When that girl told me I could stay here, everything got good again."

Reggie and Miller stared at Turner, but they weren't nearly as surprised as he was.

"Miriam told you that?" Turner asked. She had made what should have been his decision, but maybe this wasn't the best solution. He knew Miriam never considered the long term consequences of her split-second decisions. She'd probably invited Eddie to live here with as much thought as she'd given to which shoes she'd wear that morning. His expression must have revealed his annoyance. Eddie studied the floor.

"You don't gotta do this," he said, softly. He swallowed hard and appeared on the verge of tears.

"No, no, that's not it. I wanted to ask you. It was supposed to be my surprise," Turner said with as much sincerity as he could muster. Putting his arm around the old man's shoulder, he added, "I got the spare bedroom. It's yours." And now I'm completely fucked, Turner thought. On top of everything else that just happened, he was about to have a department commander pissed off because he was interfering in his family's business.

"Moved my stuff already . . . wasn't much . . . don't got much. Think I'm gonna rest a bit," Eddie said, and shuffled down the hallway to the bedroom across the hall from Turner's. Daryl got up from behind Reggie's feet and trailed faithfully behind the old man.

Turner watched until the bedroom door closed, then dropped wearily onto the couch.

"Maybe when me and Reggie get fired, Miriam will let us move in with you, too," Miller said, enjoying Turner's discomfort.

"She was trying to help," Turner said, attempting to sound satisfied with the situation.

Reggie had been jotting something in his notebook as he drank. He finished the beer and put the notebook in his jacket pocket.

"We've got to get back on Conner's mother," Reggie said. "She's our best connection to him."

"It's not our game anymore, Reg," Turner said, giving each of them a fresh, ice cold bottle.

"Yes it is," Reggie insisted.

"Besides, I don't think she's involved." Turner figured he was a pretty good judge of character. It would've tweaked his ego if Beverly Conner had fooled him that badly.

"Somebody blew your cover. My vote's for Conner's mommy since she was the last one to have contact with him," Miller added.

"Doesn't matter, we're off it," Turner said, knowing that walking away wouldn't sit well with Reggie's sense of justice and balance in the world. Turner hated not finishing what they'd started, but he didn't want to encourage whatever crazy scheme Reggie and Miller had cooked up. He needed time to figure out a smart plan to get the investigation back.

"I'm setting up on her tomorrow," Reggie said.

"Metcalf won't let you do that." As soon as he spoke the words, Turner knew it was the wrong argument. Neither Reggie nor Miller had any real concern about Lieutenant Metcalf. "I think I've got a way we can still work this case," Turner said. "Just don't do anything stupid until I can put the pieces

102

together." He didn't have a plan, not even an idea for one, but knew they trusted him and would wait.

"You think Conner killed Goodman?" Miller asked.

"Why would he do that? Goodman was his buddy," Turner said.

"Or maybe Cullen did it," Miller added.

"That doesn't make sense either," Turner said. "You saw how close they were at The Tavern. They liked each other."

"Maybe Goodman wanted out, or Cullen got greedy and didn't want to share the fifty thousand. It's okay when nobody knows who you are, but how long can you survive when everybody's looking for you." Reggie had given this some thought. "Goodman was the closest thing to being a real cop. He had the most to lose."

"That's cold," Miller said. "Hanging your best friend."

"I should try to talk to Beverly. She might want to help." Turner didn't really believe that, but it made more sense than following her around.

Miller still had some double vision from his injury. He curled up on the couch to close his eyes for a few minutes and immediately fell asleep. The emergency room doctor had given him painkillers that didn't mix well with the alcohol. Turner figured Miller would be unconscious for hours, so he threw a blanket over his snoring, drooling friend and worried that his quiet refuge was turning into a Motel 8.

He needed sleep, too, but the beer wasn't working. His mind couldn't stop calculating the possible scenarios that culminated in Goodman hanging like Miriam's underwear from a shower curtain rod. Reggie's greed theory was the most plausible, but Turner had seen Cullen and Goodman at the bar the night he and Miller followed them. They seemed like close friends. It just didn't work. So, that left the next best guess . . . Goodman wanted out of the Valley boys' gang and Ian Conner only gave lifetime memberships.

"Somebody has to be helping Conner hide," Reggie said. He and Turner were sitting in the kitchen now, drinking coffee. "The obvious choice is his mother."

Beverly Conner understood cops better than her son, and she knew the city. Turner hated to admit he was wrong about her, but it made sense.

"We'll drive out to Santa Clarita and talk with her," he said.

He convinced Reggie that it was foolish to think the two of them could follow her for very long without being detected. She knew him, and as good as he was, even Reggie would get burned if he did it by himself. Turner wondered what Weaver was doing. The surveillance boss was a company man, and he still had the other squad to supervise, but Weaver had to feel some sense of responsibility for what had ~~happened~~. When the time was right and if he needed help. T~~urner deci~~ded to use Weaver's guilt to his advantage. Tech~~ Crime~~ and Reggie were still assigned to Internal Affairs. Fir~~st find~~ Conner before more innocent people died might be the only way they could salvage their careers.

They finished a pot of coffee and a couple of slices of toast before Turner took a quick shower. They were ready to leave when Miriam called.

"Are you okay?" she asked. "I meant to call earlier, but it got really hectic."

"I'm fine, it was just a scratch. Miller's got a few stitches, but he'll be good as new in a few days." He told her most of what had happened, leaving out their discovery of Goodman's body.

"In our news release we're not saying where you guys work," Miriam said. "My boss said not to release your names . . . just say you're in a special task force."

Turner thought she sounded distracted. "You alright?" he asked.

"I know you're probably upset about Eddie," she said. He tried to interrupt to say he didn't care, but she wouldn't let him talk. "He can't live in some old peoples' home with strangers. His house is so cold and empty, and there's no food. He was so unhappy I just couldn't stand it, so I told him he could move in with us."

Turner didn't know why but it bothered him when she said, "move in with us," and then immediately felt bad because he wanted her to think of this place as her home. She'd heard Eddie's sad story and her gentle nature kicked in. She brought him home, the way she'd take in a stray kitten.

"I'm not angry, Miriam. I want him to stay with us." Turner couldn't be angry with her, but he feared this stray would eventually cause him some serious headaches.

"I promise I'll be home early to make us all dinner," she said, and wasn't upset when he said he'd be back too late for dinner. After he hung up, he realized she'd never asked why he'd be late.

"What's wrong?" Reggie asked.

"Nothing," Turner said. "It's funny when you miss someone how you only remember the good times."

"You remember what you want to remember."

Turner studied Reggie's face. The gaunt eyes were sunken behind a mask of dark circles. "You doing okay?"

"Why?"

"I never thanked you for last night. That could've been ugly."

Reggie grabbed his jacket off the coatrack. As he straightened it to cover his holster, he stood over the couch where Miller slept with the blanket pulled up to his nose.

"Miller was lucky," Reggie said. "Guy's a genius with drugs, but doesn't know shit about tactics."

"They gonna make you see the shrink?" Turner asked. He knew officers involved in a shooting had to see the department psychiatrist, but he wanted Reggie to talk about it.

"What do you think?"

"You worried about it?"

Turner realized he was pushing, but Reggie wouldn't talk unless he was pushed. A few years ago, his friend had stood on the brink of a meltdown, and Turner wasn't about to let it happen again. Apparently, there were signs then, but he never saw the despair and isolation his friend had endured. Now, he pestered and annoyed Reggie, asked questions, made him talk until he got angry and sullen, but Turner had decided that allowing him to slip back into that black hole wasn't an option.

"I killed an asshole that deserved killing. Why would I worry about it?"

"You shouldn't." End of discussion.

Turner ached to steal a couple of those notebooks to find out what was really going on in that complicated mind. One thing was certain—Reggie wasn't going to tell him.

They got to Beverly Conner's place in a couple of hours. Turner didn't call; he was afraid she'd refuse to see him. If her work hours hadn't changed, this would be her night off. When he saw the red Camaro parked in front of the barn, he was almost disappointed. For some reason he wouldn't attempt to understand, he was hoping she wouldn't be here.

Before they got out of the car, Reggie took a miniature recorder out of his pocket and stuck it in the breast pocket of Turner's jacket.

"It's on," Reggie said.

"Where are you going?"

"She's not gonna say anything useful with me hanging around. Don't worry, I'll be where I can keep an eye on you."

"Great," Turner said, sarcastically. The only thing worse than having to talk to the woman was having to talk to her alone.

She didn't open the door for what seemed like a long time. Turner was about to leave when suddenly she was standing on the porch. Her freshly scrubbed pale skin was luminescent under the glow of a single yellow light bulb. Without makeup her eyes seemed smaller, kinder. Her red hair was flat and damp as if she'd just washed it.

"He's not here," she said. She wasn't angry. There was no emotion in her voice. "Your detectives already looked."

"I came to see you."

She laughed without smiling. "Sure you did."

"I want to talk."

Beverly stared at him as if she were looking at a stranger. She held open the door and gestured for him to come inside. He did, and stood uncomfortably in the middle of the living room. She sat on the couch, lit a cigarette and waited.

"Talk," she said, exhaling a puff of grey smoke.

"I won't apologize for lying. Your son's involved in some serious crimes." He stopped. She was examining the threads on the couch. "I don't think you knew what he was doing, but you might be able to help us stop him."

"Why would I do that, even if I could?" she asked, glancing up at him.

"Because he's involved in killing innocent people."

She crushed the half-smoked cigarette in an overflowing ashtray, got up and stood in front of him. That tobacco smell was in her clothes and hair, her stale breath.

"Look Turner, if that's your real name, I'm not mad at you. I've got a shitty record with men, so it doesn't surprise me you turned out to be a lying bastard, but you're wrong about Ian. My son might be a lazy bum like his father, but he's no criminal."

Her eyes narrowed, and she crossed her arms. She was protecting her kid, but it was more than that. She was getting back at Turner the only way she could. Beverly Conner had more backbone than her son, and her body language was loud and clear. She would've punched him in the mouth if she could. His instincts were always better than most detectives. Turner knew when it was over, when a person might keep talking but wouldn't be saying anything he wanted or needed to hear.

"Be careful," he said, on his way out the door. He hesitated on the threshold, holding the door open. He didn't want her to hate him, but when he looked back and saw her hard stare he realized nothing he said was going to make her believe her kid was evil. Turner couldn't make her understand what he knew for certain—that a man like Ian could harm his mother as easily as a stranger.

The car was parked behind the barn, but Reggie was nowhere in sight. So much for keeping an eye on me, Turner thought. A few seconds later, Reggie came from the side of the house and unlocked the car doors.

"Get in," he ordered, and started the engine.

They were off the property before Reggie spoke. He drove to the fast food restaurant where they had gathered the first day of the surveillance. It was open twenty-four hours, so he ordered hamburgers for both of them and parked in one of the lighted spaces. Turner waited patiently. He knew his partner had something to tell him, but he had learned to let Reggie do it at his own pace. Usually, whatever he had to say was worth the delay.

"Thanks for dinner," Turner said, hoping to ignite the conversation fuse.

"I searched Ian's room while you were talking to his mother."

Turner stopped chewing and swallowed. "Okay."

"There wasn't much, but he'd jotted down a couple of locations with sketches. I copied them and took some keys that might belong to storage lockers."

"No guns?" Turner asked.

"He'd cleaned up pretty good, but his phone stored a lot of numbers on a caller list."

"It's something," Turner said. He gathered their garbage and tossed it in the dumpster as they drove out of the lot. He called Miriam and woke her. She asked where he'd been and got very quiet when he told her. He explained that Reggie was with him, and how Beverly Conner hated his guts. She became talkative again, explaining what they'd had for dinner, how much better Miller was and how well Eddie was doing. Turner listened quietly, still thinking about the cold indifference in Beverly's eyes. When Miriam finished, Turner told her not to wait up for him. He would talk to her in the morning.

"You staying tonight?" he asked Reggie.

"No, Miller snores."

"Stop at JR's. It's on the way."

It was almost midnight, but Turner still wasn't sleepy. He was hoping a shot of Jack Daniels would make him tired. He had liquor at home, but for the first time since he bought the house, he really didn't want to be there. JR's was a dingy bar on the pier in Redondo. The tourists avoided it, but he loved the smell of wet wood and the shabby booths nearly hidden in the darkness. The dedicated drunks drifted in here after midnight. Turner didn't drink that much but he liked their quiet, unobtrusive company.

He and Reggie found an empty booth. The adjacent sliding window was stuck open, but they were wearing heavy jackets, and the fresh ocean air felt clean and good. There were other patrons at the bar, but they were silent shadows in the dimly lighted room. After his second drink, Turner started to relax, the tension fading in his foggy brain. Reggie was one drink ahead of him, but didn't seem affected by the alcohol.

"You ever just let yourself get crazy, Reg?"

"All the time, haven't you noticed?"

"Not that kind of crazy. I mean uninhibited, tell people what you're really feeling."

"No."

"You need to do that. It's healthier."

"Most people would rather not know."

"I want to know."

"No, you don't."

"How the hell do you know what I want to know?"

"Because I know you . . . you're like me."

Turner laughed. "Now you're scaring me."

"I'm right."

"Probably . . . I'd rather do it than talk about it. By the way, you're not crazy."

"According to the shrink, I'm not."

"You still dream about that kid?" Turner wanted to take back the question as soon as it came out of his mouth. Sober, he never would've mentioned it.

Reggie hesitated as if he were deciding whether or not to respond and then said, "Every night."

"Too bad."

"In thirty-five years, I never saw anything that sick. Now I see it every night of my life."

"It's good you killed the bastard," Turner said. He was sorry he'd made Reggie think about the gory incident. A two-year-old child had been slowly hacked to death by a woman's live-in, hallucinating boyfriend. Reggie responded to the call by one of the neighbors about a child screaming. Reggie shot and killed the naked man who was under the influence of PCP, and had attacked Reggie with the same machete he'd used to mutilate himself and kill the child. The gruesome scene made several paramedics vomit. It happened five years ago, but the baby's agony still haunted his friend.

"I shot him, and he was gone in seconds. That baby suffered for hours. I should've made him die the same way that kid died."

Turner ordered two more drinks, hoping the alcohol might dull the memories. He knew one thing for certain—cops shouldn't dream.

ELEVEN

The remainder of the evening and the early morning hours were a hazy memory. Somehow Turner arrived home, but had no idea when or how Reggie delivered him. It was Saturday so he could've slept in, but his head was throbbing, and the pain kept waking him up. Finally, he got out of bed, took four Advil, then lay on top of the sheets with his face buried in the pillow. Someone was moving around and making too much noise in the kitchen. He took the other pillow and put it over his head to drown out the sound. In half an hour, he was mobile, still fuzzy-headed, but the pain was gone.

Miriam claimed she made breakfast. Something she rarely did. Eddie was walking the dog so it might've been the truth. The couch was empty, and Miller was nowhere in sight. A plate of bacon and eggs was waiting for him on the table.

"Heard you in the shower," she said. "It should still be hot." She didn't look at him, concentrating on scrubbing a frying pan. Miriam was always so careful about the way she looked, but this morning her shirt was wrinkled and her hair was pulled back in a messy ponytail. There were dark circles under her eyes.

He poured himself a cup of coffee and sat as far as he could from the food.

"Maybe in a few minutes," he said, sipping the hot black liquid that might make him feel human again. "It looks good," he lied, trying not to look at the runny eggs.

She dried her hands, tossed the dishtowel on the counter and glared at him. She seemed upset.

"It's there if you want it." There was a nasty tone to her voice this morning. He tried to remember if they'd quarreled last night. He didn't think so.

"Everything okay?" he asked.

"I know you're not happy about Eddie staying here. He said you looked irritated when he told you. I thought it was the decent thing to do."

"It's alright. I just wish we'd talked about it first."

"Maybe this wasn't such a good idea," she said, nervously pulling on her ponytail.

They weren't still talking about Eddie. "What?" he asked, but he knew and was embarrassed to admit he'd had the same feelings lately.

"I care about you. I really do, but we're so . . ." She sighed and seemed frustrated.

"Different," he said, before she came up with something worse.

"While we were separated, I had a bad experience with . . . this guy, and thought maybe you and I should try again." She stopped fidgeting and sat across the table from him, covering her face with both hands. "I'm so fucked up," she whispered. He started to get up, but she lowered her hands and motioned for him to stay where he was.

"Forget about Eddie. It's not a problem," he said, wanting her to feel better.

She closed her eyes, appeared to be trying to calm herself and asked, "Do you care for Ian's mother?"

Ian, he thought, not Officer Conner. It sounded odd, too familiar, but then that was her way. She treated strangers like friends.

"She seems like a nice woman who happens to think I'm scum." They both understood he hadn't really answered the question, but she couldn't be jealous of Ian's mother. He barely knew the woman. Miriam was one of the most confident women he knew, but there was an edginess about her now he hadn't noticed before their breakup.

"She's not that nice."

"What do you mean?"

"I mean she's not nice."

"How would you know?"

"I dated her son."

Turner took a large swallow of coffee and burned the roof of his mouth. He swore, but it wasn't the hot liquid that angered him. He took a moment before saying anything. He wanted to be calm, not upset her.

"Why didn't you tell me?"

"I was afraid what you'd think."

"What's wrong with you? How could you not tell me something like that?" The façade crumbled. He was livid and couldn't hide it.

"I'm telling you, now." She folded her arms and stared defiantly at him.

"When's the last time you talked to Ian . . . or saw him?" Although he was furious, he tried not to raise his voice.

"I'm outta here," she said, yanking her jacket from the back of the kitchen chair, so hard the chair toppled. She stopped in the doorway for her parting shot. "By the way, Beverly totally controls Ian. He doesn't piss unless mama lets him."

The front door slammed against the wall, and a few seconds later he heard the lawnmower noises from her Mazda Miata engine leaving his driveway. His live-in girlfriend had just admitted what . . . having sex with a possible killer, the guy he was investigating; and the crazy way she was behaving made him believe Miriam's relationship with Ian Conner might not be over.

He needed to clear his head and forced himself to drink more coffee, but it wasn't helping until Eddie returned and mixed up some concoction he swore would cure any hangover. It didn't taste that bad, tomato juice and something sweet with spices. It made his head feel better, but the sick feeling in his gut wasn't alcohol related. Eddie seemed to understand that Turner wasn't in the mood for discussion or advice, so he went quietly into his room and closed the door. Daryl, like all good dogs, could pick up the scent of distress, and he trailed behind Turner as he paced around the empty house.

He was fuming, and it kept him from thinking clearly. He wanted to believe he couldn't be fooled that easily. He told himself Miriam wasn't that way. She was just naïve. He wondered how long she'd been with Conner. He'd told her everything about the investigation. Was she the one who warned Conner that IA was watching him? Finally, he sat on the couch, watched the Basset hound drool on his favorite cowboy boots and realized he wasn't upset because Miriam had lied to him. He was pissed off because he hadn't been smart enough to know she was lying to him.

He needed to get out of the house, do the one thing that always calmed his nerves. He would go to the office and try to work. He needed to think about everything that had happened, try to calculate how much damage had been done. He dreaded telling Weaver about her; worse yet, admitting to Lieutenant Metcalf that his girlfriend was Ian Conner's girlfriend, and she knew everything about their investigation.

Reggie was standing in the hallway talking with Dr. Tom when Turner arrived at the Chinatown office. The nervous psychiatrist quickly disappeared around the corner as soon as he saw Turner moving in his direction. Not surprisingly, there were chicken bones in the ashtray near the elevator.

"Professional visit?" Turner asked, grinning at Reggie. It was his way of saying that those private thoughts revealed last night in JR's didn't matter. That's how they survived.

"He doesn't think I'm crazy either."

"That's a comfort. What are you doing here?" Turner asked. He was hoping he'd be alone a while to think before he had to tell anyone about Miriam, but he found himself spilling the whole story before they'd opened the door.

Reggie listened until Turner had finished and then said, "Dr. Tom just told me Metcalf was in our office this morning and left with a box full of paperwork. It's too bad about your girlfriend, but I think Metcalf might be a bigger problem."

Turner agreed but couldn't stop thinking about Miriam. "I'm afraid she told Conner we were watching him." He said out loud what he'd been worrying about since he left his house.

"Did she move out?"

"All her stuff's gone. She must've packed while I was sleeping."

"Odds are she told him."

"She's too smart to get involved with a guy like Conner."

"It's not really an intellectual thing, partner."

Turner thought about how different he and Miriam were, how difficult it was for them to live together, and yet, he was attracted to her and cared about her. Reggie was right. Intellect had nothing to do with it.

"She knows everything I know about this investigation," Turner said.

"At the moment, that's not worth much."

Turner told him what Miriam had said about Ian's mother. They would spend some time looking at Beverly Conner, digging a little deeper into her background and acquaintances; but first Reggie wanted to run the numbers he'd recovered from Ian's phone directory and check the locations Ian had scribbled on the notepad. The locations were movie theaters. Reggie ran both addresses in the department computer and found related crime reports. He called and had Jenny, the record clerk, fax the reports to him. Takeover robberies had occurred just weeks apart. Four men with masks and guns forced the managers to open their safes minutes after the nights' ticket and concession receipts were deposited.

"How much did they get?" Turner asked.

"Victims estimated the total take was close to $40,000."

"Vogel's back at RHD. Check with him, see if there's more of these movie theater robberies. Any good descriptions?"

"Not really," Reggie said. "Victims were too scared to look."

Turner started running the phone numbers. He wasn't surprised to find several calls listed from The Tavern bar, Cullen and Goodman's house in the Valley, and the apartment in West L.A. Two of the numbers came back to addresses he didn't recognize and three from a number he knew too well, Miriam's cell phone.

"Maybe we could get Weaver's other squad to watch her," Reggie said, after Turner showed him the numbers.

115

It was a smart thing to do, but Turner balked at the idea. It wasn't just the sex; she'd been his friend. He knew she'd been stupid, but Miriam wasn't a criminal like Conner and the rest of his thugs. She did things without thinking and trusted people she shouldn't. He didn't want to hurt her, but eventually he had to admit Reggie was right. They needed someone to lead them to Conner.

"Nobody's working RHD over the weekend except the callout team," Reggie said. "We'll follow up on Monday."

They decided to check out the two addresses that Turner didn't recognize from Conner's phone list since both locations were in downtown L.A.; but before they could lock up the office, Weaver walked in on them.

"What're you doing here?" Weaver asked. He seemed upset and in a worse mood than usual.

"Nice to see you too, Boss," Turner said. "What're you doing here on a Saturday?"

"Did Lieutenant Metcalf give you permission? You shouldn't be in our office."

"We don't need permission to come to our office," Turner said, not doing a good job of controlling his temper. "We work here."

"You're assigned here until the investigation's over. Nobody wants you to work on anything."

"You give up looking for Conner and his asshole buddies?" Reggie asked, calmly.

"I don't have to look for him. I got him."

"Bullshit," Turner said.

"He showed up at Hollywood station with his lawyer this morning."

"You arrested him?"

"For what? We can't prove anything. The guns are gone; his partners are dead. We have shit."

"Fuck," Turner said. He couldn't believe what he was hearing. "What about the assault rifle."

"He says we're wrong. All he had was a hunting rifle. He had no clue what Cullen and Goodman were up to."

"So, we go back on him, link him to their crimes, find the weapons, the rest of his asshole friends . . ." Turner was angry, but he wasn't ready to give up.

"We don't do shit. He's suing us."

"Suing who for what?" Turner asked, incredulously.

"All of us for harassment, so we leave him alone."

"Not likely," Reggie said.

"That's an order from the old man himself. You wanna argue with the chief."

"Just how did we harass him?"

"Spied on him . . . went into his home . . . annoyed his mother, causing her extreme anxiety. Those are the ones I can remember, but there's more." Weaver's tone had softened, as if talking about it had released some of the tension.

"Are you buying into this?" Turner asked. "You know what we did and why. You think Reggie didn't see those rifles?"

"Fuck you, Turner. The two of you and Miller, you act like a bunch of maniac cowboys . . . killing cops, leaving shooting scenes, going off on your own. I don't work that way. There's rules . . ." Weaver's voice trailed off. He was irritated, but seemed disappointed too. He folded his arms and glared at Turner. "You're a good detective, a natural leader. I expected more from you."

Great, Turner thought. He didn't think it was possible, but he felt worse than he had a few minutes ago. Still, there was no way he was going to apologize for doing what had to be done. Instead, he needed to stifle his emotions and appeal to Weaver's basic cop instincts. He believed the supervisor was a good man who wanted to do the right thing.

"Boss, we all know Ian Conner's dirty, and this lawsuit thing is just another way to keep us off his back," Turner said. "We need to keep working him." He explained how they got the phone list and addresses and the keys to storage lockers. Before Weaver could finish his tirade on the perils of harassing Conner's mother and consequences of illegal searches, Turner showed him the faxed copies of the movie theater robbery crime reports they'd linked to the addresses.

Weaver sank into the chair behind his desk.

"The sonofabitch is pulling robberies and he's got the balls to walk in the front door of Hollywood station and sue us." When a splotchy blush appeared on Weaver's face and bald spot, Turner figured he had him. "Where's Miller?" Weaver asked.

"Home, nursing a headache," Reggie answered.

"Good, leave him there. You're still assigned here," Weaver said, waving the faxed reports at them. "Conner's not that smart. Find something."

"Why are we still assigned here?" Turner asked. When Weaver hesitated, Turner guessed the answer and was right. Metcalf had initiated a personnel complaint against him and Reggie for an assortment of offenses ranging from neglect of duty to failure to follow the orders of a supervisor. For now, Metcalf wanted to keep them in IA under his control.

It wasn't a shock to any of them when Weaver checked the file cabinet, and all the paperwork related to the Conner investigation was gone. They were surprised that other case files were missing, their last couple of investigations including everything on the transvestite-loving Sergeant Gomez. The fact that Gomez's file wasn't there bothered Turner. The information on Ramona Sanchez's sister Helen was in that folder, and he felt responsible for keeping her involvement confidential. It should be safe with Lieutenant Metcalf, but he worried about who else might be looking through that file now that it was out of their office and housed in Internal Affairs. He should call her, give her a heads up, but remembered she didn't have a phone. Reggie agreed to go with him to her motel on Gower. They decided Monday was soon enough to get serious about dealing with Conner and his mother. Besides, Turner figured he needed a day or two to sort through the gloom and anger Miriam had left in her wake.

TWELVE

It was dark before they reached the rundown motel on Gower. Most of the building appeared deserted, but the lights were on in Helen Sanchez's second floor apartment. She didn't seem surprised to see Turner, but hesitated before letting him and Reggie come inside. Turner felt as if he might be interrupting something, but he could see she was alone. He noticed that the boxes were still full and piled in the hallway, nearly blocking the bedroom door. There might even be more of them since their last visit.

"I was hoping you might've moved by now," Turner said. He sat on the couch, and she stood in front of him looking as if she wanted to say something, but didn't. "You okay?" he asked her, and then glanced at Reggie who was leaning against the kitchen door. He introduced Reggie, thinking she might be uneasy because she hadn't really met him the first time.

She shook hands with Reggie. "I remember you," she said, and sat across from Turner in a chair covered with a clean white sheet. "I want to call you," she said softly. "I'm glad you come."

"What's wrong?" Turner asked. He was worried that someone had already tried to contact her.

"There is a street woman who lives near the bus stop. I am told she maybe saw what happened to my sister."

Turner felt a slight twinge of excitement. Reggie sat on the couch beside him as Helen told them about a homeless woman who was pestering the neighbors about a shooting she had seen. The woman was an alcoholic and mostly incoherent, Helen said, but she claimed to have seen a man shoot a young woman at the exact location where Helen's sister had been killed.

"Did you talk to her?" Reggie asked.

Helen shook her head. "I'm too afraid. She's loca," she said pointing at her forehead. "Crazy, you understand?"

"We understand. Is she still hanging around the bus stop?" Turner asked.

"Yes," Helen said. "I see her tonight when I come from work."

Turner told her they would talk to the woman. He tried to explain what had happened to the information she'd given them and why it might be safer for her to move out of her apartment.

"I was hoping you would've moved by now," Turner repeated.

"I need money from my sister. It is not possible now."

"How much is the new apartment?"

"No," Helen said, looking upset.

"The police department will pay. It's not our money. You're a witness, and the department will pay to keep you safe until we catch your sister's killer." Turner knew Reggie would go along with his lie.

"Happens all the time. Is this all your stuff?" Reggie asked, picking up one of the boxes.

Helen seemed confused, uneasy. She wouldn't accept charity, so they tried to make it appear that she was obligated to take their help. She didn't argue and helped them load the boxes into the trunk of Reggie's car. They settled her bill with the apartment manager and drove to an address she had given them on La Mirada. It was a duplex, and the back unit that she and her sister had planned to move into was still empty. Turner and Reggie had enough money between them to pay her rent for two months.

Helen's new, furnished home was slightly larger than the old apartment. It had two bedrooms, a decent clean kitchen and bathroom, and appeared to be cockroach-free. She stood in the living room, dazed by how quickly she had been uprooted from her old life.

"Ramona would like this," she said. Her eyes filled with tears, but she didn't cry. She lifted one of the boxes and carried it into the bedroom.

"So are we going to claim her as a dependent or what?" Reggie asked when the bedroom door closed. "At least you didn't move her into Eddie's room."

"I didn't know what else to do. Maybe in a couple of months we can find her some cheap housing she can afford that's better than that dump on Gower."

"Maybe she's not our problem," Reggie said.

"She's definitely not our problem, but I'm worried what Conner might do if he thinks she's his problem."

They waited until Helen settled in, and promised to let her know if they learned anything from the crazy homeless woman.

They drove the short distance to the bus stop on the corner of Melrose and Gower. Reggie parked on Gower, and they spotted a makeshift cardboard shelter before getting out of the car. Two television-size boxes had been cut open and pushed together for protection against the cold. A dirty blanket was tied over the opening. Turner knew someone was inside before he looked. The smell of human body odor nearly knocked him to his knees. This stench was a hundred times worse than the one in the alley the night they caught Sergeant Gomez with his favorite transvestite.

Behind the blanket an older woman was passed out, sprawled on the ground like a discarded thrift store mannequin covered in several layers of filthy, threadbare clothes. When yelling didn't get any response, Turner poked at her with a broken broomstick he'd found sticking out of a dumpster. Finally, she sat up, an old walrus rubbing her eyes, scratching her arms and legs, unable to comprehend what was expected of her. The skin on her face and hands was as dark and rough as old shoe leather. She pulled a knit cap from her coat pocket and covered her matted, thin grey hair.

Turner was trying not to breathe through his nose and stepped back as Reggie leaned closer to the opening of the shelter.

"What's your name?" Reggie shouted at her.

"Why?" Her voice was hoarse, barely above a whisper.

Reggie showed her his badge. She laughed at him. "In five minutes, I'm gonna take everything you've got here and burn it," he threatened.

121

She stared at him for a few seconds and said, "Tiny."

"Real name."

"Maggie Brown," she said in a stronger voice. She coughed several times, spitting out yellow mucus before rolling over to stand up. She was taller than Reggie and outweighed him by at least twenty pounds. She stretched and shook her head trying to clear the alcohol fog. Turner stepped back. He knew how far lice could jump.

"Did you see somebody get shot, Maggie, or are you just a drunk old liar?"

"A drunk old liar," she said snorting and coughing. "But I seen that poor Mexican get killed."

"Did you see who killed her?" Turner asked.

"Pig," she said, looking from Reggie to Turner. "You got a smoke?"

"Maybe," Turner said. "Can you tell me what he looked like?"

"Two of 'em. The littler one, he done it."

With very little prodding, Maggie described Cullen and Goodman. Turner was relieved the two killers were dead and couldn't harm Helen Sanchez, but he was also disappointed. He was hoping that one of them would have been Conner. But the big redhead was too clever to do his killing in daylight in the middle of the street.

Reggie called Hollywood Homicide and gave them Maggie's name and location. They would interview her again, show her pictures of the two cops and clear their homicide. Turner had Reggie take him back to the office to pick up his car. He wanted to go home. He was weary and couldn't stop thinking about Miriam. He hated the idea of her possibly sleeping with Conner while she was staying with him. A shower would wash off the stench of the homeless woman, but Turner wasn't certain what it would take to wipe out the disappointment and hurt of Miriam's betrayal.

THIRTEEN

A department utility car was parked in front of his house when Turner pulled into the driveway. It was a freshly washed and polished new black Ford Crown Victoria with two emergency lights in the rear window. He figured it probably belonged to one of the brass, so he wasn't surprised to see Commander Jones sitting in his living room, sipping a Diet Coke that he must've brought with him since there was nothing but beer and wine in his refrigerator. He'd been expecting and dreading this visit since Eddie moved in. Turner wasn't in the mood to deal with Eddie's pompous son, but knew the old man was no match for his overbearing offspring.

Turner put his arm around Eddie's shoulder and shook hands with the younger man.

"How are you, Commander?" he asked, but didn't wait for an answer before turning to Eddie. "You get some dinner?" Turner asked the older man, who nodded and pointed to the remains of a takeout hamburger, fries, and an empty beer bottle on the kitchen table.

"Your buddy Miller come by, and brought me some," Eddie said, looking sheepishly at his son from the corner of his eye. Commander Jones was taller than his father and thin. His complexion was lighter than Eddie's and his hair reddish brown. Turner had never met Eddie's wife, but was told by his father that she was a Mexican stripper who'd abandoned the baby shortly after it was born. Eddie never talked about her except to say she was dead.

"Junk food is not what you should be eating, Dad," Commander Jones said. "This is exactly what I mean. Your diet is atrocious. You've got high blood pressure, and your cholesterol is dangerously out of control. And you're diabetic."

Eddie sat on the recliner and glanced up timidly at Turner. "I like hamburgers."

"What can we do for you, Commander?" Turner asked. He could feel himself getting annoyed and always talked too much when he was irritated. The usually feisty Eddie looked like a beaten old dog.

"I know you think you're helping," Commander Jones said. "But this is really a family matter. I want what's best for my father." He and Turner were standing, facing each other in the middle of the living room.

"I can take care of him," Turner said.

"That's my job," Commander Jones said.

"Sit down, Danny," Turner said pointing to the couch. He saw the man's expression change instantly. Commander Jones didn't like a lowly detective calling him by his first name and telling him what to do, but Turner decided to take that risk because he knew rank would be an obstacle to any real conversation. He sat on the couch beside Commander Jones. "Your father doesn't want to be in an institution, even a really nice one. He's not senile. He's happy here, and I can keep an eye on him for you, make sure he takes his medicines." Turner was certain Eddie wouldn't like the last part, but he knew it would please the younger man.

"I appreciate that, but I'd feel better with professional caretakers."

"I don' need no takin' care of."

Turner ignored Eddie. "I know there may be a time when that's necessary, but don't you think we could try it this way for a while. It'll save you a lot of money, and your dad will be happier."

Commander Jones stared at the floor for a few seconds. Turner had noticed his expensive gold bracelet and the Rolex watch, and hoped money would be an important consideration.

Turner never liked the man. The guy was arrogant and accustomed to getting his way, but maybe he didn't want to make his old man miserable. It was obvious Eddie was comfortable and happy in Turner's house. Daryl did his part, too. As if on cue, the hound lumbered over to Eddie, laid on his feet and immediately fell asleep.

Commander Jones shook his head. "My wife is going to lecture me tonight about not doing what I know I should do. I won't insist on anything for now, but I'm making you responsible for my father's well-being. He can stay here, but he cannot go back to his house alone. Is that understood?"

Turner and Eddie nodded.

"His stuff is already here," Turner said, relieved that the disagreement was over, and he hadn't said anything that would get him in more trouble.

"Are you certain, with all the other things going on right now in your life, that you're up to this?" Commander Jones asked Turner.

"All the other things," Turner repeated. Did Eddie already blab about Miriam?

"I understand your surveillance team may have pending disciplinary action and a lawsuit behind this Conner business."

"I can handle that," Turner said. "It's got nothing to do with what goes on here." He almost choked on those words. Miriam had made him a liar.

Commander Jones didn't appear eager to hang around. He gave a few more orders about making certain Eddie ate right, didn't drink too much and got some exercise everyday. He left a list of Eddie's medications and his doctor's name and telephone number. Half-listening, Turner agreed to every condition and regulation imposed by Eddie's son. Finally, he was gone. Turner stretched out on the couch. Eddie sighed and reached down to stroke Daryl's head.

"You don't hav'ta do none of that stuff," Eddie said.

"I won't. I'm not your mother."

Eddie chuckled. "He's my boy, but he's such a shitbird."

"He's worried about you."

"I'm worried 'bout you sometimes, but don't see me tryin' to put you in no old peoples' home."

"Maybe you should've put me somewhere before I got myself in this mess with Miriam."

Eddie was a good listener and wanted to know all the details about Miriam's departure. Turner ran down the Conner investigation, everything that had happened with Beverly Conner, the deaths of Goodman, Cullen and Ramona Sanchez, Ian Conner's reappearance, the lawsuit and finally Miriam. For some reason, he felt better talking about it. Eddie didn't react until Turner got to the part about Miriam. He was disappointed because he liked her.

"Don't believe she told that Conner anything."

"The way she stormed out of here said she pretty much admitted it."

"Don't believe it," Eddie insisted.

"Since you still don't think OJ did it, I'm not putting a lot of stock in your opinion."

"You wait, you'll see," Eddie said and pushed himself off the chair. He stopped by the kitchen doorway. "How come you don't find out who it was told you about that Conner boy to begin with?"

"What do you mean?"

"You say a snitch started you lookin' at him. Who's the snitch? What's he know?" Turner heard Eddie snickering in the kitchen. "You ain't takin' care of me. I'm eatin' all the hamburgers I kin get." His voice trailed off in mumbling and coughing.

Turner closed his eyes. Why would Conner come back? The lawsuit was a loser. Even the litigation-shy City Attorney's office would fight this one and Conner was too smart to leave a trail from the robberies.

He and Reggie could follow up on the addresses and the storage units, but Turner knew he'd been missing something, and Eddie nailed it . . . the snitch. Who gave IA the original information on Conner? Their worksheet was based on an insider's knowledge.

All of these internal investigations went through Metcalf's office. He was the lieutenant in charge of the Special Operations Section. He decided which cases they worked. There was nothing in the case package that identified the informant. Weaver might know, but if he didn't or wouldn't tell them, there was only one other possible source . . . senior clerk typist Jenny Furcal at IA, the Mexican poodle. Turner cringed at the thought of having to deal with her; besides, she might not be too thrilled with his recent behavior.

He heard Eddie rummaging in the kitchen, talking to the dog, unloading the dishwasher and putting away the dishes. Miriam was gone, but this might be okay for a while.

FOURTEEN

Around four in the morning, Turner decided that an eighty-year-old man must have a bladder the size of a grape. He heard Eddie get up at least a half dozen times during the night to use the bathroom. Eddie wasn't keeping him awake. Counting the old man's trips to the toilet was the only thing he had to do. He couldn't sleep; he was too tired to read or even watch television, but his mind refused to shut down. He was lonely and felt stupid for missing a woman who made him feel like he did. Some men could live alone, but he wasn't one of them. He liked reaching out in the middle of the night and finding a woman's soft warm body. Even in her sleep, Miriam would snuggle in close to him if he touched her. The thing, though, that was really eating at his insides was the thought of her lying in Conner's bed.

At 5 A.M., he gave up and got dressed. He couldn't control what Miriam did, but he was determined to get Conner fired and prosecuted. If she wanted to be with someone else that was fine, but it wasn't going to be Ian Conner. An hour later, the phone rang as he sulked alone in the dark living room drinking last night's coffee.

"You alone?" Miller asked.

Turner looked at the phone and then said, "What do you care?"

"Get over to IA. They're gonna interview Conner on his complaint this morning."

"What does that have to do with me?"

"I got us front row seats."

"They're not going to let me sit in on his interview," Turner said. "I'm the one he's complaining about, remember."

"Would you quit arguing and get your ass down here. Weaver's fixed it so we can hear the whole thing."

"How's your head?" Turner asked. "Aren't you supposed to be recuperating?"

"I'm done. I'm here until they send me back to Narcotics or fire me."

Turner wanted to go back to bed, but he didn't. He knew better than to do anything Miller thought was a good idea, but sleep wasn't going to happen, and he was already in so much trouble another transgression wouldn't make much difference. Conner would lie about everything, but Turner wanted to hear the lies and observe the big redhead. Body language always told him more than what a person was saying anyway. Conner showed a lot of guts walking into Hollywood station, but Turner wanted to watch his eyes and his gestures as he told his version of events. Only then could he judge how thin the pretense was hiding the guy's real level of confidence. The one thing Turner knew for certain was that anyone who was willing to go along with or maybe even order the killing of innocent people was a coward.

Miller told him the interview would be conducted at the Bradbury building on Broadway. IA had offices there, and the disciplinary boards of rights were held in several of the sunny, antiquated rooms.

Turner was there in less than an hour. He wouldn't take the noisy elevator contraption constructed out of pulleys, cables and decorative wrought iron that looked like something from a 1940's movie. Instead he walked up the marble stairs toward the second floor captain's office. The open architectural plan of the Bradbury allowed a clear view of every floor, and he spotted Reggie and Miller standing in the exterior hallway near the elevator as he turned from the landing and started up the second flight of stairs. Reggie saw him too and immediately moved in his direction with Miller a step behind.

The two men reached him before he got to the second floor.

"I screwed up," Miller admitted before Turner could say anything.

"Won't let us listen?" Turner asked. He'd anticipated this outcome so it wasn't really a question that needed an answer.

"Weaver used Miller to get you here," Reggie said. "He wants to serve you and send us home until the investigation's done."

"I didn't know. I never would've called you." Miller was so upset his face was flushed, but the scar on his scalp was an ugly purple track. They had shaved his head at the hospital, and the fresh crop of grey fuzz didn't cover the damage caused by Cullen's bullet. He saw Turner staring at the wound and put on his baseball cap. "Let's get out of here," he said.

"Why?" Turner asked. He didn't see any reason to hide. "They'll just mail it to me if they can't find me. Am I the only one?"

"You and Reg, for now. Metcalf hates me, but he's got nothing, and he's not gonna harass a guy who just got shot."

"Is Conner even here?" Turner asked.

"He's getting interviewed as we speak," Miller said, grinning now. "You're not gonna believe who the investigators are . . . Earl and Tony, our surveillance refugees. Metcalf put them in charge of our case."

"Just keeps getting better," Reggie mumbled.

"Could've been worse. They could've picked two guys who actually had a brain between them," Miller said.

Miller was right. Turner had worked with Earl and Tony in the surveillance squad for several months. They were terrible cops. Their instincts were rarely on target and neither of them knew how to do a thorough investigation. He was relieved when Metcalf took them out of the squad. Unfortunately, their integrity was suspect too. If they wanted him and Reggie to look bad, they'd have no qualms fabricating the evidence they were incapable of finding legitimately.

Reggie ushered them into a witness waiting room adjacent to one of the board rooms. There wasn't a board of rights scheduled that day so the room was empty. Miller explained that Sergeant

Weaver was on his way to Turner's house to serve him with his suspension papers, because as soon as Miller found out Weaver's real intentions, he lied and swore that Turner refused to come downtown. They should have a little time to work before Weaver found them.

Reggie had already been served. He showed Turner the suspension papers before crumpling them into a ball and tossing them in the wastepaper basket. The hallway door to the board room opened and slammed shut. The three men stayed quiet. After a few seconds, they could hear voices arguing inside the board room. There was a split wall between the two rooms. Unless they worked IA, most officers didn't know the witness room existed.

Turner recognized Conner's voice immediately. He sounded angry. Another softer male voice was attempting to calm him. Conner called him useless, stupid, finally mentioning the name Jack. Reggie wrote the name Jack Winter on the back of an old newspaper lying on the table. Jack Winter was a well-known left-wing attorney who represented nearly every anti-police lawsuit in the city. He occasionally represented police officers as long as they were suing the police department or the city. Sporadically, he won and made lots of money for himself and much less for his clients. Winter was an overweight dwarf with long, stringy grey hair, a throwback to the sixties. Turner thought he looked like Tweedledum in an ugly three-piece suit. When Winter was confused or feigned confusion, he cocked his head like a puppy, earning him the nickname Fido among cops.

Winter was trying to explain to Conner why he hadn't objected to any of the questions that had been asked. Winter said he needed to know what parts of the story were subject to scrutiny. He could then have Conner elaborate on those later. Conner wasn't satisfied. He'd wanted to go in, make his accusations and leave. He didn't want anyone questioning him. Turner could hear the arrogance in Conner's voice. Conner threatened not to pay Winter unless Turner got fired. They argued about money for a few more minutes, and then the door to the board room slammed, and it was quiet again. Turner saw their shadows pass in front of the opaque glass door to the witness room.

"Follow the yellow brick road, asshole," Miller said, breaking the silence. "Why you?" he asked Turner.

Turner glanced at Reggie. How much did he want to tell Miller about Miriam?

"Who knows," he lied. "Maybe he's pissed about me dating his mother." Turner didn't need Miller's sarcasm on top of all his other problems.

"I pulled Conner's case folder in Weaver's office. The snitch's name isn't in it," Reggie said, changing the subject.

Turner didn't want to know how Reggie managed to get his hands on the file, but since the informant's name wasn't in there, the only other source he could think of again was Jenny Furcal at IA. Jenny didn't like Miller, so he offered to wait at the Chinatown office. Turner agreed. They couldn't afford to alienate the poodle.

Jenny wasn't her usual overly aggressive self when she saw Turner. She almost greeted him, but caught herself, then tried to ignore him for a second or two, but it was impossible for Jenny not to talk. She scolded him for being rude in their last conversation, for not having a drink with her, and finally for not wanting to sleep with her. She pretended she was joking, but they both knew she wasn't.

"What do you want, Turner?" she asked, after he had exhausted his arsenal of small talk. She might've been horny, but she wasn't stupid.

Pretending he didn't want something would make her angry, so he decided to tell some version of the truth.

"It's complicated, and I don't want to get you in trouble," he said, trying to hesitate just long enough to make it believable.

After a hearty guffaw followed by a snort, she said, "Sure you don't. What is it?" She sat back and crossed her chubby arms. Her lacquered blonde hair looked like barbed wire under the office lights.

"I need an informant file."

"I need a drink and a night out."

"Tonight," Turner said, knowing after he stood her up this would be the last favor he'd get from Jenny.

"Which informant?"

"The Conner investigation," he said and saw her smile fade. She moved in closer to the desk and stared at him. "I don't think so. You're sexy. I like you . . . not enough to get fired."

"How would anybody know?"

"Metcalf keeps that particular file in his office in a locked cabinet."

"Have you seen it?" Turner asked.

"I know it exists. I haven't looked inside if that's what you mean."

"Who has? Has Weaver?"

"Metcalf's the only one as far as I know."

Turner tried to persuade her, but she insisted there was no way she'd risk her job and Lieutenant Metcalf's wrath to get that file . . . even for his handsome body. After a few minutes, when he saw Reggie edging toward the door, he realized it was pointless to continue his pleading; but before he could make good his escape, Jenny clamped onto his jacket sleeve.

"Maybe I'd try if I had a reason," she whispered, pulling him a little closer.

He gently removed her fingers from his jacket, straightened up and without a word, walked away. He wasn't playing her game any longer. If she wanted to harass him, she'd have to stand in line behind Conner and his mother, the dwarf lawyer, Miriam, Metcalf, and all the rest of them. Turner was losing count of all the people who were trying to make his life miserable. Being suspended for a few weeks was beginning to sound like a good idea. He needed to get away from this insanity, this upside-down world where guys like Conner can complain about real cops doing their job.

Preoccupied with his thoughts, he didn't pay attention to where Reggie was leading him. When he looked up they were standing in Metcalf's outer office. Reggie told the secretary, a thin serious woman who refused to look up from her computer, that he had to see the lieutenant right away. She explained that he'd gone out with Sergeant Weaver to serve papers on Detective Turner. When Reggie insisted, she looked up and saw Turner.

"You're here," she said.

"Can we wait in his office?" Turner asked.

"Let me call first to see if he'll be back," she said, picking up the phone.

"I don't mind waiting," Turner said as he entered Metcalf's office.

"No, don't," she said, and then softly, "he doesn't like people in there while he's gone." Turner and Reggie were already inside and had closed the door. "I'm calling him right now," she shouted from the other side of the door.

Turner tapped the top of the wooden file cabinet. "Open it," he ordered. Reggie took a couple of paper clips from Metcalf's desk and popped the lock. The second drawer had a dozen informant packages, and every informant had been given a number. They quickly read through the paperwork in each package. In his third file, Reggie found their snitch. The informant's one and only case had been Ian Conner. Reggie copied all the personal information, replaced the package and locked the cabinet again.

They left Metcalf's office, startling the nervous secretary. She stood quickly and tried to block the hallway door.

"I talked to the lieutenant . . . be here in ten minutes . . . very grateful you came on your own . . . very positive thing." She continued to babble as they walked around her, leaving the anxious woman standing in the doorway. "Aren't you going to wait?" were her last words as Turner and Reggie stepped into the elevator.

It was five minutes from Parker Center to the Chinatown office, but Turner figured that was the first place Weaver and Metcalf would look for them. Finding a place that wasn't crawling with cops in downtown Los Angeles was difficult. Reggie knew a Mexican restaurant on Sunset that had dark booths and good food. He called Miller, telling him to meet them at La Tortuga in east L.A.

The lunch crowd had already dispersed. The three men easily found an empty booth in the back. Turner remembered Reggie had dated the owner's daughter several years ago. Her old man, still lamenting the fact that she had chosen to marry a lazy ex-gangbanger over the serious cop, hovered close by and insisted they sample a variety of tasty dishes on the house.

While they ate soft carnitas tacos and drank Corona beer, Reggie showed them the notes he'd copied from the informant's folder. The snitch was a woman. Her code name was Sapphire. There was a contact phone number but no address. Her real name wasn't in the package. She had called IA and refused to identify herself when she offered the information on Conner. Miller took his cell phone out of his jacket pocket and called the informant's contact number. It was disconnected.

Although most of the information she provided had been included in the squad's worksheet, Turner noticed one item she'd mentioned that wasn't there. It was something that probably wouldn't mean much to anyone but him. Sapphire had described Conner as a mama's boy "who doesn't piss unless mama lets him."

FIFTEEN

The more Turner thought about it, he was convinced Miriam was the snitch. She was curious by nature and smart. If she'd spent a lot of time around Conner, sooner or later she'd see or hear things that bothered her and probe for answers. After Turner repeated her parting words, Reggie and Miller agreed that Miriam was probably Sapphire and, therefore, not likely to be the one who blew their surveillance. They decided it was best if Turner talked to her alone. Although he wasn't eager to confront his ex-lover, he realized she might not have told Internal Affairs the whole story simply because too much information could've identified and implicated her.

Turner called her at work and was told she'd taken some vacation time. He called her apartment and got the answering machine. There were other contact numbers for her at his house, so he left Reggie and Miller at the restaurant and drove home.

The house was empty when he arrived. Eddie and the dog were out somewhere, probably wandering around the neighborhood. Lately, he worried when they went for their walk. Both of them were old, and neither one had any sense of direction. Turner had put a tag on Daryl's collar with his phone number and address. He tried to get Eddie to wear an ID bracelet with the same information, but the old man refused. As long as the dog and Eddie were never separated, he figured they should both get home again.

His old address book was in the desk in the den. Turner found a phone number and the address for Miriam's father in Calaveras County. It was at least a five-hour drive, but he decided to go there rather than call. Why give her an opportunity to avoid him.

She didn't have any close friends in Los Angeles. She'd grown up and gone to school in northern California. Turner had lived with her long enough to know when Miriam wanted to get away for a while, she'd always go north. He thought about asking Reggie to come with him, but finally made up his mind to go alone.

Turner packed a change of clothes. He still had the city car, but didn't want to explain what he was doing three hundred miles from home if he had an accident. His 1999 Chevy truck was a piece of junk, but it would do for this one trip. If he left right now, he could be there early in the morning. He checked the refrigerator, and there was plenty of food for Eddie. Several cans of Daryl's dog food were stacked on a shelf in the cupboard. His two companions would survive nicely until he got back. He left a note taped to the television screen, the one place he knew for certain Eddie would see it.

Miriam's father's cabin was in Arnold, a small touristy mountain town surrounded by a variety of pine and redwood trees, a dozen wineries, and images conjured up from the writings of Samuel Langhorne Clemens. It was rental property after Christmas, but this time of year, Miriam or her father usually stayed there for a week or two. It was nearly 2 A.M. when Turner pulled off Highway 4 in Arnold. He didn't know the street names, but had been here a couple of times with Miriam and thought he could find the place again. As soon as he drove away from the street lights on the main road, everything outside his truck disappeared into the darkness. All he could see was the strip of asphalt directly in front of his headlights. Bad idea, he thought and made a U-turn. There was a small motel near a shopping center where he left the highway. He would stay there until daylight and try again.

The night clerk at the Primrose Motel studied him for several seconds before admitting she had a vacancy. Turner saw his image in the mirror behind the front desk and knew why. He hadn't shaved all day and was wearing his comfortable shabby jeans and an old leather jacket that had a couple of tears in the seams. His thick military-trimmed, salt-and-pepper hair was getting too long and starting to curl. He'd lost some weight lately, and with the stubble on his face and the dark patches under his tired bloodshot eyes, he looked like an escapee from some motorcycle gang. He joked with her about the long drive from Los Angeles, and she finally relaxed a little and smiled at him. She dropped the key into his hand and pointed at a room across the parking lot. Before he left the lobby, he heard the door to her office close and lock.

His room was small and smelled of Lysol and bleach. The wall heater was turned off, and he had to light the pilot to get it started. The bed was slightly bigger than a camping cot and not as comfortable, but it didn't matter. He wrapped himself in the bedspread and lay on top of the sheets.

The sound of a car horn woke him the next morning. He hadn't bothered to close the curtains, and when he opened his eyes the sun nearly blinded him. It was warm and felt good. It would've been nice to stay there, safe in his blanket cocoon, and not have to face the complicated mess his life had become, but it wasn't in his nature to hide. He'd slept in his clothes and boots, but was rested and ready to finish what he'd started. The bathroom was even less inviting than the rest of the room, but he needed a shower. A drain was under the shower head, but there wasn't a curtain and nothing kept the water from the rest of the bathroom. When he was finished, everything was wet including his one and only towel. It didn't matter; he was clean and hungry.

It was almost noon by the time he finished breakfast. He gassed up the truck and drove away from the main highway again. He recognized most of the landmarks now, and after a couple of wrong turns managed to find her father's cabin. Like many of the homes in the neighborhood, the cabin was surrounded by pine trees and sat on nearly an acre of land. A spacious deck led to the front door. Turner knew there was a rear deck with a great view, a large stack of firewood, and a table and chairs where during better times he and Miriam drank wine and watched the sunset.

He knocked and waited. No answer. He walked around to the back of the house and up the stairs onto the back deck. He knocked again with no response. He pushed the sliding glass door, and it opened. Typical, he thought. Miriam refused to believe there were bad people in this world who preyed on naïve and careless victims. After nearly thirty years as a cop, he was certain evil existed. He had looked into the dead eyes of those who could hurt and kill the innocent without regret or remorse. It always bothered him when he thought how vulnerable Miriam was.

The living room looked as if it had been ransacked: dirty dishes were on the coffee table, soda cans and empty bottles on the floor, clothes thrown everywhere. All the lights were on, and the television was too loud. If he hadn't lived with Miriam, he might've been worried, but the house had all the signs of her typical habitat. He lowered the volume on the TV and called her name as he walked through each of the messy rooms, but she wasn't there. He stepped out onto the back deck and could smell wood burning from a neighbor's fireplace. The air was cold without a breeze. He took a deep breath—an instant tonic—compliments of Mother Nature.

He heard the neighbors' dogs barking before he saw her bundled-up figure emerge from the dense woods behind the cabin. She froze when she saw him standing on the deck, and then grabbed the ends of the scarf around her neck with both hands like a frightened child. He called out to her and could see she was straining to recognize him.

"It's Mike," Turner shouted.

She continued walking toward the house, stopping just under the deck. Looking up and breathing heavily she said, "You scared me. I wasn't expecting anyone."

"I can see that . . . cleaning lady's day off?" he asked, opening the sliding door for her.

"Fuck you," she said, dryly. "It's my house. When or if I clean is none of your anal retentive business." Miriam threw her coat and gloves on the kitchen chair. "How did you know I was here?"

"Lucky guess." He waited until she came back into the living room and then asked, "Does Conner know about this place?"

Her cheeks and nose were red from the cold, and her long brown hair was in a single French braid. She could've passed for an adolescent.

"What's it to you?" she asked, picking up debris from the floor and couch. Her voice cracked a little. He didn't think it was from the cold.

"He's not stupid. Eventually, he's going to figure out you were the informant."

She denied knowing what Turner was talking about and fussed with the dirty dishes until the tears flowed. At first, she tried to hide them, but finally she couldn't control her emotions any longer, sat on the coffee table and cried. He wanted to put his arms around her, make her feel safe but didn't. He needed the truth, and fear was a great motivator.

"Ian doesn't know about this place," she admitted when the crying stopped. "You're the only one I ever brought here."

"Good," he said, and felt a twinge of pride in spite of knowing their relationship was finished.

"He's insane. He hurts people." Her bloodshot eyes looked directly at him for the first time. "He hates you."

"Tell me everything you know about him, or I can't help," Turner said, sitting on the couch in front of her.

Miriam wiped her tearstained face with her sweater and moved to sit beside him. She told him how she met Conner at the Hollywood desk after she and Turner had gone their separate ways. She was lonely and Conner could be charming. He had a lot of money and took her to nice places like Las Vegas and San Francisco. He bought her expensive gifts, jewelry and things for her apartment. When she started questioning where he got his money, their relationship soured. One night, he was sleeping at her apartment, and she heard him on his cell phone in the middle of the night. He was talking to someone about what sounded like a botched robbery, involving a movie theater. Someone had been killed. She couldn't hear all the conversation, but she was certain Conner had planned the crime. After that there were other calls, lots of calls. It became clear to her he was dangerous.

"That's how he got his money. He was stealing," she said.

Miriam insisted she'd tried to break up with Conner after she found out about his crimes, but he wouldn't leave her alone; she was too scared to tell anyone. She knew Conner's mother hated her. Beverly had made it clear she thought Miriam was a loser who would hurt her son. Miriam was desperate, so she became intentionally nasty to Beverly knowing she would force her son to end the relationship. After one particularly bitter argument between the two women, Conner reluctantly told Miriam he was done with her. However, he continued to follow and harass her if she dated other men. He even called her at work warning her to stay away from Turner. Her eyes filled with tears again as she explained her real reason for asking Eddie to live with them. She didn't think Conner would do anything with a witness there.

Miriam was certain Conner didn't know how much she knew about his activities, or he never would have allowed her to walk away; but now, after the IA investigation and surveillance, he probably suspected she was the snitch.

"Nobody, except Beverly, ever got that close to him," Miriam said. "He's got to know it was me, and you saw what he did to Goodman."

"He killed Goodman? You know that?"

"I know Goodman wanted to leave. They argued at Beverly's place. I was going to work and heard them in the barn. Ian told him there was only one way he'd ever get out. I knew what he meant."

Turner watched her as she told her story, wanted to believe she was distressed and frightened enough to be giving him some version of the truth. There were signs. Miriam always bit her fingernails, but a few of them were bloody. She obviously hadn't been sleeping well, and now at least there was an explanation for her drastic weight loss. When she seemed drained of any useful information, despite every instinct telling him it would be a very bad idea, he pulled her closer and held her tightly. She hugged him back, squeezing so hard it hurt his ribs. He carried her into the bedroom, put her on top of the unmade bed, covered her with a comforter and stayed with her until her crying stopped and she fell asleep.

He hadn't intended to allow himself to feel this way about her again. He hoped it was just pity, but knew better. You can't pick the people you love. It just happens. Intellectually, his ideal woman would be nothing like Miriam. She'd be strong and intelligent, someone with common sense who'd love him as much as he loved her. Miriam was selfish and made bad choices, but there were those moments when her smile touched his soul. He couldn't explain it, maybe it was chemistry or magic, but he knew he'd never willingly walk out on her.

It took a couple of hours, but he managed to pick up most of the debris scattered around the cabin. He heard her heavy breathing as he washed the dishes and swept the floor. When the place was reasonably clean, Turner found an open, half full bottle of pinot noir from one of the local wineries sitting on the kitchen counter. The winery was one of her father's favorites. Miriam's father liked good wine, and he had introduced Turner to some of the best wines he'd ever tasted. He emptied the bottle, filling a large wine glass, put on his leather jacket and sat on the back deck. Turner didn't know how long he'd been out there, but he'd finished the wine and was leaning back in his chair with his feet on the railing when Miriam came outside bundled up in a ski jacket and fur-lined boots, carrying another glass and a full bottle.

"Want company?" she asked with that smile.

"If you share," he said, holding up his empty glass.

She filled both glasses and pulled a chair closer to his.

"I'm an idiot," she whispered.

"You made some bad choices. It happens."

"Happens to me a lot."

He laughed but didn't disagree. She was wearing her gloves and knit cap and held the glass with both hands. It was a clear night and the full moon bathed the deck in low light. Turner saw the puffs of air as she spoke.

"You cold?"

"Feels good. That was the first real sleep I've had since I left your house. How's Eddie?"

"Missing you."

"Is he the only one?"

Turner let his feet slip off the railing and sat up. He leaned across her chair and kissed her soft, warm lips. She put her arms around his neck. He stood, took the glass out of her hand and led her back into the cabin.

SIXTEEN

Their lovemaking wasn't long or intense, a few pleasurable moments of passion followed by hours of spooning naked under the heavy blankets. With his arm tucked around her breasts, Turner felt her rhythmic breathing. He'd slept a few hours, but was awake before sunrise, hungry, re-energized and ready to drive back into the city.

Miriam didn't stir until nearly 7 A.M. By the time she finally shuffled out of the bedroom in a long flannel bathrobe, he'd eaten breakfast and was waiting to talk with her before he left. It would be a temporary separation, but she seemed surprised he was leaving. Turner explained that she would be okay as long as she stayed in Arnold. When Conner was in jail, he would come back and bring her to his house. She had two weeks left of her vacation, and could take some paid sick time after that until it was safe to return to Los Angeles. She didn't like being alone in the cabin, but agreed it was the smart thing to do. She'd call her dad and ask him to come up for a few days to keep her company. Turner knew her well enough to be confident she'd be too frightened to go anywhere Conner might find her.

Turner was back in Redondo Beach by late morning. He'd called Reggie and asked him to meet at JR's. The bar was nearly empty that early in the day, with a few homeless regulars playing gin with the bartender. By the time Reggie got there, Turner was finishing his second beer. He recognized the sheepish grin as Reggie slid into the booth. It usually meant his partner had just done something that amused him, but had pissed off somebody else.

"Weaver's guys are following me," Reggie said, after ordering the house draft.

"They're surveilling you?"

"Looking for you."

"So, you led them here."

"Had to. These guys couldn't find a liquor store in South Central L.A. Let 'em serve you the papers, so we're rid of them."

Turner didn't like the idea of department business intruding on his favorite bar, but knew Reggie was right. He didn't need a shadow. Turner repeated Miriam's story while they waited for Weaver to arrive with the suspension papers.

Thirty minutes later, Weaver entered the bar and found them in the booth near the broken window. Looking smug, he slapped a piece of paper on the table in front of Turner.

"Sign it," Weaver ordered, handing him a pen.

Turner took the pen and signed a paper that stated he would be suspended until an investigation into the Cullen and Goodman killings was finished. Weaver gave him a copy and turned to leave.

"I like your new grey Taurus," Reggie said, and when Weaver stopped, he added, "The silver Toyota and Honda aren't bad, but I'd change the green Chevy and the Buick."

"You missed one," Weaver said, wryly.

"Metcalf's Camaro was so obvious I didn't mention it. Shouldn't he be doing this instead of hiding in the parking lot and letting his bun boy do his dirty work?"

Weaver took a few steps back toward the booth. His face was flushed. "Fuck you," he shouted, pointing at Reggie. "You wanna be cowboys; you live with the consequences. Stay away from me and my squad."

"Doesn't bother you that Conner's corrupt, and he's playing you and IA for fools?" Turner asked before Weaver could leave. As Weaver reached the door, Turner shouted, "I talked to the Conner snitch." Weaver stopped with his hand on the door. He returned to the booth. The two bums and the bartender watched him as if he were the plastic ball on a ping pong table.

"You're full of shit," Weaver said, leaning on the table. "If you know, who is it?"

"Sapphire."

Weaver straightened up. His expression told Turner the man's brain had short-circuited. He looked confused, surprised, and interested all at the same time.

"So, you got your hands on the informant package. That doesn't mean you know Sapphire's identity."

"I met with her."

"Who is she?" Weaver asked, sitting beside Reggie.

"I can't tell you."

"Bullshit," Weaver said, getting out of the booth again. "More bullshit."

"She's hiding. The guy terrifies her. She thinks he killed Goodman, and she overheard him talking about a bunch of robberies."

"Will she work with us?" Weaver asked. In spite of his anger, he knew an opportunity when he saw one. "Can we put a wire on her?"

"I don't know," Turner said, truthfully. He wasn't certain how much Miriam would be willing to do, but he didn't like the idea of getting her anywhere near Conner. "At some point, she'll testify," he said, but didn't know if that was true. Her name would come out eventually. If Miriam didn't reveal her relationship with Conner, Beverly or her son certainly would when and if Miriam testified.

"I gotta get back outside. They're waiting," Weaver said, but the heavyset sergeant didn't move. He stared at the two men sitting in the booth as if he were trying to make a difficult decision. "Don't go to the office unless I call you," he ordered. "Metcalf's in and out all the time now. Dr. Tom doesn't patrol anymore since Miller stopped feeding him, so the lieutenant's not afraid to come," Weaver said, trying not to smile. He got serious again. "We'll talk some more, but stay out of Metcalf's radar. He thinks the two of you and Miller should be fired, and he'll use Conner's complaint or anything else he can to do it."

"What about the snitch?" Turner asked.

"I've gotta think," Weaver said.

He left, and the spectators at the bar went back to their card game.

Reggie ordered another beer and said that while Turner was in Arnold, he had received a call from Vogel who was back at Robbery Homicide Division. Vogel had been doing some additional background on the addresses Reggie had confiscated from Conner's bedroom. He confirmed that they were movie theater locations that had been robbed, but one of them was interesting. The owner was killed in the robbery, but it looked like an execution. He was cooperating with the robbers, but they shot him anyway. The wife was standing right next to the victim, but they didn't harm her. The theater only showed classic movies and didn't make much money. A developer had offered the owner a lot of money for the site, but he'd refused to sell. The owner had a passion for old movies and was getting a small inheritance, so he could get by with very little profit; but the wife was much younger with expensive tastes. Vogel found out it was common knowledge she was badgering him to sell.

"You think this might be like Cullen's deal in the Hollywood Hills, a murder for hire?" Turner asked.

"It's not the kind of place you'd rob for lots of cash. They only got a couple of hundred there, while at the first two locations, they got thousands."

"It's smart," Turner said, thinking out loud. "There's a string of movie theater robberies. Nobody's gonna look for a motive other than robbery."

"Nobody except Vogel."

"Did he interview the widow?" Turner asked.

"He's gonna meet us for lunch at the Mexican place in East L.A. He can tell you about the interview."

It was nearly noon. Turner paid the bill and took his copy of the suspension papers. He knew he hadn't done anything wrong, but the accusation made him angry. He was no angel, but his dealings with Conner and his two criminal cop buddies were

146

solid, honest police work. Lately, it seemed like the only time he ever got in trouble with the department was when he did his job. The bad guy complained, and Turner had to defend doing what the city paid him to do. He drove too fast chasing a cop killer, or fired his weapon too many times at someone who was trying to kill him, or spoke too harshly to an ex-con. They wanted the end result, but didn't have the guts to acknowledge what it took to get there.

Turner worried that someday guys like Metcalf might succeed in eliminating all the diligent street cops who trudged through the messy, dangerous trenches every day, and managed to get the job done the best way they could. If it ever happened, God had better protect the good people in this city because the LAPD wouldn't have cops with the ability or desire to do it any longer.

Vogel was waiting for them when they got to La Tortuga. The lunch crowd had thinned to a few upper management types in business suits with the time to gossip about co-workers while sipping another margarita. Vogel asked about Miller, but Turner could see the nervous detective was relieved his ex-partner hadn't come. Miller's over-the-top behavior was something Vogel probably didn't miss after he left the surveillance unit.

Unfortunately, his interview with the theater owner's wife hadn't revealed much useful information.

"Every instinct tells me she set it up, but she's a good actress," Vogel said. "I couldn't get her to change her story or shake the grieving widow thing."

"If it was a hit-for-hire, she'd have to pay the killer. Where'd the money come from?" Turner asked.

"Not their bank accounts, I checked," Vogel said and added, "somehow she stashed the money or sold a family heirloom or something."

"So we've got nothing," Reggie said.

"Not exactly," Vogel said, grinning. "There's a high-end antiques store adjacent to the theater. They have a surveillance camera that swivels and intermittently catches the front of the theater."

"They still have the tapes?"

"Yep, we got 'em just before the thirty-day destruction date."

"Does it help?" Turner was annoyed. He hated being spoon-fed information.

"Don't know. Lighting's not very good. We're trying to enhance the quality."

"Conner should be easy enough to identify. How many big, overweight redheads go into that place?"

"Haven't seen anything that matches his description, but we have a possible match that night on Goodman."

Turner sat back, disappointed . . . the dead guy again. Conner was smart enough not to get his hands dirty.

"Did you show her a photo lineup?" Reggie asked.

"She didn't pick out anybody, but I noticed something when she looked at Goodman's photo." Vogel hesitated as if searching for the right words to explain it. "She got kind of depressed or something."

"You think she knew him?" Turner asked.

"I think so."

Turner remembered Goodman was a handsome young man. The theater owner's attractive, greedy wife was in her fifties, and her husband was seventy-five. The frustrated woman might have had more than a business relationship with Goodman which would explain the absence of payoff money. Turner thought it was worth a trip out to Santa Clarita to search the apartment Goodman and Cullen shared, and then a visit with the grieving widow was certainly in order. He wasn't certain anyone except the surveillance squad knew Goodman had another place. Vogel admitted that he'd forgotten about it, but said he'd searched the apartment in West L.A. and determined it was nothing more than a crash pad.

Turner needed to stop by the house first, change clothes and make certain his roommates were surviving without him. When he arrived, Eddie was digging in the front yard and shoveling dirt onto the driveway. He told himself to calm down as he parked his truck on the street. It wasn't that big an inconvenience, but one he didn't need today. Daryl was sprawled out near a freshly dug hole that was already over a foot deep. With sweat dripping from his forehead, the old man was wearing a stained New York Yankees ball cap, a worn t-shirt under a pair of overalls and his old, green rubber garden boots. In spite of his annoyance, Turner had to smile. The scene looked like the ghetto version of a Norman Rockwell painting. Turner was cold with the breeze biting at his face. He had a sweater under his jacket but could still feel the chill.

"You're gonna get pneumonia, and your kid's gonna blame me." Turner was standing behind Eddie, but the old man didn't stop digging. Daryl rolled over for his belly rub. "You upset about something?" Turner asked when he got tired of petting Daryl and being ignored. "I left a note."

Eddie stopped digging and glared at him. "I don't care if you ain't here. Don't need no babysitter. Look at that," he said, pointing at his house next door. There was a new bright red "For Sale" sign on the manicured front lawn.

"Sorry," Turner said, touching the old man's shoulder. "I didn't notice, but you're living here now."

Eddie pulled away, wiped his sleeve across his eyes and started digging again. "Stealin' my home."

"Danny's doing what he thinks is best for you."

"My boy does what's best for his own self." Eddie's shovel hit the ground so hard, Turner thought it would break.

"You trying to tunnel over there and blow it up?" Turner said, gently removing the shovel from Eddie's grip.

The trace of a smile almost broke through as the old man tightened his lips. He took a deep breath and put his hands on his hips.

"No, smartass, I'm plantin' a tree so that old dog and me has shade this summer."

Turner gave him back the shovel. "Don't break any bones or rupture anything important."

He should have offered to finish digging and made the old man go into the house, but Turner knew the therapeutic value of physical labor. Sometimes he wished he'd gone with his first love and become a carpenter. A lot of stress was pounded away at the end of a claw hammer. The adrenaline kept accumulating in police work with few opportunities to vent.

The house was in reasonably good condition. Turner wasn't tempted to open the door to Eddie's room. Peanut butter sandwiches and potato chips seemed to be his roommate's meal of choice for the last few days, so he made a bowl of tuna salad and cut up some fruit and left it in the refrigerator.

He took a long, hot shower and put on clean Levi's and his new boots, hoping to impress the widow. The phone at the cabin had the message machine on when he called earlier, so he tried again. This time Miriam picked up right away.

"I'm bored. Can't you come back for a few days," were her first words.

"No, call your dad."

"I did. He can't come until tomorrow night. I want to go home."

Turner exhaled. It was frustrating to care about someone who drove you crazy. "I'll show you the pictures of Goodman hanging in his tub. Maybe if you see what Conner can do you'll stop whining."

"I don't whine. I'm lonely."

"You're alive."

She was quiet, and finally agreed it was best if she stayed hidden. He gave her a brief update on the investigation, and they chatted about the house and Eddie's son and how good it would be when she could move back. She seemed different, more open, more optimistic about their future. Turner wanted to believe her willingness to go beyond just good sex and make a life together. "We'll see," he said to himself after hanging up the phone.

SEVENTEEN

There's always one house on the block where the shades stay closed, and every neighbor wonders what goes on inside. Turner stood on the front porch of Reggie's bungalow and felt like the kid who finally sneaks a peek. As far as he knew, no one on the job had ever seen the inside of his partner's home. Reggie guarded his privacy, but after many years, Turner got the invitation.

It wasn't what he'd expected, definitely not some eccentric bachelor's pad. The sand-colored walls were soothing background for the sleek black leather furniture. The rooms were small, but neatly decorated with a clean modern look. The place looked like a page from one of Miriam's *Better Homes and Gardens* magazines. A large impressionistic oil painting of downtown Los Angeles hung over the couch. He liked it because he figured the jumble of dark colors and shapes was probably the way Reggie saw the city.

While he waited for Reggie to take a shower and finish dressing, Turner studied the built-in bookcases that lined every wall of a small den off the dining room. The collection was mostly history books and biographies. One shelf was filled with small notebooks like the one Reggie carried everywhere. It was tempting, but he didn't pick one up and thumb through it. Like most cops, Turner was curious. He wandered around the house, looked in the tidy kitchen, and discovered that the spare bedroom was used as an art studio—complete with a cluttered drafting table and paint-spattered drop cloths protecting the hardwood floor. There wasn't a television, radio or computer anywhere in sight.

"Nice place," Turner said when Reggie finally emerged from his bedroom.

"Sorry it took so long. I was sleeping when you called."

"You do this?" Turner asked, pointing at the picture over the couch.

"Therapy."

"Does it help?"

"Not much, but I like it better than writing. You ready?" Reggie asked as he did a chamber check on his .45, slipped it back into the holster and covered the weapon with his shirt.

Turner thought the bungalow would give him a better picture of his friend, but the guy remained an enigma, like his painting, a cluttered mishmash that never quite came into focus. He never doubted Reggie's strength and courage, but there was darkness beneath the surface he couldn't ignore, an uneasy feeling that life intended something awful for Reggie. He never asked, but was pretty certain Reggie felt the same way because the man lived and worked without those natural fears possessed by ordinary men contemplating old age. Turner figured he was probably a shit for exploiting his friend's willingness to put himself in harm's way, but he was nervous about the possibility that Conner could get away with all the mayhem he'd created. That meant Miriam's life would be hell, so he'd take advantage of Reggie if that was the only way.

The traffic was light, and it took a little over an hour before they parked in front of Goodman's apartment building. The resident manager didn't hesitate to give them the key to the one-bedroom unit on the third floor. She had just taken the job a few days ago and wasn't aware one of her tenants was dead. Goodman was paid up until the end of the month, so there hadn't been any reason to talk to him.

It was a well-maintained building. The hallway walls were freshly painted with sconce lighting between the doors. Potted ficus trees were set at the top of each stairwell and skylights flooded the top floor with natural light.

They stood in the hallway for several seconds after Turner opened the door. The few pieces of furniture had been turned upside down. Lamps, books, photos, newspapers, and magazines were strewn over the floor. The kitchen lights were on and the refrigerator was open and empty, with an assortment of rotting food decorating the linoleum. Most of the contents from the cupboards and drawers had been dumped.

"If this was Miriam's place, I wouldn't worry," Turner said, finally stepping inside and over a table lamp. "But in this case I'd say somebody's already been here."

"The widow?" Reggie asked as he put a chair upright.

That was a possibility, but Turner couldn't picture a middle-aged woman doing this much damage.

They moved cautiously through the apartment checking each room to make certain they were alone. The bedrooms and bathroom were in similar disarray. Dresser drawers were emptied. Clothes were pulled from hangers and left in the middle of the room in a messy pile. In what appeared to be Goodman's bedroom, Reggie picked up a flimsy woman's nightgown and a couple of bras.

"If it was her, she wasn't real interested in getting all her stuff," he said.

Turner found pictures of Goodman with his buddy Cullen and an older woman taken at the Police Academy in Elysian Park. Some of the divisions had their summer picnics at the Academy. The price was right and the grounds were nice. She was obviously older than Goodman, but she was a strikingly beautiful woman, tall with Marilyn Monroe blonde hair and a twenty-year-old's figure.

"She left too much evidence of their relationship. I don't think this was her handiwork," Turner said.

"Maybe she hired someone really stupid to do it."

"No," Turner said. "If this is the widow, she and Goodman got their picture taken at a company picnic. There's no attempt to be discreet about it."

Reggie shoved the bedspread onto the floor and sat on the mattress. "Could've been Conner. Maybe Goodman had something worth getting killed for."

"Like what?"

"Money . . . compromising stuff . . . I don't know."

"Maybe the widow knows."

"There's only one way to find out," Reggie said, pushing himself up.

Turner tossed a handful of photos on the dresser. Conner might be an asshole, but he was clever, too. There wasn't one picture or anything else linking him with these guys. They did all the nasty stuff, and the redhead kept his distance. The big guy wasn't going to get his hands dirty. Putting him in prison wasn't going to be easy either, unless they caught a break or one of his buddies got really scared or pissed off and lived long enough to tell the story.

He called Vogel and told him what they'd found at the apartment. Vogel agreed to drive over and try getting prints, but they all knew that would be a waste of time. Vogel had talked to the widow that morning, and she'd reluctantly agreed to meet with Turner as long as he got to her house before 8 P.M. that night. She was flying to San Francisco and had a taxi coming at exactly 8 P.M.

Her address was less than a mile from Goodman's apartment, and they had almost an hour before her deadline.

Turner was about to hang up when Vogel stopped him.

"I forgot to tell you. I found a storage locker. Remember the keys from Conner's room? One of them was for his storage locker."

"What was there?"

"Nothing, it was empty. The manager said the lock had been cut off a couple of weeks ago. He was going to file a crime report, but Conner told him not to bother . . . that there was nothing in there but some old books."

"His mother's got an empty barn. Why would he need a storage locker?"

Vogel laughed. "Does this seem like the kind of guy that pays to store old books?"

After Vogel hung up, Turner told Reggie what he'd said.

"That could explain why he surfaced again," Reggie said. "Somebody's got something that belongs to him, and he wants it back."

"Maybe he found it in here."

"Maybe," Reggie said. "Let's see what the widow's got to say."

The widow's place was a sixties-style ranch home painted that lime green no one wanted any longer. It was the biggest house on the street and had a long front yard with a circular driveway. Turner parked in front of the entry porch where the motion lights immediately illuminated the car. The lines of the house had faded into the evening shadows, and a chilly breeze reminded him there was still a touch of winter in the brisk air. It was dark inside the house. There was always the possibility that she'd lied and left earlier in the evening. He was annoyed and felt his irritation growing the longer they stood there and no one answered the doorbell.

Reggie looked in the front windows and went to the side of the house. He returned after a few minutes, picked up a ceramic rabbit from the porch and broke a pane of the small decorative glass in the door. From Reggie's expression, Turner knew it would be pointless to try and stop him. He wasn't certain he wanted to.

"I think she's dead," Reggie said, as he carefully reached inside the broken glass and opened the door.

They searched the house before entering the master bedroom where the middle-aged widow was sprawled on the floor in her bra and panties with an extension cord tied so tightly around her neck it cut into the skin. Her manicured nails were bloody and broken from fighting for her life. Pieces of red chipped acrylic nails were lying around her. It was made to look like a burglary and attempted rape. A few dresser drawers were searched. Her purse had been dumped on the bed. The wallet was empty, no cash or credit cards. Her bra and panties had been pulled down, but no real attempt had been made to molest the woman. Turner was almost certain it had been done for effect. He'd handled a lot of burglary calls and probably more than his share of rapes because his partners always requested that he talk to the victims. Turner had a way of putting both women and men at ease. They would tell him details they were too ashamed to tell the other cops. This didn't look like an attempted rape. Rape is violent and angry when a woman fights back like this one did. There's damage . . . cuts, bruises, more blood and torn clothing. She was strangled. Rape was an afterthought. Somebody searched, but not the way a burglar would. This person searched in a panic as if he were looking for something specific. He could be wrong. It was instinct, not science.

Turner phoned Vogel who notified the local detectives that RHD would handle the homicide. In less than an hour, the yellow tape was up, and uniformed officers were keeping the neighbors and media away from the house.

"Other than where you broke in there's no other point of entry," Vogel said when he finally had a chance to talk to Turner and Reggie alone. "She either knew the killer or he got in through an open door or window. Considering how fucking cold it is, I doubt she had a window open."

"Those phony nails are like a weapon. Be great if she got a few gouges in the guy's face or arms," Turner said.

"SID will check for someone else's blood or skin on the pieces of phony nails, but don't get your hopes up. It looks like she broke most of them on the floor or trying to grab this bed frame." Vogel pointed to scratches in the mahogany leg of the bed.

"She doesn't look that strong." Reggie was kneeling near the body looking at the neck wound. "No contest," he added.

Vogel looked around the room and motioned for the two men to follow him away from the bedroom door. The confident detective was transformed into the nervous and tentative surveillance-squad Vogel again.

"I got a buddy on the shooting team," he whispered. "He told me they found a hole in Cullen's body they can't account for."

"We fired a lot of rounds. He could've been hit before Reggie finished the job."

"Were you firing a rifle? It was a .308 round from a high-powered weapon . . . direct hit in the ten ring. Standing up was probably a reflex. He was dead when Reggie gave him the coup de grace." A light film of perspiration was forming on Vogel's forehead.

Turner and Reggie exchanged a brief look. They both had a pretty good idea where that round had come from, but once again they had no way of proving it.

"Does it make sense?" Turner asked. "Why kill him?"

"Potential witness," Reggie said.

"But if Conner was watching, he had to know we were there. Why not warn Cullen, just stop him before he got to the parking lot?"

"Maybe he wanted Cullen dead but didn't trust us to do it."

"You think that whole murder-for-hire thing was just a way to kill Cullen?" Turner wasn't certain he agreed. "Sheffield would've been an accomplice. That old man was scared shitless."

"What if it was legitimate at first, but at some point Conner sees it as a way to dump a liability?" Reggie seemed more certain of his theory now.

"He wanted both Cullen and Goodman dead?" Turner asked.

"He wanted us to kill Cullen, but at the last minute he wasn't gonna take a chance we'd fuck it up."

By the time the department figured out the surveillance team hadn't killed Cullen and started looking for other suspects, the murder weapon could be sitting at the bottom of the Pacific Ocean or buried under a ton of cement in any one of a dozen developments downtown, Reggie further calculated.

"If you're right, you know what that means?" Turner felt a little uncomfortable as he remembered how he got involved in the Sheffield investigation, the disgraced Sergeant Gomez and his cousin Helen Sanchez telling him about the Sheffield's murder-for-hire. If Reggie was right, one or both of them could be an accomplice to murder.

"Gomez helped set up Cullen," Reggie answered without hesitation.

"He's a sleazeball, but I can't believe Helen knew about any of this." Turner didn't want to think he could have misjudged her that badly. She appeared to be a strong, principled woman. He'd believed and trusted her, helped get her into a new home. If she wasn't involved, moving her to the new apartment might be the only reason she was still alive. People with any link to Conner were dying at an alarming rate.

They left Vogel to finish up at the widow's house, but it was late and Turner was too tired to drive back to Redondo Beach. They decided to get a few hours sleep at a nearby motel.

The next morning, as Turner was driving toward Helen Sanchez's apartment, Weaver called him on his cell phone and asked to meet with him at the surveillance office in Chinatown. Normally, it wasn't easy to decipher what Reggie was thinking, but when Turner made a U-turn to go downtown, it was obvious his friend wasn't pleased. Reggie probably would have ignored the request and continued his investigation. He had little use for supervision, and usually got away with handling matters his own way because he worked specialized divisions and was really good at what he did. Although he wasn't always happy with the people in charge, Turner tried to respect the chain of command and follow the rules. He did what he thought was right, but knew if he wanted to act like a sergeant or lieutenant, he had to get the job first. So, despite Reggie's displeasure, he was going to meet with Sergeant Weaver before he talked to Helen Sanchez.

He got lucky and found a parking space in front of the building even though the sidewalks were packed with tourists today. Dozens of Chinese men and women dressed in traditional bright red and yellow silk clothing mingled among the crowd. Several men carried what appeared to be pieces of a dragon costume. Some sort of celebration had apparently just ended and confetti covered parked cars and the street. He hadn't seen Chinatown this busy for a long time. The houses and apartments north of César Chávez were packed with Asian families, and by the look of these sidewalks most of them had wandered down to participate in the festivities.

A couple of stairs led to the front door of the office building. It was shady and a place to rest. He slipped between sweaty bodies and stepped over packages to get inside the lobby with Reggie one step behind him.

When they got off the elevator, Turner half expected to see Dr. Tom lurking near the sand-filled ashtray, but the hallway was cold and empty. He tried the door to the psychiatrist's office. It was locked and the lights were off.

"Coal mine canary's not working today," Turner said.

"Lucky lieutenant."

Weaver and Lieutenant Metcalf were waiting in the cramped surveillance office, but they weren't alone. Tony and Earl were the investigators handling Turner's case, and had both been reassigned to permanent jobs in IA when the surveillance squad was disbanded.

No one offered to shake hands.

While the lieutenant sat behind Weaver's desk with a detached, I'd-rather-be-anywhere-else expression, the sergeant began by saying that Tony and Earl would interview Turner; but before Weaver could finish his carefully worded explanation, Miller arrived and interrupted him. He greeted Turner and Reggie and ignored everyone else. Turner thought he heard the lieutenant groan.

"We're in the middle of something, detective," Metcalf mumbled.

"You're out of this," Weaver said, attempting to herd the bigger man out of the room. He was angry, patches of red appeared under his day-old beard. "I told you to stay away from here."

"I know, Sarge," Miller said, smiling. "But I figured these guys might need a rep. Department says they're entitled to representation of their choice." He put his arm around Turner's shoulder. "How about it, Mike, am I your choice?"

"Yes," Turner said, afraid to say more because he wanted to laugh. The lieutenant's pencil-thin mustache nearly disappeared as the frustrated man sucked in his upper lip. Turner knew Miller was the last person he should pick as his rep because the irreverent narcotics detective pissed off just about everybody. But in this case, that might be exactly what was required. Conner's bogus allegations deserved to be ridiculed.

Weaver turned his back on Miller and explained how the interview would be conducted.

"You're the only one left in this investigation, Turner," Weaver said, looking embarrassed. Turner guessed this was something the sergeant really didn't want to do. "Conner's saying you inappropriately fondled his mother. That's the only allegation left. All the other stuff's not misconduct and it's been dropped."

Turner didn't know if that charge could get him fired, but it certainly would keep him from getting another special assignment. The department frowned on molestation of any kind. He looked at Reggie who didn't seem surprised and Earl who glared back at him. "You saw what happened in the barn," he said, challenging the tall, skinny black man. "Any touching was on her part. Tell them," he ordered.

"Back off, Turner," Tony said, taking a step forward. "He'll tell his story. You tell yours." Turner ignored him. Tony was bigger than him, but they both knew it was an empty gesture.

"I know what I know," Earl said, weakly.

"It's actually scary how much you don't know," Miller said, smirking.

Turner sat on the corner of Weaver's desk. He noticed Reggie's expression hadn't changed. His friend was staying out of this. It could've been because he'd been cleared of any wrongdoing, but Turner figured the real reason was he didn't care. Department discipline meant no more to Reggie than the price of doing business the way he believed it had to be done. Turner, on the other hand, was angry. Earlier in his career when he'd gone through some bad times, he deserved department scrutiny, but not now. He was smarter now and played by the rules—mostly. Even if he did cut corners, it would take someone smarter than these guys to catch him. Earl was trying to make points with the lieutenant and climb the career ladder at his expense.

Miller leaned closer and whispered in his ear, "I told you to leave that old woman alone."

EIGHTEEN

The interview was quick but unnerving. The questions were limited to Turner's interaction with Beverly Conner, but the answers were complicated. Did he grab and kiss her? Not exactly. He tried to explain what Earl had seen or thought he'd seen. She kissed him, and then he put his arms around her; that sounded lame even to him. Yes, he'd removed the transmitter when they left the restaurant, but it wasn't to hide anything. He didn't like people listening in on his conversation. It was difficult to clarify his thinking at the time. His biggest mistake, Turner explained, was allowing himself to be placed in that position.

"I'm not an undercover officer. I don't enjoy pretending to be someone I'm not," he said.

"Didn't you go back to her house after Ian Conner left?" Tony asked, looking at Metcalf after every question.

"Yes, but not to harass her," he said with annoyance. "I just wanted to find her son."

"You threatened Mrs. Conner after she refused to cooperate," Tony said, pointing at Turner.

"Bullshit," Miller said, immediately. He hadn't participated up to this point. "Did Beverly Conner tell you that?"

"It doesn't matter how I got the information . . ."

Miller interrupted him. "I want you to tell me exactly how you know Turner threatened Ian Conner's mother. Did she tell you that?" Miller asked.

"She didn't have to," Tony said. He'd stopped looking at Metcalf.

"What does that mean?" Miller was only a few feet from Tony now, glaring menacingly at the man.

"She was too traumatized to mention it," Tony said, trying to sound confident. "So I thought . . ."

"So, you lied and put words in her mouth," Miller said, raising both arms and looking at the ceiling as if he were dismayed.

"No, I just thought . . ." Tony hesitated, looking back and forth from Weaver to Metcalf.

"You thought there's no proof so I'll just lie and hope nobody catches me," Miller said, finishing Tony's sentence.

"I could see she was too upset to talk about the incident. It's a legitimate interrogation technique to make up facts, put them on the table to make a suspect nervous. If Turner believed she had accused him, he would confess because he'd think I had evidence that I didn't really have, but . . ." Tony's words stopped like a car running out of gas.

Even the bored lieutenant had to look up as Tony struggled through his convoluted rationalization.

It was over in less than an hour. Turner told the truth but had a bad feeling about the outcome of this investigation. Ian Conner had done a masterful job of keeping the department's attention off himself and onto the actions of the surveillance squad.

"Conner's a sleazebag. I can understand him lying, but Earl worked with us. He knows me. I'm not like that," Turner said, after brooding for several miles in silence while Reggie drove them back to Redondo Beach. Miller had invited himself and was stretched out in the backseat. He didn't have to work that night and knew Reggie and Turner well enough to expect the next stop to be JR's.

"It's the department management code. Do the honorable thing . . . unless it messes up your next promotion," Miller said.

"They couldn't pay me or scare me enough to turn on my partner," Turner said emphatically. He had kept his mouth shut on more than one occasion to protect the man or woman working beside him. Turner wouldn't tolerate corruption, but couldn't destroy someone's career who made an honest mistake trying to do the job.

"Never do it for fear or money," Miller said dryly, "but the opportunity to be a lieutenant . . . now that's something worth a betrayal or two."

"Beverly was angry, but I can't believe she'd go along with this."

Miller grunted. "What'd you base that on . . . a little hug and some tongue licking in the barn?"

Turner ignored him. He still trusted his instincts.

Even after they had a couple of beers at JR's, Turner couldn't relax. He was restless and wanted to go home. Also, he was about five minutes and one more sarcastic remark away from choking Miller. He told Reggie to take the car and drop Miller at his house. Reggie understood. Although Miller was smart enough never to provoke him, Reggie had stepped in on more than one occasion to shut down the narcotics detective's annoying cynicism. Reggie said he'd be back early the next morning to help interview Helen Sanchez.

Turner walked the half dozen blocks from the bar to his house trying to get the Internal Affairs investigation out of his head. Just before spring was the best time of the year to live near the beach. It was still chilly in the early evenings, so the onslaught of sun worshippers hadn't started yet. The locals jogged on the bike path or walked their tiny, yappy dogs dressed in designer sweaters on the sidewalk above the path and away from the nasty gusts of ocean air. He laughed to himself thinking about the last time he brought Daryl here. The Basset hound looked like a helicopter when the wind got under his long floppy ears and spun them like rotor blades.

As he got closer to home, Turner couldn't see the ocean, but it was one of those nights when he could smell it. Eddie was on the front porch, bundled up in a parka and knit gloves. The dog was asleep under his chair.

"What're you doing out here? It's freezing," Turner said, sitting on the bench beside him.

"You been carjacked?"

Turner explained what had happened to the city car and asked again, "You waiting for me?" He studied the old man's face for some clue to his strange behavior.

"Nope, watchin' my place."

"Why, what's going on?"

"Nothin'."

"Is Danny over there?" Turner asked. He knew Eddie's son drove him crazy. The old guy couldn't forgive him.

"Hell, no. That boy don't come 'round here no more. Don't have nothin' to say to me."

Turner didn't want to get dragged into that discussion again. "You hungry?" he asked, changing the subject.

"I got supper done. I jus' gotta heat it up . . . made some a my Texas chili 'n' cornbread."

Turner smiled. "Great," he said, but he was cringing inside. Eddie always gave Daryl a bowl when he made chili, and the dog had explosive diarrhea for a week.

"That pretty lady been callin' all day. She's bored. You bringin' her back?"

Turner didn't want to talk about that either and persuaded Eddie to go inside so they could eat dinner. He couldn't get the old man to tell him why he was watching the empty house. There probably wasn't any good reason, and he was eager to talk to Miriam. He wondered how many other people she'd called and told them where she was.

She answered on the first ring, complaining again about her isolation in the mountain cabin. She swore she hadn't called anyone except Eddie.

"I thought your dad was coming?"

"He can't leave until morning. Why don't you come up? I'm horny."

Turner laughed. "Tempting offer, but I can't." He could sense her pouting. It was one of those things that made him uneasy about their relationship. Her childish spontaneity was attractive when he was in the mood. Other times it made him feel like her father and caused him to long for a more independent mature woman. There was a reason he'd never been married. Love was a complicated emotion that usually required more energy than he was willing to invest. He repeated all the reasons why she should stay in the cabin so he could continue to work on putting Ian Conner in prison without worrying about her safety. She complained about the loss of her freedom and other conditions that Turner couldn't control. Finally, out of frustration, he told her to stay put or she might get killed. He didn't know if that was the truth, but he didn't want to find out. If he was right about Conner, the man was a psycho and more than capable of deadly violence.

"I know how dangerous he can be," she whined, "but I hate being alone more than I'm afraid of Ian."

"That's stupid. It's only one night. Go to bed and your dad will be there in the morning."

Miriam remained agitated, and lamented her bad luck. Finally, she hung up on him. Turner was relieved. It was difficult to be sympathetic when she behaved like a spoiled brat. Her father had indulged her; he could deal with her tantrums tomorrow.

He didn't have long to think about Miriam's situation. The phone rang before he could put it down. It was Reggie. He had driven by Helen's new apartment after dropping Miller at his condo. She was gone. The apartment manager told him Helen had moved out several days ago in the middle of the night with her few possessions. She was paid up so he didn't know whether or not he should try to rent the place again. Turner knew. She wouldn't be back.

Undeterred, Reggie said he had tracked down an address for Alex Gomez. The disgraced sergeant was living on his small pension in a rundown hotel in East Los Angeles.

An hour later, he and Reggie were driving up the Harbor Freeway toward L.A. Gomez would most likely know the whereabouts of his attractive cousin. His willingness to help was another matter. As soon as Vogel had told them Cullen had been shot by an unidentified weapon, Turner began to doubt Helen Sanchez's story and wondered if her reasons for bringing them into the murder-for-hire scheme may have been more complicated than avenging her sister's death. Did she know Cullen had been targeted for elimination and did she know Ian Conner? Those were the questions he needed to ask her. Gomez was weak; he was their link back to Helen.

The hotel was four blocks from the old Hollenbeck station on First Street. Reggie admitted one of his buddies in Hollenbeck had told him about the strange sergeant living in the dilapidated four-story hotel.

The skinny, jaundiced man who answered the door bore little resemblance to the uniformed sergeant they captured in the alley just a few weeks ago. Turner guessed some sexually transmitted disease passed on by one of his drag queen conquests had ravaged his body.

"What do you want?" Gomez said in a surprisingly strong voice. He tried to block the doorway, but Reggie easily nudged past him into the stuffy room. It smelled of pine air freshener.

"Where's your cousin?" Reggie asked. Without waiting for an answer he opened the bedroom door and looked around. He quickly checked the kitchen and a small laundry room before returning to the front room. Turner waited at the door until Gomez relented and let him enter.

"Satisfied?" Gomez asked, sitting on a couch covered with a blanket that had patches with brightly-colored ponies. Two folding chairs and a pole lamp were the only other furniture in the drab room.

Turner stood over him. "No, where is she?"

"You should know. She said you moved her."

"Why's she hiding, Alex?" Reggie asked from the kitchen. He was examining the label on a pill bottle.

"Put that down," Gomez shouted, pointing at Reggie. He coughed uncontrollably until the tears trickled down the sides of his face. "You've no right," he whispered when he could talk again.

"They don't prescribe this unless you're pretty bad, Alex," Reggie said, ignoring the outburst.

The sick man sank into the corner of the couch. He ran his finger over a red pony with a yellow mane and tail that pranced over the edge of the blanket. "I'm a dead man," he said. "Get the fuck out of here."

"No," Turner said.

"I don't know where she is," he almost pleaded.

"Yes, you do," Turner insisted. He felt sorry for the dying man who was squirming and rubbing the wrinkled skin on his arm. It was difficult to believe Gomez was only in his forties. He'd become a pathetic old man. Boxes of adult diapers were stacked behind the television, and a walker was near the front door.

Reggie took one of the chairs and moved it closer to the couch. He sat with his knee nearly touching Gomez's leg. "We know you and Helen lied about Ramona's killing," Reggie said matter-of-factly. Gomez started to protest, but Reggie put his hand on the sick man's leg. "Don't," Reggie said. "If you lie to us again, we'll let her die."

Gomez grunted some noise that sounded like resignation. "What's it to me. She's not gonna die."

"How do you know?" Turner asked.

"She's smarter than him, smarter than all of us."

Turner didn't speak. He waited. Reggie was quiet too. They would let him tell it his way.

Gomez wiggled to get comfortable. "She's the one pushed him, found the jobs. What a sweet setup . . . clean houses, hear stuff, snoop in personal shit. He goes back and robs them. People don't keep records of who cleans their house, pay in cash . . . cops never make a connection."

"That doesn't explain her sister getting killed," Reggie said.

"Cullen killed Ramona and made the mistake of letting Helen find out."

"Why'd he kill her?"

Gomez groaned as he tried to adjust his position again. He asked for one of his pills and a glass of water. Turner got it for him and asked again, "Why?"

"He said Ramona heard and saw too much. He was afraid she'd ID him if she ever got questioned. Helen was furious. She told you about Sheffield's murder-for-hire so you'd kill Cullen."

"How could she know that?" Reggie asked.

"She couldn't; so she paid a shooter in case you screwed up, or he surrendered."

"Is that why Goodman was killed?" Turner asked.

"Probably, if he helped Cullen."

"You know Conner?"

"No."

"How'd you know they were working together?" Turner could hear the frustration in his own voice. He was tired of finding dead ends when it came to connecting Conner to all this mayhem.

"Don't know him. Know she has a cop partner . . . cold bastard according to Helen." Gomez laughed and coughed a little. "She oughta know."

"What's that mean?" Turner asked.

Gomez hesitated a second and then shrugged. "Why not," he said. "It's a story I heard from the folks in Mexico. Her dad was shot and her mom raped and killed by this police colonel in Juarez. The colonel never saw or knew about little Ramona or Helen, who's a teenager at the time. Helen was gorgeous beautiful then. She dresses up in some trashy outfit, arranges to have someone introduce her to the colonel at a bar, and she gets him to invite her to his hotel room. She has sex with him, and when he passes out she cuts his throat and then hacks him up pretty good . . . did a Mafia number on his manhood." Gomez shakes his head and coughs quietly. "Somehow she drags his naked, mutilated body to the third-floor window and rolls it out onto the street. That night the rest of the family hid her and Ramona in an oil tanker and got them out of the country."

Turner tried to reconcile the picture of the soft-spoken, classy woman he met with the bloody teenage avenger Gomez described. Actually, it wasn't all that unusual. He remembered a case where a distraught wimpy CPA had used a double-barreled shotgun to blow off the head of his six-year-old son's molester.

If Gomez was telling the truth, Helen and Conner would make a formidable team. Cullen, Goodman and the widow might have found that out the hard way. Turner felt himself getting nervous again about Miriam. Conner didn't know how much Miriam knew. If he did think she was the informant, was she enough of a threat for him to go after her? He watched Gomez take a sip of water, wiping his mouth with the back of his hand. He scratched the grey stubble on his face as a thin stream of liquid flowed from the corner of his mouth and under his chin. He could barely swallow.

"You think she might have gone to her partner?" Turner heard Reggie ask.

"No, she doesn't trust him." Gomez groaned again and took another pill without water. "I've got to rest," he said.

Turner wrote his home number on the back of his business card. "Call me if she contacts you." He placed it in the man's sweaty palm.

Gomez nodded and closed his eyes.

"Shouldn't you be in the hospital?" Reggie asked, staring at him.

The emaciated man looked up at him. "Hospital's for sick people, not dead men." He pulled the blanket around his shoulders and stretched out his legs on the sofa. His breathing was loud and labored. Turner tapped Reggie on the arm and motioned for them to leave.

They were in the car driving with the windows open for several minutes before Turner could get the odor from the apartment out of his nostrils.

"Not our best witness," he said, thinking out loud.

"He's not going to make it through the night," Reggie said. "You see his eyes?"

Turner had. The smell of death was on Gomez and it triggered unwelcome thoughts of mortality. As he got older, Turner worried more about all the ways he could die. Surprisingly, those dangers associated with the job didn't bother him. Things like cancer, heart attacks and strokes did. Police work might kill you, but it would be fast and bloody, not slow and humiliating like the death Alex Gomez was facing. He didn't like thinking about a time when he wouldn't be in control.

"You listening?" Reggie asked him. "Where you been?"

"Thinking."

"Forget him. You can't fuck drag queens and not pay the price."

Turner smiled. He wasn't thinking about Gomez. He was thinking about himself. "Did you ask me something?"

"No, I told you I was going to the Conner place," Reggie said.

"Great, another perfect ten in my career swan dive."

"If you're right about Beverly Conner," Reggie said, "she's pushing this complaint because she's afraid of her asshole son. We'll offer her a way out."

"I can't afford to donate rent on another apartment."

"Offer her witness protection and then the county pays her room and board."

"I don't think I should go there."

"Nobody ordered you to stay away from her. Did they?" Reggie was comfortable operating in the grey zone. Turner would do it, but had just enough management mores to feel guilty. Tony should have ordered Turner to stay away from Beverly until her complaint was resolved, but didn't. He was about to take advantage of Tony's careless oversight.

"It's kind of implied," Turner said, grinning.

"He gave you an order, or he didn't. It's not your job to read his mind."

"Can't argue with that," Turner said. He could, but once Reggie made up his mind, it was pointless. His only other option was to let his partner go alone, but he couldn't do that either.

It was close to 9 P.M. when they arrived at the Conner property. In this sparsely populated rural area, house lights were solitary beacons in a sea of darkness. After entering the driveway, Reggie drove in a straight line toward the hazy light that disappeared behind a curtain of dust kicked up by the tires. It gave the place an other-worldly appearance. Reggie was good at remembering landscapes and had to retreat only once to avoid a pile of dead tree limbs.

Beverly's vintage car was parked near the house. Driving with his headlights out, Reggie pulled in behind it. Turner got out and immediately checked in the barn. He could smell the animal before he saw the handsome sorrel quarterhorse staring back at him from the last stall. The barn wasn't an empty, cobweb-filled warehouse any longer. Oat hay covered the floor. Bales of sweet-smelling alfalfa and timothy were stacked in an empty stall, and a wheelbarrow overflowing with horse shit with a shovel protruding from the middle had been left by the door. There was no sign of the covered yellow Corvette or Ian Conner.

A few moments later, Turner stood on the front porch of the house staring at the rusted screen as Reggie reached around him and rang the doorbell. In this case, he didn't mind his partner taking the initiative. His apprehension in confronting Ian's mother was building by the minute. It was always difficult for him to be indifferent to a woman's feelings when he liked her. Beverly Conner was understandably protecting her son, but she was street smart too, and he hoped by now she had realized something had gone terribly wrong with her kid. Despite Miriam's description of the woman, his instincts told him Beverly had been used by Ian, and beneath her hard exterior, she was as frightened as Miriam . . . maybe more. Beverly had a better grip on reality.

She opened the door wide, apparently not intimidated by what or who she might find on her porch at this late hour. Turner was surprised at her appearance. She had lost a few pounds and was wearing tight work jeans, dusty cowboy boots and a baggy sweatshirt. Her red hair had grown a little and was pulled straight back away from her face. She didn't appear to be wearing any makeup, but was prettier than he remembered. She unlatched the screen and moved to one side so they could enter.

"Sorry to bother you," Turner said. He was looking into those wonderful green eyes, but didn't detect any of the hatred that had been there the last time they talked.

171

"I just opened a bottle of something red. Want some?" she asked, walking toward the kitchen. Reggie declined, so she brought back the bottle and two glasses.

"Is that your horse?" Turner asked. "He's beautiful."

Turner saw Reggie ease around the room and slip into the hallway.

"Don't bother, detective. He's not here and won't be back." She wasn't upset and sounded resigned. "You're welcome to look in his room, but he pretty much cleaned it out."

Reggie disappeared down the hallway, and Turner heard a door open and close.

"Did he leave voluntarily or get told to go?" Turner didn't see any reason to avoid the subject. They both knew why he was here this time.

"I wasn't crazy about Miriam—" she said and then hesitated. "Sorry, I know she's your friend, but clingy, selfish people make me nuts. I didn't tell my son to dump her. I just didn't like her. That was his decision. This other woman is a different story." She handed him a glass of red wine and put the bottle on the coffee table.

"What other woman?" he asked, but was still thinking about Miriam and wondering why he almost said she wasn't his girlfriend.

"The Mexican bitch, I call her. I won't have her in my house."

"Helen," he said, taking a healthy swallow.

"You've met her? They packed up and left a few days ago. Took all his stuff and anything of mine that wasn't nailed down."

"Where'd she go?"

"Don't know, don't care, glad she's gone." She came across the room and sat beside him on the couch.

She put her glass on the table, and stared at the floor. "Look, I'm sorry about the complaint thing. I was mad at you and worried about Ian. I hope it didn't cause you any trouble." She cautiously glanced up at him.

It was the expression of a little kid who got caught doing exactly what she intended to do. It had caused him a lot of

172

trouble, but he said, "No, not really." He put his hand under her chin and gently lifted her head until she was looking directly at him. "Did you tell the IA investigators I grabbed you and kissed you against your will?" he asked.

"Hell no, who told you that?" she asked, moving back a little. "What I said was it's unprofessional to make a woman think you cared for her just to get information on her son."

"I'm not that good at pretending, Beverly." He said it, and was surprised as well as a little relieved because it was true. He wasn't shocked that Earl had exaggerated what he saw and Tony went along, adding his creative touches. Lieutenant Metcalf wanted a certain outcome, and they were going to give it to him regardless of the truth.

"If you need me to testify for you or anything, I'll do it," she said. "I'm not mad at you anymore. I know Ian and that woman are up to something. I don't want them in my house, but you gotta understand he's still my kid."

"What did you see?" he asked quietly.

"Guns, shady-looking people, whispering whenever I came into a room . . . I'm not stupid. They're up to something. I just want him to stop before he hurts somebody or gets himself hurt," she said anxiously.

"If I'm right, he's already done some bad stuff," Turner said. He couldn't make himself tell her the details. She wanted . . . expected him to fix it. He'd heard that familiar pleading in mothers' voices when he became their only hope to take away the pain, make everything right or avenge their loss. In their minds, he was Gary Cooper and Clint Eastwood. Their expectations usually went well beyond what was reasonable or doable for any cop.

"You will try to help him?"

"I'm gonna arrest him, Beverly."

After a long silence she said, "I understand." She was near tears, but wouldn't cry. "Just don't hurt him." Reggie came back and sat across the room in an overstuffed chair near the rustic brick-covered fireplace. "Can we be alone for another minute?" she pleaded, looking at Reggie.

"No," Reggie said.

As much as he wanted to be alone with her, Turner was thankful it wasn't going to happen. A little voice in his head kept reminding him about the personnel complaint. Actually, he doubted his cautious partner had ever been out of eavesdropping range.

"Did anybody come to the house that you can recall?" he asked, wanting to change the subject and trying to sound as if he hadn't heard her request.

"I don't know," she mumbled, obviously not pleased, but then added, "besides Helen, just the dwarf."

"His lawyer?" Turner asked. He described Jack Winter, and she was certain it was the same man.

"He seemed more interested in the Mexican," Beverly said, disdainfully. "They always had their heads together whispering something in Spanish. Do you like Buddy?"

"Who?" Turner asked.

"My horse."

"He's beautiful." He guessed she was done talking about her son.

"I get his younger sister next week. She's a rescue like him, and tomorrow a lovely little donkey will be in the first stall."

Turner laughed. "When you go country, you main line."

"Come back after I get Sissy, and we'll go riding." She stood and offered to shake hands.

He got up. She had revealed all that she wanted him to know and was dismissing them.

"I'd like that," he said, touching and gently squeezing her hand. Her skin was mostly soft, but he could feel the calluses. The bartender had definitely become a horse rancher. He and Reggie stepped onto the porch. The door closed behind them, and they were alone.

"You're welcome," Reggie said, walking slowly away from the light back into the darkness.

174

NINETEEN

At 5 A.M., Turner was awake. He wanted to sleep more, but as usual, couldn't shut off his brain and stop thinking. He finally got out of bed and tried to get to the kitchen without turning on the lights. Reggie had stayed over and was asleep on the couch with Daryl curled up under the coffee table. He could see under the bedroom door that Eddie's light was still on, but the old man always fell asleep without turning off his television or the lights.

Turner figured he couldn't make coffee without waking up everybody, so he slipped on his running shorts and sweatshirt and decided to take Daryl and walk, maybe jog, to the beach. JR's was always open at daybreak, and he could have a cup of coffee with the early rising beach bums and dedicated drunks.

It was just before sunrise. The air was cool, but there wasn't much breeze. Nice walking weather, he thought. Why spoil it by running and getting all sweaty. The dog liked to run, but he was happy just being out, and Turner didn't mind slowing down to accommodate the Basset hound's stubby legs. Daryl trailed a few feet behind him, stopping occasionally to observe stray cats, but there was a little bounce in his step this morning. They were both enjoying the early morning outing. Turner's cell phone was in his sweatshirt pocket, but he'd wait a couple of hours to give Miriam a call. She wasn't a morning person, and he didn't want to piss her off again. A light marine layer was drifting in off the ocean. The moisture settled on his face and hair. He loved that seaweed and wet sand smell in the morning. He passed the harbor and noticed the crews from several fishing boats were

175

already unloading the day's catch. His father loved the ocean and always said if he hadn't been a cop he would've been a deep sea fisherman. Turner enjoyed fishing too, but he got seasick. Too bad, ocean fishing would have been a great way to make a living. Being a cop was better. Two weeks on a boat and he'd probably go crazy with the peace and tranquility. He needed excitement . . . guns, car chases. It was an addiction, as real as any junkie's habit, the ultimate adrenaline high.

Beverly's face kept creeping into his thoughts, so he tried to think about what he would say to Miriam to calm her down. Maybe when her dad got there, she would be better. He found himself comparing the two women. Beverly was a little older than him; Miriam was much younger. Beverly smoked and drank hard liquor; Miriam drank boutique wines and wouldn't eat meat. Sex with Miriam was great. Beverly had a woman's body. He guessed a man could lose himself in Beverly's body.

He was standing outside JR's before he realized how far he'd come. It was crazy. As soon as he put Ian in jail, Beverly would never talk to him again. Her son would always be the ugly red-headed gorilla standing in the corner of their lives. Regardless of the outcome, she would never really forgive him. That depressing thought came about the same time he was beginning to accept the inevitable, that although he loved Miriam and had no intention of leaving her, they wouldn't be together much longer. Miriam was an immature child in a woman's body who couldn't sustain long-term relationships. He always knew that, but hoped this time it might be different. It wasn't.

He poured a mug of black coffee from the pot behind the bar in JR's, filled an empty peanut bowl with water for Daryl, and sat in his regular booth. He put the water bowl on the floor under his table. Daryl drank noisily and spilled half the water before lying down on Turner's foot and falling asleep. One of the bums lifted his head off the counter and was about to come over to beg for money until he recognized Turner. He did a U-turn and fell back into his former position. That day's paper was lying on the table so Turner pulled out the local news section to see if the LAPD had been involved in anything interesting overnight. Occasionally, one of his buddies would get into a shooting or a big case that made headlines. There was a tiny paragraph on the back page about the movie theater widow being found dead in her home. No mention was made of Turner or Reggie. Vogel was quoted as saying they had no suspects, but it appeared to be a burglary.

He'd just grabbed a stale donut and another mug of coffee when Reggie arrived. Reggie helped himself to the same breakfast before sitting in the booth. Daryl immediately got up and moved closer to Reggie's feet.

"Miriam's father called a few minutes ago," Reggie said after a sip of coffee. "He got to the cabin, and she was gone."

"She's probably hiking. Did he check the trail?" The donut began churning in his stomach. He didn't know if it was anger or worry.

"She packed and left before he got there, probably late last night."

They drove the dog back to the house, and Turner changed clothes. He went alone to her apartment, using his key. He didn't think she'd been there, but with Miriam it was difficult to tell. Dirty dishes with moldy remnants were in the sink, and a layer of green pond scum had grown in the half-filled glass coffeepot. The apartment overall was relatively clean, and the bed was made. There was no current mail on the entry table, her regular dumping spot, so it was probably still downstairs stuffed in her box. He opened her refrigerator. As usual, it was empty except for ice cream and an assortment of aluminum foil-wrapped restaurant leftovers. At least she wasn't stupid enough to come home. He called his house, and Eddie said she hadn't been there either and hadn't called. It had been at least eight hours since her father arrived at the cabin, plenty of time to make the drive back to L.A.

He called the police building downtown. She hadn't gone back to work. Her boss said he expected her back next Monday, in another week. The captain had talked to her three days ago.

Miriam said she was anxious to come back and would see him then. She'd seemed fine, he said.

Turner pushed a couple of pillows out of the way and sat on her couch. He realized he didn't know any of her friends or if she even had friends other than the people at work. They never talked about those things. She had an address book, but she kept it in her purse. He didn't know where to begin to search for her. Maybe that was good. Maybe Conner wouldn't know either.

As a last resort, he called her father at the cabin. Miriam's dad always liked him, felt that Turner was a good influence on his daughter. He hadn't been told why his daughter had been staying at the cabin. He surmised she and Turner were having problems, and knew that Miriam was unable to face or deal with unpleasant realities. He complained to Turner it wasn't in her nature to confront problems; she'd rather hide out in the mountains.

"Sir, I need to know if you have any idea where she might've gone," Turner asked, when the older man finally gave him an opportunity to speak.

"Her place," he said, matter-of-factly.

"I'm at her apartment now. It doesn't look like she's been here." He was embarrassed but asked the next question anyway. "Does she have any friends she might stay with?"

"Don't know. Sometimes stays with my mother . . ."

Turner got the address and hung up. It was a long shot. He didn't think Miriam would put her grandmother in danger, but knew she wasn't always the most considerate person when it came to having her own way. If she thought Conner didn't know about her grandmother, she'd probably take a chance and go there. Turner also knew if anything went wrong, Miriam would protect her grandmother like a hellcat. She wasn't a coward or a bad person. He'd decided if Miriam ever grew up she'd make a terrific woman, but was finally realizing he wouldn't have the patience or time to wait for that to happen. At this moment, he just wanted her to be safe.

The grandmother lived in the City of Sierra Madre in the San Gabriel Valley. She owned a tidy four-plex on Baldwin Avenue at the base of the foothills. In the sixties, those lush low mountains had been home to hippies, anti-war vets, and a "Who's Who" of cults, but the high cost of housing meant better police service and no more camping in the rich people's backyards.

The entry way of the building had a panel with four door-bells, one for each apartment. Miriam's last name, Friedman, was on every name tag with a different first initial. Great, Turner thought, the old woman rented to all the relatives. He looked up at the security camera almost hidden in the eaves and pushed the button for apartment one. An elderly voice asked what he wanted. Turner smiled at the camera, gave his name and said he was looking for Miriam. The voice told him to wait. The front door buzzed and he opened it.

Apartment one was to the right as he entered the building. Grandma was holding the door open for him. She was a short stocky woman with white hair tied back in a neat knob-like bun. With her dark-rimmed glasses, she reminded him of his third grade teacher, a nasty little Dominican nun who'd predicted a dire future for him.

"Sit," she ordered, pointing at a chair with an ugly green and yellow flower pattern. It was an old lady's room with too many knitted throws and porcelain things on every shelf. When he sat, he thought the chair had a faint odor of moth balls. She introduced herself and said, "My granddaughter's changing her clothes." With her back to him she mumbled, "I'm supposed to believe you haven't seen her in her PJ's."

In less than five minutes, Miriam appeared from the back of the apartment. She was wearing tight black jeans tucked into black boots and a heavy, blue turtleneck sweater. She looked rested and pretty. The fresh mountain air had left a little blush in her cheeks. Her long auburn hair had some new red highlights. She kissed her grandmother on the cheek and then stood by the door.

"Let's go for a walk," she said, leaving before he could answer. He said goodbye to the older woman and followed Miriam out to the street. He started to ask if she was alright, but she

179

interrupted him. "I don't want a lecture. I'm not going home. It's safe here. Nobody knows about Nana."

"I found you."

"My dad probably told you. He likes you; he won't tell some stranger."

Turner shook his head in dismay. It was useless. She was stubborn and reckless. He realized they were walking up Baldwin toward the mountains.

"Where are we going?" he asked, looking around at the quiet streets and beautiful landscape directly ahead. There had been plenty of rain that winter, and the hills were flourishing with new growth and wildflowers. The crisp air was filled with the smell of wet grass and new spring blossoms. Typical of this city, there weren't any traffic signals and only the occasional passing vehicle.

"A walk, I told you. We need to talk."

He'd heard those words from her on another occasion. The last time, she'd explained they were a bad match and walked out leaving him unhappy and lonely. This time, he almost welcomed the little speech she was about to make. She wouldn't exit in a rage, and she couldn't disappoint him. The smells and the silence surrounding them had lulled him into such a peaceful state that he barely listened to her words. It didn't matter. In the end, they both wanted the same thing. He would just take in the view and when she was finished, agree with her.

THEY WANDERED across the narrow quiet street the way they had all morning. His eyes were almost closed as he breathed deeply, enjoying the silence after they'd agreed to the separation. She seemed lost in her thoughts of work or moving somewhere Conner couldn't bother her.

He didn't notice the truck until almost the last few seconds. There were no screeching brakes, no horn. It had come down the hill without a sound. Turner glanced up at the last moment before it hit them. He felt the steel hood crushing her against

180

him as he grabbed her arm and rolled across the front bumper dragging Miriam behind him. His head banged off the pavement, his right knee jamming into the roots of a massive oak tree on the corner. His pants were torn and bloody, and the impact stunned him for a moment. When he looked up, Miriam was lying beside him with blood oozing from her head and nose. He took off his outer shirt and held it on the head wound. Her left arm was twisted and bruised. She was moaning, but conscious. He saw the heel of her boot had broken off. The neighbors began trickling onto the street, carrying blankets, and clean towels trying to help stop Miriam's bleeding.

Turner heard the sirens and tried to stand, but his leg wouldn't hold his weight; he was dizzy. A grey-haired man with sunglasses helped support him and attempted to convince him he should sit down again.

"Where's the truck?" Turner asked, trying to focus on the street. "Did they stop the truck?"

The old man looked both ways on the quiet street. "Must've took off," he said.

The ambulance arrived and the paramedics rushed to Miriam. They worked on her for several minutes before one of them asked Turner if he was okay and examined his injuries. The paramedic explained they would transport her to the Methodist Hospital. They carefully placed Miriam on a board, then onto a stretcher before loading her into the ambulance.

Turner, with the old man's assistance, climbed inside too and sat beside the paramedic who adjusted Miriam's IV and monitored her vital signs. He thought about phoning her grandmother and father, but didn't. He would tell them when he got to the hospital and knew what to say. He noticed a policeman standing outside the ambulance and called to him, told him about the truck. He tried to describe what he could remember which wasn't very much. None of the neighbors except the old man had seen it, and there was no sign of it now. Neither Turner nor the old man had seen the driver.

His head and knee ached. Turner leaned back against the ambulance wall and watched Miriam. The skin on her face was scraped and bruised, her hair matted with blood. An oxygen mask covered her nose and mouth, but her breathing was raspy and labored. Her left hand clutched at the sheet. He touched it and whispered her name, but she didn't respond.

Crazy thoughts raced through his mind. Had someone followed him from Miriam's apartment and seen an opportunity to eliminate a possible witness. He didn't know how good the local cops would be at figuring it out and finding the truck. He left a message for Reggie, who called him back in a couple of minutes. His partner would search the area for the truck Turner described as big, black with tinted windows, and probably a Ford or Chevy.

EIGHT HOURS later, the emergency staff at the hospital had stabilized Miriam, and she was in a private room. Turner didn't need to call anyone. The neighbors had notified the grandmother and driven her to the hospital. Miriam's father arrived a few hours later. They would stay with her. The doctor said her injuries were serious—a broken arm and ribs, some minor internal damage, hairline fracture behind her ear, and the one injury Miriam would hate the most, a broken nose—but she would fully recover. Turner was more fortunate. He was bruised, and he'd probably had a mild concussion, but his leg wasn't broken. His knee twisted when it hit the tree, but a couple of weeks in an Ace bandage should fix that. The doctor explained that Miriam had gotten the worst of the impact, and her body had protected him, acting as a sort of buffer.

"That makes me feel like a shit," Turner said.

"Don't. If you hadn't pulled her away, she'd be dead," the doctor replied. He was a young, arrogant Asian who appeared to be right out of medical school. "The truck didn't get a solid hit because she was moving or being dragged by you. You probably saved her life. Feel better?" he asked, turning away and checking his pager as if the whole thing should have been obvious.

Turner sat on one of the uncomfortable benches in the waiting area. Actually, he did feel better. He couldn't be content being safe and escaping serious injuries if it cost Miriam that much pain and suffering. He knew it was a matter of ego, but he felt better thinking he kept her from getting killed.

He was dialing Reggie to come and pick him up, when his partner appeared outside Miriam's room. Turner didn't like hospitals and was eager to get home, but before he could slip away, her father spotted him and came away from her bed with tears in his eyes. He was grateful and generous, offering his car, his home, his money or anything else Turner might need or want. Turner declined. The only thing he wanted was rest, and he promised the distraught man to check in on Miriam later. His primary concern at the moment was the real possibility that the hit-and-run wasn't an accident. He'd talked to Weaver and convinced him to put a team outside her room until someone tracked down the driver. Maybe it was foolish, but he didn't believe in coincidence.

As they navigated the maze of hospital hallways to get to the parking lot, Reggie told Turner that a couple of hours before he'd arrived at the hospital, he and some of the uniformed officers had found the truck parked at a shopping center in Arcadia, just a few miles from the hit-and-run scene. Reggie had convinced officers from two police agencies to search every large public parking lot within a two-mile radius, but he was the one who eventually located the black Chevy truck with front-end collision damage and traces of blood on the bumper. The local police had it impounded and when they ran the license plate, discovered the vehicle had been stolen earlier that morning from one of the outer lots at the Santa Anita racetrack. Turner wasn't surprised Reggie was the one who had located the truck. His partner had the uncanny ability to think like a criminal.

The doctor had given Turner an anti-inflammatory drug and painkillers, but it seemed as if every inch of his body was sore. He needed to get home and rest before he could think straight again. The crutches might assist him in getting to Reggie's car, but when he got home, a couple of beers would ease the pain better than any pill.

He doubted forensics would find prints or any other valuable evidence inside the truck, but the good news was one of the officers had confided to Reggie that Sierra Madre's only major street had traffic cameras, and both parking lots—where the truck was stolen and where it was dumped—had security cameras.

AFTER SCOLDING Turner for getting hurt and not protecting Miriam, Eddie announced that he'd saved some lasagna and garlic bread for dinner. Turner realized he hadn't eaten all day and was really hungry. He and Reggie finished the leftovers and after Turner took a shower, they settled in for a couple of beers. He pushed back on the recliner to elevate his leg, but the throbbing pain didn't ease until he'd finished his second beer. He couldn't remember how many he'd had after that, but woke up the next morning in his chair covered with a blanket. The pathetic moans emanating from the vicinity of the couch told him Reggie had spent the night, and probably drank a few more beers than he had.

It was difficult to bend his leg, and it still had some swelling this morning, but a lot of the pain was gone. The rest of his body felt like the morning after he'd played a long, hard game of tackle football against some really big guys. The dog and Eddie were gone, but the smell of fresh-brewed coffee wafted in from the kitchen. Reggie must have smelled it too because he rolled over and fell off the couch. He lay there a few seconds before sitting up and sliding back onto the cushions.

"Want coffee?" Turner asked, no stranger to a painful hangover.

"In a minute," Reggie said. He stood and went into the bathroom. The shower was running a few seconds later, and when he came back into the living room his hair was wet and dripping water onto his shirt.

"Did you bother to undress?"

"I think so." He walked unsteadily into the kitchen and returned with two mugs of coffee, giving one to Turner. "It'll take time to go through the tapes from all those cameras," Reggie said, sipping the steaming coffee before dropping onto the couch. "You wanna take a few days . . . mend . . . visit Miriam?"

"We were breaking up again when the truck tried to make us road kill."

Reggie was quiet for a few seconds and then said, "Her dad still likes you."

Turner laughed and his ribs hurt. "Great," he said looking over his shoulder to be certain Eddie hadn't returned. "Just what I need; another old guy to fill up my social calendar," he said, adjusting his position to get comfortable. "What are you gonna do?"

"Follow Jack Winter until he leads me to Helen Sanchez."

"I'm going with you," Turner said, and pushed his chair into a sitting position. He wasn't good at being incapacitated. He hobbled into the bedroom, searched through his closet and found an old elastic knee brace he'd left in his workout bag when he used to play racquetball. He pulled it on, and although he still had a slight limp, he could walk. He dressed, wearing long sleeves to cover the bruises on his arms. The more he moved around, the better he felt. It was late enough, so he called the hospital before they left to get an update on Miriam. Her father said she was sleeping and feeling much better. She had eaten breakfast, and would make a decision later that day on the plastic surgeon to fix her nose. He sounded concerned when he mentioned his daughter was considering doing some other touch-ups since the nose would look so good. Turner thought his tone wasn't as warm or friendly this morning, and surmised Miriam must have revealed that their shaky relationship was finished. For some reason, that made Turner feel as if a burden had been lifted from his shoulders. He didn't have to pretend anymore and give that nice old man a false sense of hope that his daughter had finally grown up.

185

"There must be something wrong with me," Turner said as they drove away from the house.

"Want me to make a list?" Reggie asked.

"I'm serious. I'm over forty years old, and I still can't seem to make a connection with the right woman." He looked over at the silent Reggie who was staring out the front window, definitely the wrong guy to give him advice on women.

The biggest surprise of the morning came when Weaver called on his cell phone. He was at the hospital, but Lieutenant Metcalf had ordered the squad to cease its unauthorized surveillance of Miriam's room. The lieutenant felt it was a waste of time and resources. On the other hand, Sergeant Weaver had become a believer. He didn't put much stock in coincidence either, and there were too many crimes connected, albeit indirectly, to Conner. Ian Conner was a shady character whose acquaintances were either suspect or dead. Weaver finally admitted if Reggie said he saw an automatic weapon in Conner's hands that morning, Conner had an automatic weapon. Reggie didn't make that kind of mistake. So, despite his inclination to mindlessly follow the chain of command, Weaver was going to find a way to watch Miriam. His squad would do it off duty if necessary, but Turner had better connect Conner to something criminal as soon as possible because he didn't know how long he could keep what he was doing from Metcalf.

If she was still alive, Helen was the key to catching Conner. Her cousin was dying, but even if the guy lived, Turner doubted that Alex Gomez would ever be willing to repeat what he'd told them.

JACK WINTER'S office was in a strip mall at the corner of Fountain and Ardmore in Hollywood, stuck between a nail salon and a Persian fast food restaurant. Although Turner and Reggie were parked in a lot across the street, an afternoon breeze filled their car with the aroma of roasted chicken and a medley of Middle Eastern spices.

They observed a procession of street people and parolees wander into the lawyer's office throughout the morning. It was easy to single out those men on parole. They were usually pretty bulked up from all those hours they worked out at the taxpayers' expense, had an assortment of gang tattoos and that distinctive prison swagger. When they left Winter's office, several of them sat at the restaurant's outside tables drinking coffee and smoking.

Eventually, the lawyer wandered out with his shirtsleeves rolled up and joined them. Two young women from the nail salon in low-cut tank tops and spandex pants greeted several of the men, and both women bent over to give Winter a kiss.

"It's like visitors' day at San Quentin," Turner said. He was looking at the scene from the passenger side, rearview mirror. Reggie watched from his mirror. They were parked behind another car so there was little chance anyone from across the street would notice them.

"Without the bars," Reggie said.

He and Reggie stayed in the car and watched the office all day. Winter would occasionally come out to get coffee or a sandwich. He'd chat with different clients who continually occupied the outdoor seating area. The lawyer would stand and visit a while, drink his coffee and then return to his office. An hour or two later, he'd come outside again and do the same thing. Finally about 8 P.M., the tables were empty. The restaurant closed at nine. Winter's lights stayed on until almost eleven when his black Porsche Carrera was the only car in front of the mall. The lot across the street was empty too, so Reggie had to park on Ardmore on the other side of Fountain away from the street lights.

The office lights went out just as Turner was beginning to wonder if the attorney lived in his office. Winter came out the front door carrying his briefcase and what looked like an overnight bag. He set them down, locked the office door and used a rope to pull down the security grates on the door and window. He padlocked the grates to a connection on the sidewalk, and loaded his briefcase and bag into the front trunk of the Porsche.

They followed him to the Burbank airport where he boarded a Southwest plane for San Francisco. That plane was technically full, and the next flight was in half an hour. Reggie talked to the manager for Southwest, and five minutes later—while a pretty stewardess had Winter preoccupied with his first class internet ticket—Turner and Reggie boarded the plane and sat in the last two empty seats at the back of the plane.

Asking Reggie how he managed to get them onboard never crossed Turner's mind. He just accepted the fact that it had been done, and they were on their way to San Francisco. Forty-five minutes and two beers later, they landed at the San Francisco airport and watched Winter climb into a rented white limo. They followed him in a cab for thirty minutes up Highway 101 through the downtown area's busiest streets, and finally stopped at the luxurious Mark Hopkins Hotel on Nob Hill where the attorney talked to the doorman as if they were old friends. A bellhop took his bag, and Winter followed him onto the elevator without stopping at the front desk.

Reggie watched until the elevator stopped at the penthouse. They took the next elevator, but couldn't get out on that floor.

Reggie pushed the button to go back down to the lobby. "It's gonna be a long night," he said. "Wanna get a room?"

"My Visa couldn't handle the tips in this place."

They decided to rent a car and then find an inconspicuous place to watch the hotel until Winter went out or somebody they knew arrived. It wasn't a great plan, but the best they could manage with just the two of them and no expense account. The city was considerably colder than Los Angeles, and unlike L.A., the downtown area was alive with pedestrian and vehicle traffic all night. Homeless bodies curled up in doorways, over grates or anyplace they could find a draft of warm air. It was easy to hang out; there was plenty of company.

At dawn, they were sitting on a park bench in the shadow of the Grace Cathedral across the street from the sumptuous hotel, drinking coffee and finishing warm croissants from a bakery Reggie found on California Street. Turner had taken off the knee brace during the night, and this morning his leg ached from the cold and dampness. He untied his shoe and pulled the brace back over his swollen leg, then hobbled around the bench a few times to loosen up the muscles. The knee still hurt, but he'd taken a couple of pain pills with the coffee, and it was at least tolerable.

The cable car creaked and strained down the center of the street with only a handful of early morning riders. Turner watched groups of older Chinese men and women congregate on the grass in front of him. They stretched their bodies performing some strange yet graceful ritual of movements.

The smell of urine escaping from the gutters and the pungent odor of an occasional unwashed body emerging from the hedges around him were less troublesome than the cold. An icy wind cut through Turner's flimsy southern California clothes, but Reggie seemed unaffected by the chill. The sun wasn't having much luck cutting through the thick layer of fog, so Turner had made up his mind to look for a department store to buy thermal underwear just as Winter exited the front door of the hotel. He was alone and without his briefcase or bag. He stood on the sidewalk and glanced both ways. After a few seconds, he walked downhill toward their park. The little man was dressed casually in an olive green pullover sweater, khaki pants and brown high-top tennis shoes. His shoulder-length grey hair was pulled back in a ponytail, and around his waist he wore a black leather fanny pack. There was a little bounce in his step that made Turner grin as he and Reggie stepped behind the trunk of a large tree and waited until he passed them on the other side of the street.

"What's wrong with you?" Reggie asked.

The lyrics "Hi ho, hi ho, it's off to work we go," kept replaying in Turner's head. Miller would get it; Reggie would just think he was stupid. He said, "Nothing."

They followed him for about fifteen minutes before Winter stopped at a busy coffee shop for breakfast. Turner was cold, but sweating. The pain kept him about half a block behind Reggie, and he only caught up when Winter sat at one of the outside tables. The little man didn't seem bothered by the cold. Fortunately, there was a juice bar across the street where they could stay warm and have an unobstructed view of the lawyer. The waitress had just taken Winter's order when a tall, overweight, dark-skinned man with shiny black hair sat at his table. They shook hands, but neither man seemed particularly happy to see the other one. They talked until the waitress returned. When the dark man put his elbows on the table, Turner could see that both his forearms were covered with tattoos. The dark man watched silently while Winter ate a huge breakfast. Turner felt his stomach growl. He wanted that omelet and those sausage links. His puny croissant was a poor substitute for the thick sourdough toast dripping with butter and grape jelly that Winter had just devoured. The dark man and Winter drank coffee when the plates were cleared away. They seemed to be arguing, but the lawyer didn't appear to be upset. At one point he raised both hands as if to say he'd given up. The dark man scribbled something on a napkin and stood. Winter read it, put the napkin in his fanny pack and continued drinking his coffee, ignoring the man's departure.

"We need some help," Turner said. "Who do we follow?"

"I think that's one of the guys I saw at the Conner place with an automatic weapon," Reggie said.

"Stay with him?"

Reggie got up and asked, "You got your cell phone?" Turner nodded. "Good," he said, nearly out the door. "Winter's yours. Do the best you can. I'll take the big guy."

The lawyer didn't seem that eager to leave. He sipped his coffee and took the napkin out to look at it again. He removed a cell phone from the fanny pack and called someone. The waitress brought his bill, and he paid before she left. It must have been a big tip. She was gushing all over him as he turned away, continuing his phone conversation. He left the table almost half an hour later still talking on the cell phone. At one point, he held up the napkin as if reading from it. Finally, he put the phone and the napkin into the fanny pack and walked slowly back toward the hotel. Turner was grateful. Sitting all that time had stiffened his knee again. He didn't know how much longer he could abuse his injured leg and hoped Winter was returning to his room. He'd lost sight of the little man when he reached the park and then caught a glimpse of the green sweater disappearing inside the Mark Hopkins.

An elderly Chinese woman in a hooded sweatshirt and baggy pants stared at him as Turner grabbed the back of the first bench he could reach and limped around to sit. His knee was throbbing, so he swallowed two more of his pain pills without water and lifted his leg to rest it on the bench. It felt much better as soon as he stopped walking, and within a few minutes, with the help of the drugs, the pain subsided. The old woman watched him cautiously, a curiosity in the park, until he smiled at her. Then she spun around on her odd-looking silk pink slippers and scurried away across the grass.

It was almost another two hours before Reggie called. He had followed the dark man to the airport, and they were on a plane headed toward San Diego.

"I'll meet you there," Turner said. He thought about Winter, but had a feeling the lawyer had completed what he'd come to do in San Francisco. Also, he was beginning to worry that this entire trip might have nothing to do with Conner or Helen Sanchez.

"Go back to L.A.," Reggie said.

"We might be spinning our wheels following this guy."

"I got a name off his ticket info. It's Rigoberto Gomez, and he's using Sergeant Alex Gomez's address. Go back to L.A. I'll call."

TWENTY

After standing in long lines at the airport for tickets and security checks, and the cab finally left him in front of his house, Turner wanted to sleep for a week. Unfortunately, Miller was waiting in his kitchen wanting to know everything that had happened. Reggie had called him to make certain Turner got home okay. Eddie seemed upset and didn't say much.

"I look worse than I am," Turner said, putting his arm around Eddie's shoulder. He was trying not to limp and sound nonchalant. "All I need's a little rest."

Now that he was satisfied Turner wasn't badly injured, Eddie led the dog back to his bedroom and closed the door. Turner felt something was wrong with the old man, but it was difficult to think straight. He figured he could deal with Eddie later on when they were alone.

He'd taken too many pain pills during the day on an empty stomach, so he finished two peanut butter sandwiches and half a quart of milk before he reached the point in his story where Reggie had followed Rigoberto Gomez to San Diego.

Miller followed him to the living room where Turner crawled onto his lounger and covered himself with the blanket. He intended to sleep until Reggie called again, but Miller continued pestering him with questions about Helen Sanchez and Alex Gomez.

"She's hiding and Alex Gomez is probably dead by now," Turner said, finally frustrated with his friend's persistence.

"Is she with Conner?" Miller asked.

Turner twisted in the chair trying to get comfortable. "I don't know, Miller. Wait until we get the video. If Conner's in the truck, we'll track him down and maybe get her too." He closed his eyes, wanting to sleep.

"I'll talk to Vogel; he'll snatch that midget."

Turner sighed and sat up. "No, bad idea."

"Why? Give me five minutes alone with the dwarf. He'll tell me everything."

"He's a nasty little shyster who lives to sue cops. You're his dream defendant. Don't go near him."

"It's your call," Miller said, obviously disappointed. "Just don't wait so long everybody disappears again."

Turner started to say something, but Miller was gone. There was little doubt in his mind the guy would attempt to do something stupid. Luckily, Vogel was as timid as Miller was crazy. Any scheme Miller cooked up usually required someone else to do all the dirty work. He was too clever to compromise his own career, and Vogel was too scared to do anything that hadn't been sanctioned by his boss. Turner doubted that even Miller could badger the RHD detective into something as brainless as arresting a lawyer to question him about a client.

Turner couldn't remember falling asleep, but the living room was dark when he finally woke from a dreamless slumber. It was as if he'd been drugged, that heavy confused awakening that leaves you wondering where you are and what really important appointment you missed. The digital clock on the end table said it was 5 A.M. He had slept fully dressed for nearly twelve hours. When he pulled back the blanket and rolled up his pant leg, he saw that the swelling in his knee was nearly gone, and there wasn't any pain when he moved it. Cautiously, he edged off the recliner and put his weight on the leg. It was stiff but felt much better.

It surprised him when he flipped on the light switch in the kitchen and saw Eddie asleep at the table, his face buried in his arms. Turner switched off the lights again and quietly backed out of the room.

"Not sleepin'," Eddie said, without looking up.

"Wanna be alone?"

"Don't need no lights. Otherwise don't matter."

Turner noticed the coffee was made and filled his mug. "Want some?" he asked, holding the pot. Eddie didn't look or answer. He sat across the table from the old man. "Wanna talk?"

"Not 'specially, but you gonna keep pestering me 'til I do."

"Is it Danny? Did your son do something?"

"How old's your daddy when he passed?" Eddie asked, lifting his head. His eyes were bloodshot and watery, set in dark sunken circles. He probably hadn't slept all night, but Turner couldn't smell any alcohol on his breath.

"Sixty-one, you know that."

"Most people I know from the job's gone."

Turner leaned back in the chair. He was eager to call Reggie and find out what was happening in San Diego, but knew he couldn't rush Eddie. Eventually, the old man would reveal what was bothering him. He just had to keep asking.

"So, what's wrong?"

"Better t'die before you get stupid."

"You're one of the smartest guys I know. What's this about?"

"I know that little girl's up to no good. I shoulda told you," Eddie said, rubbing his bony hands together.

"Miriam?" The separation had been too easy. Turner had this nagging premonition she wasn't done with him. "Tell me now."

"She says don' tell Mike; can't do no good, but I know that big geeky-lookin' red-haired Howdy Doody's a rotten pile a shit."

"He was here?" Turner asked as calmly as he could. The thought that Ian Conner was in his home made him want to hit somebody.

The old man nodded.

"When?"

Eddie thought for a moment and then said, "The day 'fore she left . . . wanted somethin' she swears she ain't got."

"What?"

"Couldn't make out all the words. He's yelling; she's whisperin' and I'm tryin' to pretend I ain't hiding in my room. Says somethin' of his been stole. Must of believed her, 'cuz after a while he goes away." He hesitated before admitting, "She's cryin', makes me promise not to say nothing . . . says if you know, you go after him and get yourself hurt."

"You should've told me." Turner was furious, but not with Eddie. Miriam was a shit magnet. She had a way of attracting trouble and didn't care who got dragged in . . . her father, her grandmother, Eddie . . . him. It didn't matter as long as Miriam got what she wanted, or what she thought she wanted.

"My boy's right . . . I'm jus' too old to think straight."

"Your boy's an asshole. There's nothing wrong with you. Miriam had no right involving you in her mess."

It took a few more minutes, but Turner was able to console the old man and convince him to rest. Sleep was a wonderful drug, and Eddie needed something to restore his confidence and feisty attitude. Turner had detected a hint of his old friend when he called his son an asshole. Eddie had grinned at this description, and his eyes sparkled like a kid on Christmas morning.

When he heard steady snoring coming from Eddie's room, Turner took Daryl out for a short walk and tried to calm down before driving to the hospital and confronting Miriam. He was livid about Conner being in his home, and obviously Miriam knew more than she was revealing. Her fear of Conner went beyond the possibility that she was an informant. She had something—or Conner thought she had something—he wanted back. Maybe that hit-and-run was intended to damage her just enough to scare her into giving it up.

He'd walked all the way to the beach before he realized how far he'd gone. Daryl was panting, but Turner's knee felt great. He found a drinking fountain and managed to get enough water cupped in his hands to revive Daryl, before they returned to the house where the dog immediately curled up near the foot of Eddie's bed and fell asleep.

Turner took a shower and was on his way back to the hospital in Arcadia before lunch. He tried not to think about how pissed off he was. The walk had helped, but every time he imagined Conner being in his home, he felt his blood pressure rising. He knew if he was going to get any cooperation from Miriam, he needed to stay calm. His irritation would only serve to make her defensive, stubborn, and less willing to tell the truth.

Miriam was awake, sitting up watching television news when he got there. Her nose and face were heavily bandaged; her hair had been shaved, and her left arm was in a cast from her wrist to above the elbow. She looked worse than the last time he'd seen her. He wouldn't have recognized her if she hadn't waved at him. The rage that had festered in his gut since he'd talked with Eddie gave way to pity. She'd lost some more weight and was wrapped in several hospital blankets. He leaned over, gave her a gentle hug and sat on the bed.

"Got my nose job," she said in a dry throaty voice.

"You look like something they dragged out of a pyramid."

She grunted. "Don't make me laugh. It hurts." She touched the bandages near her eyes. "Insurance's paying . . . so I fixed one or two problem spots."

"Good for you," he said and knew it sounded sarcastic. He didn't think he meant it that way.

She pulled the blanket closer around her neck. "What do you want?"

"Wanted to see how you're doing."

"Terrific, can't you tell?"

"Eddie told me about Conner's visit to my house."

Miriam fixed her bloodshot gaze on the ceiling. The gauze wrapped around her face shifted a little, revealing the purple and black bruises under her eyes. It looked painful, and for a moment he felt sorry for her again.

"Eddie was trying to help me. He loves you like a son . . . better."

"I'm not mad at Eddie," he said.

She rubbed the cast on her arm. "It itches. I can't scratch." She reached over to a control box hanging on the bed and pushed a button. "I have to lie down," she said, wearily. A nurse came in and gently pushed past Turner to help Miriam slide down in the hospital bed. They were quiet until the woman finished examining Miriam's bandages and finally left.

"I knew he had the storage place, but I didn't take anything," Miriam said, staring at the television screen.

"What did he have?"

"Money . . . jewelry . . . pictures."

"Pictures?" Turner couldn't imagine killing people for a photo album.

"Expensive art, sculptures."

"Stolen, of course," he said.

She sighed and scratched at the bandages wrapped behind her ear. "Goodman told me about the place. He showed me photos of stuff and asked if I thought it was valuable. They had a fucking Erté stuffed in a hundred-and-fifty-dollar-a-month locker."

"What's Erté?"

"Do cops read anything besides the Penal Code? He's a famous artist with a very distinct Art Deco style. His work is worth a fortune."

"And you never suspected these things might be stolen?"

"I'm not stupid, Turner." She fell back against the pillow and rubbed the bandages covering her forehead. "But I'm an idiot," she whispered. "He spent a lot of money on me and I never asked any questions. Then, when I finally got curious, he dumped me."

"Did Beverly know?" He wasn't certain why he asked that question. It would make Miriam angry, but he needed an answer.

She didn't respond for several seconds and then said, calmly, "That woman wouldn't believe anything bad about her kid. It was kind of funny. She thought I was taking advantage of Ian; all the while he's making a fool of her."

"What happened to the money and other stuff in storage?" he asked.

"I figured Cullen or maybe Goodman took it."

"They're dead and Ian's still searching."

"I don't have it," she said in a hoarse, dry voice. "He's trying to kill me, and I swear to God I don't have it." She touched his arm as she spoke. Her hand was too warm. He worried that she had a fever and pushed the button again for the nurse. "You've got to help me," she whispered, but wasn't asking. With her last little bit of energy, she demanded his help.

He stayed until the nurse came. She took Miriam's temperature and hung a saline bag for an IV. Before the needle was in her arm, Miriam was asleep, her battered, surgically altered body barely a ripple under the clean white sheets, a helpless, perfect victim for Conner.

Turner believed her. Maybe she was too scared to lie this time. Miriam just wasn't a good liar. Normally, she wasn't afraid of anything either, but the surgery and the injuries had taken the fight out of her.

Weaver's surveillance team was stationed outside the room. The two men said they were using their vacation hours to guard Miriam because Weaver had asked them to do it. Lieutenant Metcalf wasn't happy about the arrangement, but couldn't stop them from hanging around Miriam's room on their own time. They assured Turner someone would stay with her. Weaver had managed to get Patty back into his squad, and Miriam could move in with her as soon as she was well enough to leave the hospital. Turner wanted this to be over before she left the hospital, but had no idea how he'd make that happen.

TWENTY-ONE

He drove by JR's bar on the way home. He hadn't intended to stop, but made a U-turn when he spotted Reggie's car parked beside Miller's in the front lot. His first thought was that can't be good . . . a stick of dynamite and a match in close proximity with no adult supervision.

They grinned at him when he located them in his favorite booth.

"What took you so long?" Miller asked. "We figured this would be your first stop after the hospital."

"You talked to Eddie," he said. The old man had filled them in on the whole depressing story, so Turner didn't feel obligated to reveal any of the messy details.

"Did she tell you what we're looking for?" Miller asked, impatiently tapping his fingers on an empty glass.

Turner shoved him over and sat in the booth. "Money and stolen stuff," he said, waving at the bartender to bring him a beer. "What did you get in San Diego?" he asked Reggie.

"Rigoberto's got a place downtown, him and a woman . . . not Helen, older," Reggie said. Turner was listening but couldn't help noticing his friend looked tired, worn-out weary. With his day-old stubble, sunken, bloodshot grey eyes, and his wrinkled, stained shirt, Reggie could've passed for one of the regular derelicts who inhabited JR's. He was wearing the same clothes he had worn in San Francisco a couple of days ago.

"You need some sleep and a shower," Turner said, interrupting.

Reggie ignored him and continued, "Alex Gomez is dead. They delivered his body to a San Diego funeral home. Guy in charge there says Gomez's brother is taking him south for burial."

"Why San Diego?" Miller asked. "Why not right into Mexico?"

"Red tape, paperwork?" Turner asked.

"Don't think so," Reggie said. "Consulate takes care of all that. Rigoberto's delaying, waiting for something or somebody."

"What makes you think that?"

"The body won't get shipped until the day after tomorrow, and the family's arranged private transportation."

"So?" Miller was getting impatient.

"The Mexican government will do it for nothing," Turner said, figuring out where Reggie was going.

"So?" Miller repeated.

"His relatives are dirt poor. I'm guessing there's more than bones in that coffin or soon will be."

"You think Conner and Helen are moving the money and stolen stuff in the coffin," Turner said.

"I think Helen and Winter might be," Reggie said.

Miller groaned. "Okay, I've officially got a headache. What happened to Conner?"

"She ripped him off," Turner answered for Reggie. It was finally starting to make sense. "Stole Conner's stash and split."

"Don't think so," Reggie said. "I'm guessing Cullen or Goodman or maybe even Miriam took it." He glanced up at Turner for just a moment before continuing. "It doesn't matter. Somehow Helen figured out where it was and got the lawyer to help her hide it. Conner got screwed by the only two people he actually trusted."

"You think Helen's in San Diego or already across the border?" Turner asked. "My guess is she's too clever to let the stuff out of her sight," he said before Reggie could answer.

"It must be worth a bundle for her to risk ending up like Goodman or Cullen," Miller said.

Turner remembered the colonel Helen had killed in Mexico, "I've got a feeling Conner's the one who needs to be afraid."

"I gotta sleep a few hours," Reggie said. "Then we'll go back to San Diego."

After a meal of hamburgers, fries and beer at JR's, they all decided to stay at Turner's house overnight and leave before

200

dawn. From Redondo Beach, it was less than a two-hour drive to downtown San Diego. They could be there before breakfast.

Miller fell asleep in the recliner five minutes after they got to the house. Reggie wanted to take a shower but made the mistake of sitting. On his way to Eddie's room, Turner noticed Reggie already curled up on the couch, snoring softly with his hand dangling over the side resting on the dog's head.

The old man was awake, lying on the bed watching television. He wasn't interested in what was happening in the other part of the house, but wanted to talk with Turner. He'd called his son and had asked him to bring all the information on the assisted living place to Turner's house tomorrow. There was that awkward moment of silence when Turner knew Eddie was waiting for some reaction, but he wasn't certain what he wanted to say. If he interfered again, Eddie's son might not be as forgiving as the last time. He shouldn't be in the middle of this anyway.

"You want to do that?" he asked, knowing it sounded a little testy. After all, he had incurred Danny's wrath by letting his father move in. And then there was going to be that big I-told-you-so smirk all over Danny's face when his father moved out.

"Might be best," Eddie mumbled, staring intently at some annoying toothpaste commercial.

"Bullshit."

Eddie glanced away from the television, and calmly asked, "You gotta problem with that?"

"No, I've gotta problem with you."

"Fuck you, too," Eddie said, still remarkably composed.

"You're right. It's none of my business. If you want to go someplace where you can't take a piss without permission, and the only excitement is betting on which old guy is gonna die next, why should I care."

"Didn't say I was goin' nowhere."

"Great, if you don't go now, your kid's gonna blame me for changing your mind."

"Why'd you care what he thinks?"

"He's a commander. He can mess with my life."

"Ain't like you got much career left to mess with," Eddie said, with just a hint of sarcasm. He slid closer to the edge of the bed. "I can jus' pack up my stuff an' be gone."

Turner took a deep breath. This wasn't right. "You've got a place here as long as you want. What I meant to say was you're my friend; I want you to be happy. My house may not be as clean or as well-run as some institution, but it's wrong to stop living before you're dead."

"I don't wanna be no burden to nobody."

"I know life's not predictable or neat. You can forget to lock the door or to turn off the stove or lose Daryl on one of your funky walks—I don't care. I just don't want you to quit," Turner said, without thinking. To his surprise, he really didn't want the old guy to go even if it meant incurring his son's wrath.

Eddie scooted back on the bed and picked up the channel changer. "Good," he said. "I ain't goin' nowhere. Get outta here so I can watch my cable news in peace." Turner got as far as the hallway, and Eddie called him back.

"Wanna fight some more?" Turner asked, peeking into the room.

Eddie used the remote and turned down the volume on the television. "That's wrong what I said 'bout your career. You're a good cop . . . better than your daddy ever was an' he's the best I ever seen. Anybody can study books an' kiss ass like Danny did and get to be boss. Being a good cop's tougher. Can't learn that in no book, gotta do the roadwork." The volume came back up, and he leaned against the pillows, staring at the screen again.

Turner stepped back into the hallway and closed the door. It was nice to hear Eddie say the words, but he always knew he was a member in good standing. He'd earned his status as a respected, working cop, and knew his dad, the only man whose approval ever mattered, would've been proud. His dad and Eddie were naïve about how the department was managed, but they always recognized and admired a fellow worker bee. Unlike Eddie and his dad, Turner needed responsibility and knew he could take on more, but he also knew you don't always get what you want and sometimes it's easier to settle for what you have.

In a couple of hours, the house was quiet. Even the television in Eddie's room had been turned off. Reggie had taken a shower and was back on the couch asleep despite Miller's snoring. The pungent odor of red tide saturated Turner's bedroom. It was a chilly night but he'd opened the window because the smell of the ocean always seemed to clear his head. He was wrapped in the bedspread propped against the pillows, staring at the full moon and sipping Rémy Martin when the phone rang. The noise startled him, and he grabbed it before it woke everyone in the house. Before saying anything, he glanced at the clock radio on the night stand. It was 2 A.M. His first thought was something had happened to Miriam, but he was wrong. It was Jack Winter.

"How'd you get my home number?" Turner asked, not attempting to hide his annoyance.

"We need to talk." The little man had a surprisingly strong voice with just a hint of a Boston accent.

"Why?"

"Not on the phone, meet me at your bar."

Now Turner was upset. The attorney had his home phone number and knew he drank at JR's. Did the little fuck have him followed?

"Tell me why, and maybe we'll talk."

"I saw you in San Francisco. I can help you find her."

"Her?"

"Don't play stupid. I don't have time for games."

Turner figured he would regret his decision, but agreed to meet the lawyer at JR's around 6 A.M.

The marine layer was heavier than usual, leaving the streets and sidewalks around his house under a thin coat of water. It reminded him of London without the soot. Daryl got up, but wasn't interested in venturing out beyond the front yard, so Turner jogged carefully on the wet asphalt. He'd left early enough to circle the harbor and get back to JR's before the bartender unlocked the door. His knee ached, and he was breathing hard when he arrived at the front step in his damp shorts and t-shirt. Jogging was always a good gauge of how out of shape he was. He needed to start working out again and not just for the benefit of his waistline. His thinking was better when he forced oxygen into his brain. As he got older the real question was how long his knee would endure the pounding; but he was vain enough to enjoy the fact that most people thought he was younger, and he was willing to accept a little pain if he could still attract a pretty woman like Miriam. He sat on the step, resting his back against the building. It wasn't easy getting her out of his thoughts.

He heard the unique hum of the Porsche engine before he saw Winter driving toward JR's. The car's windows were slightly tinted, and Winter looked like any other successful middle-aged lawyer until he opened the driver's door. The car had hand controls and a built-up seat so he could peer over the steering wheel. He swung his short legs to the left and slid off the seat onto the ground. His shoulder-length grey hair wasn't tied back this morning, and he hadn't shaved. He was wearing black sweat pants and a black polyester hooded jacket. He looked like an evil gnome.

Locals trickled into the lot from off the boardwalk, and from under makeshift dwellings constructed from blankets and dilapidated tents. Some of the more affluent drinkers lived in the apartments across the street. They gathered around the Porsche staring at the sleek machine until they caught a glimpse of the little man standing beside it. Most of these men lived in that twilight state between sobriety and drunkenness, an uneasy world filled with inappropriate behaviors and incongruities. They greeted Winter like an old friend.

At exactly 6 A.M., the bartender opened the front door and unlocked the security screen. Turner didn't wait for the lawyer and ordered his coffee and eggs on the way to his booth. His legs were tired, but overall the brief run had invigorated him. His good mood changed as soon as Winter sat across from him in the booth. They didn't speak until the bartender placed the coffeepot and two cups on the table.

Turner took a long swallow before asking, "What do you want?"

"Maybe I just want to help you out . . . be a good citizen." Winter pushed his coffee aside, nervously rubbed his chubby hands together.

"Now who's playing stupid?"

"Ms. Conner dropped her complaint a couple of days ago, told IA it was a misunderstanding. I've got no reason to lie or harass you," he said with as sincere an expression as a lawyer could muster.

Turner smelled the odor of perspiration, and at first thought it was coming from his own body; but he quickly recognized the distinct stink of sweat and polyester and saw the damp patches forming under Winter's armpits. It was stress sweat, not the healthy pleasant scent from exercising.

"So, what's up?" Turner asked before taking a big bite of his scrambled eggs.

"She's trying to kill me."

"Helen Sanchez?"

"You saw her cousin in San Francisco. He threatened me."

"Don't you have some kind of lawyer-client thing with her?" Turner asked.

"Conner was my client. Fuck her. Nobody threatens me." The attorney was so angry he was bouncing on the booth's cheap leather seat.

Turner finished his breakfast and sat back staring at Winter as he drank his coffee. He put the mug on the table and didn't feel that bad about the lawyer's apparent distress, but wanted to get as much information as he could because he knew the guy would stop talking as soon as he felt safe again.

"What do you mean Conner was your client?" he asked, emphasizing the "was."

"He's gone. I can't find him. His mother says she hasn't heard from him. I think that crazy Mexican woman had him killed, too, or he's hiding from her."

"Tell me everything you know about her and Conner, or we're done talking."

Winter ordered a Jack Daniels straight up and gulped it before starting his story. He knew Ian Conner was scamming the city, but took the case because it was easy money. The City Attorney always settled. The deputies in the CA's office were lazy and didn't like to litigate, and when they did go to court, they lost. In Los Angeles, the police department was always wrong, and juries always overcompensated plaintiffs for any perceived injury. Winter admitted he'd made a good living suing the department, and Conner wasn't any better or worse than most of his clients. Winter said he knew Conner and Helen Sanchez were partners, but was never told about their business. Conner introduced him to Goodman, who had asked him to help a widow with probate when her husband was killed in some robbery. Helen's gay cousin Sergeant Alex Gomez and his brother Rigoberto were Helen's protectors. She had an extended family across the border that she supported, and they would do anything for her.

Winter ordered another drink and took a few sips before continuing. Turner looked at his watch and knew they'd be waking up at the house and wondering where he was. He didn't want to interrupt the lawyer to make a phone call and hoped Reggie would come here to look for him.

"I never met Ian's girlfriend, but I knew they were living together for a while," Winter said. "He liked her, but Helen made him dump the girl."

"Why would he do what Helen said?"

"The woman's scary. Conner swears she had her own sister killed."

"Why tell me all this?" Turner asked, attempting to prod Winter into telling him something he hadn't already figured out.

"She pretty much told me she had that Goodman and the widow killed."

"She told you that."

"I asked for more money. I work hard; I deserve it. She was trying to scare me. Then her gangbanger cousin Rigoberto, he brags to me in San Francisco that Helen knows how to take care of anybody that interferes in her business. He threatened to kill me if I didn't shut up and do what she wanted."

"What's her business?" Turner asked.

"I don't know." Winter wouldn't look at Turner.

"What's your cut?"

"She paid me to do paperwork, write letters. That's all," he protested, weakly. "I did nothing illegal."

"So, why does she want you dead? You forget to mail a letter?" Turner took twenty dollars out of his pocket and placed it on top of the bill. "I think the rest is yours," he said, sliding out of the booth. "I'm busy. Call if you want to tell me the truth, otherwise don't bother me."

Winter practically leapt from the seat. He grabbed Turner's wrist to keep him from walking away. The little man's grip felt like a vise digging into the bone. Turner tried to pull away but couldn't. It hurt so much he was about to punch the smaller man and didn't care how bad it looked to the drunken bystanders, when Winter released him.

"Sit," Winter said, pointing to the booth. "I'll tell you."

Turner stood for a few minutes rubbing his wrist. He couldn't believe those stubby fingers could do that much damage.

"Sorry, I was a wrestler in my other life. Sometimes I forget how strong I am," Winter said, apologetically.

It still hurt, but Turner stopped rubbing and said, "Terrific, let's talk about this life. What are Conner and Helen up to?"

"Conner and his buddies were stealing, doing hit jobs for cash . . . bragged they were some kind of bad boy gang. They robbed a house Helen was cleaning. She helped them, gave them other places she and her sister worked, and pretty soon she was running things."

"So, where do you fit in?"

"They needed papers on stuff, and she wanted her people to come across the border without any hassle. They paid me a lot of cash to fill out some forms and write a couple of letters. She wanted me to do more . . . deal some of the stolen pieces." Winter tightened his fists. "I refused and Rigoberto threatened me."

"What happened with Conner?" Turner asked. He thought he knew but wanted to hear Winter say it.

"Helen took everything, emptied his storage place, and Conner's so stupid he blamed everyone but her. Now he's got nothing, and her relatives are hunting him down."

"Where's the stash?"

"San Diego, I think. She's unloading everything and crossing the border."

"How?"

Winter shook his head. "I didn't stick around to find out . . . haven't been home or at work since I left San Francisco. I helped her. Now I'm just another loose end like Conner and her sister."

"You got a safe place for a couple of days until we pick her up?"

Winter nodded. "Don't worry, I'm not going anywhere. I'll testify. It may cost me a small fortune, but I'm not going to jail, and I'm not gonna let some fucking wetback threaten me."

Turner glanced up toward the front of the bar as Miller and Reggie maneuvered around the cluttered room to get to him. They seemed upset until they got close enough to see Winter sitting across the table from Turner, and then they looked confused. It only took a few seconds and a long hard fix on the nervous, grubby lawyer for Reggie to figure out what was happening, but he listened intently as Turner quickly repeated highlights of the story.

When Turner finished, Winter assured them again he would be available, but Miller insisted on taking him downtown for a formal, signed statement.

"No offense," Miller said, as he waited for the lawyer to slide out of the booth. "But it wouldn't take much to kill your puny little ass."

"You'd be surprised," Winter said, leading the way out of the bar.

Turner rubbed his sore wrist. No, it wouldn't be that easy.

TWENTY-TWO

I t was easy to be a free spirit, a maverick with a devil-may-care attitude when he had nothing to lose, but when he knew he was back in the game with his reputation intact, Turner was a little tentative about not doing things the right way. He called Weaver and repeated Winter's story, explained the need to get to San Diego before Helen and her family crossed the border with the stolen money and property. Predictably, Weaver told Lieutenant Metcalf, and everything was put on hold until the lieutenant could get permission up the chain of command.

Metcalf didn't like the plan. He didn't trust Turner, but he didn't have a better idea except his usual, overly cautious approach of doing nothing and letting the Mexican authorities deal with Helen after she crossed the border. Turner argued that Helen probably had thousands of dollars, a small portion of which would earn her safe passage and protection anywhere in her own country. It was nearly noon before Metcalf's boss, the IA captain, with Weaver's prodding agreed to let four members of the surveillance squad go to San Diego. He also threatened immediate suspensions if anyone in the detail "put one toe over the border." Metcalf was satisfied because if anything went wrong, the captain had made the decision and would be responsible. Metcalf mentioned going along with the squad as an observer until Miller not too subtly reminded him that if he were present, as the highest ranking officer, he would assume all responsibility for the operation. When the time came to leave, Metcalf couldn't be located, but left word that some pressing matter had surfaced unexpectedly.

Weaver contacted the San Diego police and gave them Helen's description. They agreed to have an undercover officer watch the funeral parlor and Rigoberto's house, and would notify Weaver if the body was moved. Their officers wouldn't detain anyone unless they were about to cross the border.

The small surveillance caravan left Parker Center a few minutes after noon with Reggie in the lead car. Turner followed with Miller behind him and Weaver bringing up the rear. It would be a quick but boring ride south to San Diego. Usually they'd amuse themselves chattering and joking on the radio, but they had been driving for an hour and no one spoke. Turner knew they were upset, but he didn't care. He was willing to push the line just so far. He knew the difference between hard-charging police work and doing something your own way just because it's easier than following the rules. Doing police work outside L.A. County without notifying the boss might be more expedient, but it was dangerous and stupid.

He was hoping Helen wouldn't show up until they got to San Diego. It was important that he did the interrogation. He'd underestimated her the first time, but wouldn't make that mistake again. He laughed to himself. Maybe, he would. His track record with women was dismal. Men were a lot easier to decipher. They were pretty simple animals, and he always seemed to know when another man was lying or hiding something, but women were a complete puzzle. He trusted the wrong ones, and like most guys, was willing to forgive a lot if a woman had a pleasant face and firm body. When he met her, Miriam's laugh melted his heart until eventually she didn't laugh as much, and he noticed she was sloppy and selfish. She hadn't changed; he'd chosen badly.

Interstate 405 was flowing freely, and Reggie was cruising between eighty and eighty-five miles per hour. Even though the squad drove unmarked cars, the Highway Patrol recognized that they were the police and pulled alongside Reggie, trying to slow him down a little with hand signals to a safer speed. Reggie held up three fingers to indicate a Code-three emergency, and they backed off. Turner was glad he couldn't hear Weaver's remarks in the last car.

Reggie led them directly to Rigoberto's house. It was a one-story, patched stucco bungalow outside the downtown area in a locale that appeared to be occupied primarily by poor Latinos. A graffiti-covered liquor store was on the corner adjacent to an alley. Rigoberto's house was across the alley. Reggie warned them to stay several blocks away from the neighborhood where strangers triggered an immediate run-or-hide alert. He would park and find a place where he could watch the house and not be seen.

Before Turner could settle into a comfortable location, Reggie advised everyone that Beverly Conner's 1968 red Impala was parked in the alley behind Rigoberto's house. No one spoke, but Turner could taste his disappointment. They all knew how he felt about her, so he expected an onslaught of jokes and snide remarks, but they were silent.

The radio was quiet until Weaver cautioned, "Heads up, guys, anyone could be driving that car."

That was true, but given his history with women, Turner would take bets Beverly was inside the house.

It wasn't long before Reggie broadcast that he'd seen an older woman moving around in the house. He hadn't seen Helen, Beverly or her son. The San Diego officer who'd been watching the house for a couple of hours insisted that he'd seen the old woman, Rigoberto and two Mexican Mafia-type men in the house. He was certain they were still there.

After more than an hour with no activity, Reggie wanted to get closer on foot, but needed Turner to take the point. Turner followed his directions, walking down the alley on the other side of the street until he spotted Reggie on the roof of a dilapidated shed that gave him a direct line of sight to Rigoberto's house and yard. Shades were drawn in all the windows. A sprinkler head attached to the garden hose sprayed an uneven layer of water on the brown, patchy, weed-covered front yard. The hose leaked and a huge mud puddle was rising like a moat around the front step.

He motioned for Reggie to stay on the roof and indicated he would take a look in the house. It was a spontaneous decision that Turner probably wouldn't have made had he given it some thought. His inclination wasn't to be the guy who crawled under windows and overheard conversations. Reggie and Miller were good at that; he wasn't. He was good in a gun battle or at being the first one to go through a door. Creeping wasn't his strong point, but he'd volunteered, so he worked his way across the street and around to Rigoberto's backyard.

There was a rotting redwood fence behind the house that had several slats loose on the alley side. He lifted one of them and saw a jungle of weeds and overgrown shrubbery. His radio was in the inside pocket of his shirt. He secured it by buttoning the flap and told Reggie he was going onto the property. As he slid between the boards, a rusty nail caught on his Levi's leaving them torn at the knee. He'd tweaked his bad knee trying to twist his leg away from the nail and landed in two inches of mud. The water from the front sprinkler had seeped under the fence into the back yard.

The radio clicked. "How you doing?" Miller's voice asked.

"Just dandy," Turner said, wiping the mud from his hands onto his pants.

"Look behind you to the right."

Turner glanced over his shoulder and saw Miller crawling in his direction from the corner of the yard, covered in mud and grinning at him.

"What a shit hole, somebody should tell them there's water rationing in this state," Turner said, feeling much better after seeing Miller's condition. "You look inside the house yet?" he asked.

"About to when I spotted a fellow swamp rat," Miller said, pushing weeds aside to see the house. There was a rear door, and all the shades were drawn in the back windows too. Turner heard loud music as they kept low and ran closer. When they got to either side of the door, Miller reached out and clutched the door knob.

"What're you doing?" Turner whispered. They had no idea who was in there, and they didn't have a warrant or anything a court would say was a good reason to go inside.

"What's happening?" Weaver's voice asked in his earpiece.

"Going in," Miller said in his microphone. "Coming?" he asked Turner as he opened the unlocked door and stepped inside.

As soon as he entered the house, Turner felt a jolt of energy and his senses magnified as if someone had injected him with a shot of adrenaline. He drew his weapon, crouched down, and slid to the right. The kitchen was empty. Dirty dishes were piled in the sink and the room smelled like a pack of dogs had peed on the floor. Like always, his mind flashed through a scenario of probable cause—hot pursuit of Helen Sanchez and Ian Conner, possible homicide suspects. It wasn't great, but it was a reason, a flimsy one, but all he had to walk into someone's home without an invitation or a warrant.

They cautiously moved through every room until they reached the back bedroom. The blast of Tex-Mex music hit them as Miller kicked open the door. An overweight grey-haired woman was lying flat on her back on a messy bedspread. She wore a faded denim-blue housedress, but her feet were bare and dirty. At first, Turner thought she was dead, until he heard the wheezing as he moved closer to the bed. Otherwise, the room was empty. Rigoberto and the two Mexican men, if they were ever here, were gone.

It took several minutes of shouting and shaking to wake the old woman. Frightened and confused, she struggled to sit up, tugged at the bedspread to cover her legs and glared at the intruders. In his pigeon Spanish, Miller attempted to talk to her. According to Miller's translation, she was Rigoberto's aunt. She allowed her nephew to stay in her house while he was in this country. She didn't like him, and was afraid of his friends. They were bad men she said, and she hoped the police would arrest them. Helen was her niece. She refused to answer any questions or talk about her.

213

Turner radioed Reggie and Weaver to come inside, and they quickly searched the rooms while Miller interviewed the woman. Generations of junk filled every inch of the house. Boxes were packed so tightly under the bed, they were locked in place. Dresser drawers and shelves in the living room were stuffed with everything from baby clothes to hand-sewn wedding gowns. The rooms were so dirty and dusty that one drawer in a night-stand near the old woman's bed caught Turner's attention. It was the only one that had been opened recently. The area around the knob had been wiped clean. He pulled out the drawer and noticed the woman staring at him. She used a corner of a sheet to dab at sweat forming on her forehead and upper lip. She was responding to Miller's questions but following Turner's move-ments intently. Turner watched her as he lifted items out of the drawer and laid them on the floor. Her eyes seemed to be telling him where to search. He yanked the drawer out of the night-stand, and she stopped talking. He turned it over, and she gasped softly. A stack of pawn tickets were taped to the bottom of the drawer. Every pawn shop in San Diego and several in Hollywood had been beneficiaries of Helen's divestment. He wondered who the lucky guy was that got the Erté thing, whatever it was.

The old woman nervously made the sign of the cross over and over, mumbling something in Spanish.

"She's afraid they're gonna kill her when they see the tickets are gone," Miller said. He touched her arm and spoke softly in Spanish trying to get her attention to calm her, but she seemed too frightened to concentrate on anything he had to say.

"We'll get Vogel to take a photo six-pack out to every one of these pawn shops, confiscate Helen's stolen goods, and ID our suspects," Weaver said. "If we get lucky, some of the stuff she or her family of thieves pawned is from the dead widow's house."

"Ask her where they went," Turner told Miller.

"I already did. She doesn't know. They were here when she fell asleep."

Turner kept thinking about Beverly's car parked in the alley. How did Rigoberto and his buddies get the car, and why did they leave it here? He called Beverly's home number. There was no answer. Whoever answered the phone at the bar said she wasn't scheduled to work. He gave the pawn tickets to Weaver and went out to search the car.

The doors were unlocked and the interior was clean. No one had tampered with the ignition. The trunk was empty. There was a picture on the visor of Beverly and a gawky-looking pony. He put the photo in his pocket, called the records unit at IA and asked Jenny to run the plate. The car hadn't been reported stolen. Going back inside the house, he told Miller to ask the old woman if she knew who'd been driving the car.

"*No manejo,*" she said, demonstrating with an imaginary steering wheel that she couldn't drive. Miller couldn't make her understand, and every time he tried she acted more confused.

"Screw it," Turner said, after the fifth or sixth attempt. He would call the San Diego officers and ask them to impound the car as soon as they were ready to leave. The local police would probably offer the old woman some protection from her family, but Turner wanted to make certain she was able to take care of herself before they left her alone. She was a big woman and appeared to be at least seventy years old. She was sweating and flushed and didn't look very healthy. He tried to persuade her to get out of bed just to see if she was ambulatory, but she appeared frightened and refused to move.

"Leave her," Miller said. "She's not our problem."

"We'll tell the San Diego guys. Let them deal with her," Weaver said, impatiently. He was anxious to get back to the funeral home where he was certain they would find Helen and Rigoberto.

Reggie walked around the bed and tried to help by gently lifting her under the arms. She slapped at his hands and threw her body back on the pillows, kicking at Turner who had crawled up on the bed to help. Turner looked at Reggie and knew they were thinking the same thing. She was hiding something. Reggie drew his Glock semi-automatic and pointed it at the old woman's forehead.

"What the fuck," Miller yelled, backing away from the bed.

"Put your hands on your head and get off the bed," Reggie ordered. "Don't give me that 'no comprendo' crap."

Weaver stared at Reggie as if he had lost his mind, but didn't interfere. Turner grabbed the old woman's hands and tried to handcuff them behind her back, but she was so fat her arms couldn't get close enough. He cuffed her in front and tugged on the handcuffs, pulling her off the bed. Standing, she was nearly as tall as him. He figured she must've weighed close to three hundred pounds. He glanced at the spot on the bed where she'd been sitting and exhaled. In the middle of her sunken nesting place was a .45-caliber Smith & Wesson semi-auto pistol. Turner took the gun and moved the bedspread aside, uncovering stacks of U.S. currency.

"How . . . ?" Weaver mumbled, his question lost at the sight of so much cash.

"Hunch," Turner said, smiling at Reggie. "Wanna tell us who you really are, Grandma?" he asked.

"Fuck you," she said in perfect English, spitting on the floor. "That's my money. I saved it."

"They gotta come back," Reggie said, ignoring her. "Are your cars away from the house?" Everyone had parked at least a block away.

"Who are you calling?" Turner asked Weaver, who had flipped open his cell phone.

"San Diego."

Turner reached over and closed the phone. "Not a good idea," he said. "If they get here the same time as Helen, she's in the wind, and we'll never find her again. Sorry boss, we gotta do this one."

Weaver was quiet. Turner could almost see some serious conflict going on in his supervisor's brain. Weaver had to know Turner was right, but he wouldn't want to get into a possible gun battle in another city without notifying that jurisdiction. Turner was counting on the man's natural instinct to do good police work. Weaver couldn't help himself; he was basically a street cop.

"What the hell, captain said don't cross the border. He didn't say anything about making arrests," Weaver said. He removed his baseball cap and rubbed his bald spot. "Miller," he shouted.

"Don't get excited, boss. I'm standing right here."

"Get where you can watch the street."

Turner led the old woman into the bathroom where he closed the lid and told her to sit on the toilet. He took another pair of handcuffs and attached one end to those securing her hands and the other end to the sink pipe. She couldn't stand or sit up straight, and he hoped she couldn't get enough leverage to break the pipe connection. There weren't any windows in the room, just an air vent that he turned on before leaving and shutting the door.

That should hold her long enough to do what we've got to do, he thought. Before Turner could tell Weaver what he'd done with the old woman, he heard Miller yell from the living room that two cars were approaching the house. Reggie turned on the radio in the bedroom again and closed the door. They agreed to let everyone get into the house before attempting any arrests.

Reggie got behind the front door and would be at the suspects' backs after they entered the room. If necessary, he could use the heavy door for protection. Weaver found cover in the hallway, and Turner took a shotgun that Weaver had retrieved earlier from the trunk of his car and crouched behind an oversized recliner. Despite Weaver's strategic positioning of everyone in the room, they all knew crossfire might still be a problem if shooting started, but then it was never going to be perfect.

"It's them," Miller whispered, moving away from the window and kneeling behind the couch. "Woman . . . two Mexican assholes. Big, tattooed guy stuck something in his belt behind his back."

A few seconds later, the deadbolt clicked, and the door knob turned. Helen was the first one to enter the living room, and she walked directly toward the hallway, not paying attention to anything around her. The men were laughing and talking in Spanish. Before they could close the door, it slammed shut behind them.

They turned to see Reggie pointing his semi-automatic Glock at them. He ordered them to raise their hands. One of the men immediately did what he was told and backed away from Reggie. The tattooed muscular guy kept his hands in front of him near his waistband. Miller stood with his weapon and repeated Reggie's command, but it wasn't until the man saw Turner's shotgun pointed a few feet from his face that he reluctantly raised his arms.

Helen had hesitated only a moment before turning and running through the hallway toward the rear door. As she passed him, Weaver stepped from the bedroom and grabbed her with one arm around her waist and the other around her throat. She resisted, kicking and punching wildly at him. Apparently, he wasn't in the mood for a struggle, so he tightened the choke-hold around her carotid arteries until she stopped struggling. He let go, and she slumped to the floor like a marionette whose strings had been cut. Before she woke up, he handcuffed her, took hold of one of her arms at the elbow, and dragged her limp body into the living room, dropping her beside her handcuffed companions.

Turner had removed a six-inch, .38-caliber revolver from the muscular man's waistband and another smaller .32 from the rear pants pocket of the other man. When the suspects were secure, Weaver called his San Diego police contact and asked him to send uniformed officers and to examine the Alex Gomez coffin at the funeral parlor. He was informed that the coffin had been loaded onto the truck about fifteen minutes ago. The San Diego sergeant had tried to call Weaver, but his cell phone seemed to be turned off, so his officers had already stopped the truck and gotten permission from the driver to search the coffin. They discovered that Sergeant Alex Gomez's remains were about to be delivered to his final resting place with an estimated half a million dollars tucked inside the silk-tufted padding surrounding his freshly embalmed body.

TWENTY-THREE

It took several hours to sort through the evidence and remove all the cash secreted in the coffin. Gomez's remains were transferred to an inexpensive box, loaded onto the truck and dispatched to the dead man's family in Mexico. The old woman continued to claim she was Helen's aunt and had papers to prove she was in the country legally. She also had three outstanding felony warrants for drug dealing and was booked in San Diego.

The activity around the police station resembled that at most big city police departments, and Turner had to remind himself he was still some ninety minutes from home. The uniforms weren't blue, the cars weren't black and white, but they were cops. Familiar banter echoed in the corridors; prisoners sat chained to the bench outside holding cells. A paunchy sergeant had a pretty probationary officer in a starched new uniform cornered in the break room. Turner smiled. The sergeant thought he had the upper hand, but the young woman's big blue eyes showed no fear and lots of confidence. She'd be calling the shots, having these guys tripping all over themselves to get a kind word from her when probation was over, and she knew it. The pretty ones never cried harassment; they always had complete control. Turner nodded at the sergeant and poured the last cup of coffee from a pot on the counter. The woman's partner called her. She gathered her utility bag and activity log, gave Turner a sweet smile and left without acknowledging the sergeant.

"They get worse every class," the sergeant mumbled on his way out of the coffee room.

Turner didn't agree. He admired plucky women. That was the problem with a lot of women in law enforcement. They were afraid to be bold. He laughed to himself. He was probably the last person to speak as an authority on women.

He finished his coffee and found his way back to the detectives' room. Weaver had called Lieutenant Metcalf and arranged to have Vogel and other detectives from RHD drive down and take over the case. They would bring the arrestees, except grandma, back to Los Angeles, but Turner insisted that he interrogate Helen Sanchez first. If the pawn tickets checked out, they could tie her to the money and stolen property, but he wanted Ian Conner and had a feeling Helen knew where to locate the big redhead.

The San Diego detectives left Helen handcuffed to a chair in their interview room. Her dark hair was pulled back, but thick strands had come loose during her scuffle with Weaver, and it made her look as if she'd been caught in a wind storm. Her tailored black shirt and cream-colored pants were streaked with dirt, and the strap on her right shoe had broken off. Despite all indications she'd lost the battle, her attitude hadn't softened. She was still defiant, glaring at Turner when he entered with Reggie.

"I'll save you some time," she said, before they sat across from her at the table. "I'm not talking about anything."

"Those pawn tickets are gonna put you on death row," Turner said. He searched her face for some sign that information bothered her, but she didn't react. If the story he'd heard about her and the colonel was true, it would probably take more than a threat of execution to scare her.

The room had a musty chemical smell and no fresh air. Drops of sweat were forming on Helen's forehead, and the expensive-looking blouse was stained under the arms. Turner was about to open the door, but decided against it. She looked really uncomfortable, and he noticed a little bruise on her chin. She'd fallen hard when Weaver released the chokehold and was probably sore in a couple of places. He motioned for Reggie to leave the room with him.

"Let's leave her in there a few minutes. Maybe she'll give us a little information to get out of that miserable room," Turner said as he searched for the thermostat and set the temperature a few degrees higher.

"Not likely," Reggie said.

"I don't expect a confession, just a hint where to find Conner."

"Offer her something."

"Like what? Killers don't get deals."

"Promise to do something for the old lady. We were dumb enough to pay her rent. She'll believe you."

He didn't need much, and even Helen might be willing to share an address to get some relief and a break for her aunt. He wasn't certain just what he could do for the old woman, probably nothing, but it was worth a shot.

Helen was resting her head on the table when he and Reggie returned about thirty minutes later. After a few seconds, she sat up. Turner was relieved. He was afraid she had fainted. Her face was flushed and damp, but her eyes told him she had no intention of giving an inch. The air was unbearable in the cramped space, and he had to open the door or leave. He made his offer.

"I'm guessing you don't care what happens to you," Turner said. She didn't react. "I might be able to do something for your aunt."

Helen's eyes narrowed. "Do what, for what?" she said, still defiant.

"Tell me where I can find Conner, and I'll put you in an air-conditioned car, send you to the Sheriff's comfortable jail and not LAPD's downtown snake pit, and I'll try to get a deal for the old lady on her warrants."

Her expression didn't tell him anything, and she was quiet for several seconds before looking directly at Turner.

"I'll talk to you alone," she said, deliberately. He didn't have a chance to say anything before Reggie was out of the room, closing the door behind him.

"Talk," he said.

She leaned as far as she could over the table and whispered, "Ian is dead." It took a moment for her words to sink in, and to his surprise he felt anger instead of relief. He didn't have a chance to think much about it because she added, "He just doesn't know it yet."

The relief must have shown on his face. She laughed, a dry, hollow sound and sat back, pleased with herself.

"Where's Conner?"

She glared at him, but didn't answer.

"How did you get Beverly's car?"

The corner of her mouth twisted in a sinister smirk. "She gave it to me."

He exhaled and sat back. This was going nowhere. "What do you want from me?"

"I like you," she answered after a long pause. "You helped me, and I don't want to see you get hurt again."

"Again?" He knew what she meant, the hit-and-run. "Why would you harm Miriam?" he asked, not really expecting an answer. Her eyes narrowed, and she stared at him as if he were some subterranean life form. He wouldn't pursue it. Helen had lost her gamble. She was going to prison, maybe facing execution if they could prove she was involved in any of the killings connected to Conner, including her sister's. She was avoiding what he really wanted to know, which most likely meant she didn't know Conner's whereabouts and was hoping Turner would say something to help her locate him.

She shifted her weight to get comfortable. "Ian's not your problem anymore," she said as if she'd read his thoughts.

"What difference does it make if I get him or you do? If he killed your sister, why take the chance he might get away."

"Don't worry about my sister," she whispered, so softly he barely heard her. "She's my problem," she said, and closed her eyes, slumping against the chair.

"If you help me, I might be able to do something for your family," he offered in one last attempt to get cooperation.

She didn't respond and turned her body away from him. Suddenly, she looked old and tired, and it wasn't just her physical appearance. As soon as she talked about her sister, it seemed to drain the energy from her. Turner wondered if Winter was wrong about Helen arranging her sister's death, or even if she had some part in it. At this point in time, she blamed Conner. It might not be logical, but guilt and grief rarely were.

What bothered him most was the idea that Helen still believed she could get to Conner. It meant she had Rigoberto or relatives not in custody who were ready to do her bidding. He could almost understand what she'd had to do to avenge her parents in Mexico, but now she was going after people he cared about. Miriam wasn't evil and didn't deserve what happened to her. Goodman and the others should have been punished, but not her way. Her sense of justice was offensive and contrary to everything he believed.

She groaned a little as she twisted her body, attempting to get comfortable. He checked the handcuffs. They weren't tight, but she'd been trying to pull her hands free. Her wrists were red and bruised, the skin rubbed raw. Turner found a first aid kit in the watch commander's office, put disinfectant on the open wounds and wrapped her wrists in gauze, which made it even more difficult to slip out of the cuffs. When he finished, she didn't thank him but spit on the floor at his feet. Her behavior didn't affect him any more than a mad dog trying to bite him. That's what they do. The best she could hope for from now on was spending the remainder of her miserable life in a cage. There wasn't much he could do to make it worse.

When Vogel and his partners arrived, Weaver told Turner and the others to go back to L.A. The surveillance squad was done. RHD detectives would follow up with the arduous legwork, tracking down the pawn tickets and money, and booking the evidence and bodies. They would start matching stolen items to crime reports and identifying anyone who delivered stuff to the pawn shops. Vogel brought some good news, too. The video from Sierra Madre and Arcadia had been reviewed, and they could positively identify Ian Conner's handsome face in the hit-and-run vehicle. They had photographic proof of him, stealing the black truck from the racetrack, driving the stolen truck through an intersection just seconds after the hit-and-run, and then dumping it at the shopping mall. Three different cameras had documented his crime spree. Turner was grateful for the paranoia of wealthy communities that gave detectives the means to file felony hit-and-run and assault with a deadly weapon charges on Conner with the DA's office. He was fair game to arrest and book as soon as Turner could find him.

All of that could wait until tomorrow. Turner was tired, physically and mentally exhausted. He should've been pleased. The case had come together. The Internal Affairs investigation was over, and he had his surveillance job back, so why did he have this empty feeling. After relentless pleading from Miller, he'd promised to meet him and Reggie at JR's, but had no intention of going. He wanted to get away from all of it and was grateful to be driving home alone. He turned off the car radio and all the police radios.

The sun was setting over the ocean between broad strokes of charcoal and orange hues. He pulled off the freeway in Oceanside and parked in one of the lots along the sand where he could watch the last bit of light bounce off the waves. The smell of seaweed and salt water comforted him, forcing him to see the world as bigger than him and his problems. He could have almost the same setting at home, but he was an hour or more from Redondo and needed a dose of beach therapy now. It was difficult to admit, but that feeling might have been loneliness. Some men didn't need intimacy; he wasn't one of them. Unfortunately, the woman he seemed to want and the only one he'd felt a genuine connection with for a very long time was probably unattainable. Beverly would be unlikely to feel any love or affection toward him after he arrested, or even worse, had to shoot her asshole son. Finding her car in San Diego was still bothering him, too. If Beverly gave Ian her car, she might be involved in all of it, protecting or hiding him.

His brain was beginning to ache. How did Helen get the car? Maybe he should just drive up to Beverly's house and ask her. Weaver would be pissed if he went alone, but he needed to know. He could call Reggie, but if he did that, Miller would be there and want to go. The thought of having to deal with Miller again tonight was more than he was willing to inflict on himself or Beverly. Besides, it wasn't any big deal. He'd just go and then tell Weaver about it in the morning.

Once he'd decided to confront her, he was eager to get back on the freeway. Action, even if it was the wrong one, gave him a sense of purpose and direction. Sitting around worrying wasn't in his nature.

He'd barely reached the on-ramp when Beverly called. Strange coincidence, sympathetic vibes, whatever it was, it gave him a little chill when he heard her voice.

"It's strange," he said. "I was just thinking about you when you called."

"Why is that strange?" she asked, but didn't give him time to answer before asking, "Where are you?"

"On my way to your house. Is that okay?" he asked. Her voice sounded different, too quiet, too formal.

"No, don't go there. Meet me at The Tavern," she said, quickly.

"Are you alright?"

"Why wouldn't I be?" she asked in the same tone.

He could think of a dozen reasons why she shouldn't be alright, but he would wait and talk to her when he could see her. In a few minutes, those pretty green eyes would tell him a lot more than hours of conversation.

"I'll slip onto the 10 Freeway and be there in twenty minutes," he said. "Don't leave."

It took an hour, but she was waiting, sitting near the end of the bar, the same place he'd sat the night he met her. She was wearing tight jeans, cowboy boots and a tucked in white shirt. It was unbuttoned far enough to see a low-cut lacy black tank top under the shirt. Her red hair hung loose, nearly hiding her face. It wasn't until he got closer that he saw the bruise, an ugly purple and red blotch on her left cheek and around her eye. She'd tried to camouflage it with makeup, but that didn't work or maybe it did, which meant there was a lot more damage than what he saw.

She smiled at him as he sat on the bar stool next to hers.

"What does the guy look like who lost?" he asked, gently touching under her eye.

"I lost," she said. "It wasn't even close." She tilted her head, moving away from his hand, and avoided looking directly into his eyes.

It was a slow night. A couple of patrons were playing pool, and a retired detective who Turner recognized was at the other end of the bar. There wasn't anyone sitting near them, but she glanced in the direction of any movement—every noise caught her attention. The bartender dropped a glass and Turner noticed her hands trembling.

He wanted to say something to help her relax, but hoping she was frightened enough to tell the truth, he said, "Tell me why your car's in San Diego."

She leaned her elbows on the bar and held her head with both hands. "I'm scared they're gonna kill him." When she looked up her tears left streaks in the heavy makeup.

"Who hit you?"

"Big ugly tattooed Mexican . . . smelled worse than my horses." She sighed, wiping away the tears and makeup with one brush of her sleeve and finally looked at him. "He wanted my son. I guess he wouldn't believe I didn't know anything until he hurt me."

Turner tried to keep his anger under control. Bullies made him crazy, but she didn't need to be that certain of him just yet. Rigoberto wasn't in jail, and he fit the description. He was suspect number one, and Turner would deal with him later.

"Did he steal your car?"

"He said it was payment for not killing me," she said, nervously rubbing her hands on her legs as she talked. He cupped his hand over hers, and she stopped.

"I'm curious," he said, tightening his grip slightly. "You aren't asking why they want your son bad enough to beat you up and steal your car."

She pulled her hands away and folded her arms. "It's always about money with Ian. He has a debt or took money that didn't belong to him."

"You report any of this to the police?" There was no answer. He figured she hadn't.

"Stop badgering me. If you can't help, just leave me alone." She tried to sound in control, but her voice was breaking. She glanced up at him . . . no more tears. "Well?"

"What do you want from me, Beverly? Your son's a fugitive. He tried to run me over. If I find him, I'm gonna arrest him, and he's gonna spend his life in jail."

The tears started again, this time from anger. "I don't believe you," she said, shaking her head.

"Truthfully, the only thing that concerns me right now is how much you're involved."

"Me?" she asked, and stopped crying. She took a cocktail napkin and wiped her nose. Her expression told him everything he needed to know. She was a mother protecting her offspring, not an accomplice. "I don't want my son killed. I'm asking you to give him a chance to prove his innocence. Does that make me a criminal?"

"Might, if you're protecting him."

"If I knew where he was, I wouldn't have called you."

"Has he contacted you?" Turner asked, and she looked away. "When?" he asked.

"Same day they stole my car," she whispered. "He needed money, but was afraid they were watching me."

"How'd you get it to him?"

"Deposited cash in his bank account . . . just a few hundred."

"Where is he?" Turner asked and waited, but she didn't answer. "If they find him first, Beverly, they'll kill him."

"Why? I don't understand. What did he do?" she pleaded, and the tears started again.

The bartender, an older menacing man with steroid arms, a grey handlebar mustache and bushy eyebrows, came over to where they were sitting and leaned over the bar near Turner, but Beverly waved him away. The man stepped back, glaring at Turner with an expression that promised "if you hurt her you'll deal with me."

Turner decided to do what he'd told himself he shouldn't do—tell her the truth.

"Helen blames Ian for her sister's death. She took all the cash and stuff she and Ian stole and maybe killed for. I think she doesn't want your son tracking her down or terrorizing her family to get it back."

"Ian wouldn't kill anyone."

"If he goes to court, he'll have a chance to prove that. If Helen's people get him he's a dead man."

She sat quietly, staring at the chipped green and black marble bar top, running her finger along the black-lined veins. He waited patiently for her to work it out her own way.

"He tried to hurt you?" she asked, as if distracted by the thought.

He told her about the hit-and-run, how badly Miriam had been injured. She nodded a few times as he described in detail, maybe exaggerating a little, every one of Miriam's wounds. However, he was careful not to mention anything about her elective touch-up surgery.

When he finished, she picked up her half-filled bottle of beer and drank it in one swallow.

"He didn't tell me where he was, but when we got done talking I checked my caller list. His number had a 209 area code. I looked it up; it's in northern California."

"You still have the number?"

She hesitated for only a moment, then reached over and removed a small piece of paper from a floppy leather purse on the bar stool next to her. She held it in her hand for several seconds and then gave it to him.

There was no need for her to tell him where it was located. He knew that area code. He'd called Miriam's cabin in the mountains often enough to remember the prefix. He didn't recognize the rest of the number, but it was too much of a coincidence to believe Ian was there for any other reason. He punched the numbers into his cell phone; it rang. A woman answered. It was the same motel he'd stayed in the last time he went to the cabin. He asked about the rates and was it busy this time of year. The woman volunteered that the motel was empty at the moment, and he'd have his pick of rooms.

It was a hunch, but he called Methodist Hospital and asked for Miriam's room. The desk nurse told him her father had checked her out several hours ago. He wanted to take his daughter somewhere she could rest and recuperate.

Beverly watched quietly. "What's wrong?" she asked when he'd finished.

"You have somewhere you can stay other than your place for a day or two?" he asked. He was afraid Helen's frustrated thug cousin might come back and not be as easy on her the next time.

"No. I can't leave my animals." Now, she was worried. "What's wrong? Where is that?" she asked, pointing at the paper in his hand. The fire was back in her eyes. "Tell me," she demanded.

"I think he's somewhere around Miriam's cabin in the mountains. This number is a motel nearby, but he's not there anymore." He wasn't going to say anything about Miriam and her father.

But then Beverly asked, "Is she there?"

"I don't know," he answered, truthfully, but he'd be surprised if that wasn't her destination.

"I gotta go," he said, sliding off the bar stool.

"I'm going, too," she said, and stood in front of him.

"What about your animals?"

She closed her eyes in frustration. "I'll find somebody. It's late. You're not leaving tonight. Are you?"

"I'm leaving now."

She kicked hard at the swinging bar gate with her cowboy boot, and it flung open slamming against the wall.

"Hey," the bartender yelled from the other side of the room.

"Sorry, we're gone," Turner said, putting his arm around her and nudging her toward the door.

When they were outside, he asked, "How'd you get here?"

She had calmed down and took a deep breath before saying anything. "I'm sorry. I'm not mad at you. Ian makes me crazy, and I'm really scared."

She maneuvered through the parking lot, stopping at a faded blue Jeep Wrangler with a torn convertible top.

"It's a neighbor's . . . a piece of junk even the Mexican wouldn't bother to steal."

He stopped her as she started to sit in the driver's seat. "Get someone to feed and muck your horses, and stay away from your house until I get back."

She got into the car and started the engine. "Don't hurt my son," she said, before driving out of the lot.

It was a full moon, reminding him of the last time he and Miriam sat on the porch of her father's cabin. He might not have the same affection for Miriam he once had, but Ian wasn't going to get another opportunity to hurt her. He stood there for several minutes, staring at the sky, trying to decide what he should do. He could call the locals and have them check the cabin, but then he took a gamble that some two-man police force with ten minutes of mall security training would either get themselves or Miriam killed. He could bring in the cavalry and look like an idiot if his hunch proved wrong, or call Reggie, drive all night, handle it himself and piss off both Lieutenant Metcalf and Sergeant Weaver.

He called Reggie.

Waiting for Reggie to pick him up in Redondo Beach, Turner tried all the phone numbers he had for Miriam. No one answered at any of them, including her father's house and her grandmother's apartment. The message machine at the cabin came on after the second ring.

He was relieved to find that Miller was tired and had gone home after a couple of beers at JR's. He and Reggie worked well together. Sometimes, Miller complicated things.

Reggie had the newer city car, a Ford Mustang, so he drove. It was normally a five-hour trip, but they arrived at the strip mall in Arnold a few hours before sunrise. As they pulled off the highway, the full moon gave them barely enough muted light to negotiate the dangerous curves and read the confusing landscape. A never-ending assembly line of trees and shrubbery lined the road, every mile no different than the one before it.

Turner directed Reggie when to turn off the headlights. The last time he was here, he made a concerted effort to remember the way so he'd never have to spend another night in that miserable motel room waiting for daylight. As they approached the cabin, he immediately saw from a distance the motion lights had been activated, and the building glowed like a candle in the dark.

It was still very cold in the mountains, so if Ian was here Turner figured he'd most likely be inside the cabin. He and Reggie would approach on foot to get close enough to see inside.

They left the car a long half a block away and walked uphill in the street toward the cabin. There weren't any sidewalks or street lights, but plenty of strange noises, screeching owls and an assortment of unidentifiable animal communications. At this moment, Turner regretted that he'd grown up in Los Angeles and had begged his parents to throw away the Boy Scout application. The forest and wildlife were a complete mystery to him, and he half expected a bear to reach out from among the trees and drag him away for dinner. Reggie walked quickly, several feet from the edge of the road as if he might've worried about the same thing.

By the time they reached Miriam's driveway, the motion lights around the house had gone off and the hazy grey light of sunrise brought the cabin in full view. It appeared that the interior lights were on in most of the rooms. There was a new silver Cadillac sedan parked on the grass in front of the porch. He crouched behind the car while Reggie jogged to the cabin. Turner watched him look in every window until he'd made a complete circle around the structure.

When he'd finished, Reggie knelt beside Turner and shrugged. "Just the two of them," he said. "I could see in every room."

They discussed finding a spot to hide and watch the cabin in case Conner showed up, but finally decided to go inside. The sun was nearly up and Turner doubted Conner would try anything sinister in the light of day.

He knocked on the front door, and Miriam's father opened it. The old man was barely over five feet tall, thin and balding. His remaining grey hair was cut very short. He glanced from Turner to Reggie and without a word stepped to one side so they could enter.

"She's asleep," her father said, pointing to the couch. "Sit. You want coffee?"

"I'll get it," Reggie said.

"He's been here too?" the old man asked, watching Reggie go directly to the kitchen.

"Kind of," Turner said, knowing Reggie's familiarity with the cabin's layout came from peeking in all the windows a few minutes ago. "Has Ian Conner tried to contact you or your daughter?" he asked. He didn't want Miriam's father thinking this visit was anything but business.

"I don't know that name," her father said, and stared at the floor for a few seconds before adding, "I don't want you bothering my daughter, so I think you and your friend should drink your coffee and go before she gets up."

"Conner is the guy who tried to run her over. He called his mother yesterday from the motel down the road. You understand what I'm saying. He's trying to hurt Miriam."

Turner expected some alarm, but the old man didn't flinch. "I don't know this man, but nobody's going to hurt my daughter."

"Aren't you listening to me? He's here."

"I heard you," he said, and reached into a log bin in front of the fireplace and produced a double-barreled shotgun. He was a slight man and could barely hold the shotgun steady. He handled the weapon as if he were afraid it would go off on its own. "Nobody's gonna hurt my daughter," he repeated.

Turner shook his head. He was impressed the old man was willing to protect his family, but knew Conner was capable of taking that gun away and killing him and his daughter without a moment's hesitation.

"You need to go back to civilization where the police can protect you," Reggie said, returning with two cups of coffee. He gave one to Turner. "What happened to Weaver's men, the ones who were guarding her?" he asked, snatching the shotgun with his free hand before the startled man could react. Reggie put his coffee on the mantle and examined the weapon.

"Three things," Reggie said, leaning the shotgun against the fireplace and retrieving his coffee. "Clean it, oil it and put some shells in it, or throw the damn thing away before it gets you killed."

"I sent Sergeant Weaver's guards away," the old man said. He was proud and refused to back down. "They aren't needed anymore."

"Ian's not here to hurt me," Miriam said, stepping out of her bedroom and closing the door behind her. She'd improved a lot since the last time Turner had seen her in the hospital. Her hair was growing out and almost covered the nasty scar on her scalp. She'd actually gained a few pounds and looked healthier in loose-fitting sweat pants and a heavy sweater. Although her arm was still in a cast, most of the bandages on her face were gone. Only a small white patch covered her nose. Her pale skin had some discoloration, but nothing like the bruising he'd seen after the surgery. She was almost pretty again, but her eyes were glassy, and her words slurred a little. She appeared to be on some sort of medication.

"You look good," Turner said, standing and offering her the overstuffed chair he knew she liked. "How are you feeling?"

"Better," she said, sitting in the chair. Her father retreated to the kitchen and brought her coffee. She thanked him, and he kissed the top of her head.

Something good might have come from all this, Turner thought. These two had never been close. Miriam's father never approved of her lifestyle or her choice of friends. This affection seemed genuine.

"I think you should go," her father said, standing behind his daughter and looking at Turner. "My daughter is safe here with me. She needs time to heal."

"Papa's right. Ian came here to hide from that Sanchez woman, not to hurt me. He's confused and scared. He really loves me. That woman forced him to do bad things," she said, her voice trailing off to a whisper.

"How can you say that?" Turner asked. "He tried to run you over."

"He was mad at you, not me. He promised he never tried to hurt me."

"You talked to him." Turner wasn't surprised.

"Where is he?" Reggie asked.

Miriam scratched with one finger just inside the top of her cast. "I don't know for sure," she said, her attention riveted on the source of the itching.

"Guess," Turner demanded. He'd had enough of her irrational behavior.

"Most of the cabins around here are seasonal," she said looking up at him. "They're empty until it snows," she added, as if he were stupid. "If somebody broke into one, could be months before anyone knew."

"And you told him which ones would be vacant," Turner said. He knew he was right because it was something she would do, like inviting Eddie to live in his house without asking, or feeling sorry for Conner and believing he still loved her after he tried to kill her. Her appearance might have improved, but inside it was the same old mixed-up Miriam. No, he thought, she's worse now. She sounded and behaved as if she'd completely lost touch with reality and it wasn't just the medication.

Her father must have realized it too. Suddenly, he looked pale and a little unsteady. He sat on the couch and clasped his hands, his head bowed. His daughter's behavior might've become too unstable even for him to manage.

"Which address did you give him?" Turner asked, taking a pen out of his jacket pocket.

She hesitated until her father said, "Tell them, Miriam" in a tone of voice that made it clear he was fed up.

"The place behind us . . . go to the end of our property; it's empty," she said, softly, looking at her father as she spoke. The self-confidence and bravado were gone. Her shoulders slumped just a little, a child rebuked by someone she depended on. Turner always knew Miriam was in some ways immature and erratic for a woman her age, but he worried now it might never get any better, that she was one of those unfortunate souls destined to bump into things and live with self-inflicted disaster for the rest of her life. He wouldn't be a part of it. He'd rather be lonely than deal with the tribulations of a perennial adolescent.

234

TWENTY-FOUR

I t was early afternoon, and the sky was ominous; black clouds and a light drizzle had quickly become a full-blown mountain storm. Pebbles of hail hit the cabin for several minutes, pounding on the corrugated metal roof like tiny baseballs on a steel drum. The noise was piercing and unnerving. Miriam clung to her chair, too frightened to flee. Her father moved closer and tried to calm her. He'd succeeded until lightening struck a transformer in the front yard, and the lights went out. She buried her face in his chest and sobbed. Turner made no effort to help, but watched the scene like it was the disturbing aftermath of a disaster. He wanted to turn away but couldn't.

While the old man escorted her back to the bedroom, Turner and Reggie looked out the cabin window facing the rear of the property. A wall of juniper trees and heavy brush blocked their view. Turner glanced at Reggie, and he nodded. They knew what had to be done, but neither of them wanted to go out in the storm and risk pneumonia or worse—being hit by lightening.

Miriam's father thought all of them should get out of the cabin and back to the city as soon as possible, but he understood how dangerous it was to drive down the mountain in this kind of weather. They had to stay together until the storm passed, but he cautioned them to avoid any further contact with his fragile daughter, which was fine with Turner.

After half an hour, the thunder and lightening stopped, and only patches of light rainfall remained. The electricity didn't come back on, so the cabin was cold and gloomy, smelling like damp rotting wood. Turner suggested to Miriam's father that he might want to take his distraught daughter back to town while

235

there was a break in the storm. It didn't take much persuasion, and twenty minutes later Miriam and her father were in his Cadillac heading down the mountain. The old man had given Turner the cabin keys, instructing him to lock up when he'd finished his business. He didn't ask what they planned to do or how long they might be there. He seemed relieved to get his daughter safely away from Turner and whatever was about to happen.

Reggie took the extra radios and surveillance equipment from the trunk of his car, and gave one set to Turner. They had earpieces and microphones and could communicate if they got separated. Before they left the cabin, Turner started to dial Weaver's number, but thought about it and changed his mind. The supervisor would want them to wait and bring in the locals or the state police, and it always got messy with too many agencies involved. Turner wanted to do this himself. He was a good cop and trusted his instincts. Every time he tried to play by department's rules, Metcalf or Weaver or some other guy in a suit who'd never done real police work got in the way. There was too much at stake this time to wait around for permission to do the right thing. He needed to get Conner in custody or dead, and it didn't matter if the lieutenant or sergeant thought it was a good idea.

The steady rain resumed as soon as they locked up the cabin and moved along what they believed to be the perimeter of Miriam's property line. There weren't any fences or other markers to tell them when they had crossed onto someone else's land. It took only a few seconds before the rain soaked through their flimsy jackets, and Turner's new leather cowboy boots weren't any better match for the deep sticky red mud than Reggie's expensive running shoes. As they entered the tree line, the brush grew thinner, and the higher branches formed a natural umbrella. Luckily, they found a foot trail, probably the same one Miriam used on her daily walks. It came to an abrupt end where a ragged, narrow ravine began. They climbed into the ravine and crawled up the other side. It had rained enough to fill the gully with two feet of moving water, drenching them as they scrambled to cross. They trudged through the downpour until they reached the protection of another grove of trees bordering at last on a solitary cabin. It was bigger than Miriam's cabin and had been nicely landscaped with paths of river rock and flagstone. The storm windows were up and appeared to be secure. The garage was padlocked, but the door of an adjacent shed was ajar.

Reggie had worked his way around to the other side of the house and got behind the garage and shed. He radioed that the lock on the back door leading to what looked like the cabin's mudroom had been pried open. He was going inside. Turner tried to get him to wait until they could go in together, but Reggie wanted him outside in case Conner tried to run.

"No, wait. Don't go in without me," Turner ordered, but there was no response. He ran around the garage to the back door. It was wide open. His partner was nowhere in sight. Cautiously, he stepped inside the narrow room with the only light coming from the open door. An assortment of winter coats hung on a row of pegs set over a long wooden bench. Pairs of snow boots in different sizes were placed neatly beneath the bench. He could almost picture the family—a man, a woman, and two small children. They're not here, they're safe, he told himself as he pushed open the door to a large kitchen and breakfast area. It was dark and ice cold. The cabin had been winterized. The electricity and heat must have been off for months. When his eyes adjusted to the darkness, he saw fast food boxes and empty bags, half-eaten hamburgers and pizzas, several soft drink cups scattered over the counters.

The smell coming from a small bathroom off the living room told Turner the water was probably shut off too, and Ian was too lazy to turn it on. He crouched down in a corner of the den and tried to raise Reggie on the radio, whispering his name.

"I'm inside," Turner said. "Where are you?"

"Upstairs," Reggie whispered back. "Bottom floor's clear. Come up to the right."

Turner had to wait. It was too dark. He didn't want to use the flashlight, but it got worse as he went deeper inside the house. He unholstered his .45 and took the small SureFire light from his belt. He slipped his left hand with the flashlight under his right hand with the weapon until the backs of his wrists were touching. The light followed in sync with the movement of the gun. He found the staircase and followed Reggie's instruction. As soon as he made a right turn, he saw Reggie kneeling near the banister and shut off the flashlight.

Reggie grabbed his arm and pulled him down.

"If he's not in there, he's gone," Reggie said, motioning toward the door directly in front of them.

Turner pointed the flashlight at the ceiling on the second floor. He slowly moved the stream of light from one end of the landing to the other and stopped when he found it. Most of these cabins had pull-down ladders to the attic and directly above him was the door. If he were Conner, he'd hide in the attic or basement, two places where extra blankets, food supplies, and camping equipment were usually stored.

They did a cursory check of the bedroom, but Turner knew Conner wouldn't be there. He left Reggie to guard the attic door while he went down to the basement and did another quick search. He didn't expect to find anything in the basement either. The most likely place to find Conner would be in the attic. Nobody, especially cops, ever looked up when they searched. Conner was probably counting on it. Besides, the basement was small and packed with old furniture, snowshoes, a washer and dryer, and several pairs of broken skis. It also had about an inch of nearly frozen water sitting on the floor, another unpleasant surprise for the unsuspecting family on their return. Turner hurried back upstairs. While he was gone, Reggie had located a couple of kerosene lamps in a hall closet and placed them on the floor below the door to the attic. The glow gave them enough light to turn off the flashlights.

They couldn't find the pole with a hook on the end to pull down the ladder. Turner surmised Conner had taken it with him into the attic. A couple of wire hangers twisted together worked just as well, and in five minutes the ladder was down, and he was staring up at the black hole in the ceiling. Reggie turned off the lamps, and they waited until their eyes adjusted to the darkness again.

The last thing Turner wanted to do was go up the ladder and stick his head through that opening, but he knew it had to be done, and it had to be him who did it, so when this was over he could look Beverly in the eye and say he'd done everything possible. If Conner wanted a fight, he'd get one, but Turner would at least try to book the asshole in one piece. Reggie seemed to understand. Usually, he'd be the first one charging up the ladder, but he stepped aside and waited for Turner to take the lead.

There might've been safer ways to do this, but Turner was by nature and training a dope cop. You went in and got the stash; let the SWAT guys worry about tactics. He'd get Conner his way. The brass could second guess and criticize him later, wet their pants fretting about everything that could've gone wrong or should've been handled differently. The job would be done. He didn't have the patience any longer to deal with their hand-wringing.

He started up the ladder. A few feet from the top rung, he stopped and listened. It was quiet above him, and he could smell the stale, dusty odor of a storeroom without fresh air. He needed to climb into the attic quickly and get away from the hole as fast as he could. If Conner was hiding up there, he had the advantage of knowing exactly where Turner would be and that made him an easy target. Turner took a deep breath and pushed away from the ladder, leaping into the space above him. He rolled away, but landed on his bad knee and the sharp pain immobilized him for a moment. It was only seconds before Reggie tumbled into the attic in the opposite direction. They both stayed still waiting to hear some movement from Conner, but there was nothing and it was too dark to see any farther than a few feet.

Turner was disappointed. He guessed Conner was too undisciplined to stay quiet and hidden, so he probably wasn't up here either. He would go through the motions anyway, and drew his gun and flashlight, began in what he guessed was the corner of the attic and started to scan the room. He and Reggie took turns lighting up sections of the room, moving, and then doing it again. If Conner was in the attic, he wouldn't be certain where they were at any time. Finally, it happened. Reggie's beam illuminated a couple of small mattresses and the frame of what appeared to be children's bunk beds, and there it was, a barely audible shuffling noise . . . a shoe moving, shifting positions to get comfortable, just enough to break the silence. Reggie's light went off. From another part of the room, Turner put light on the mattresses again. The bed frame crashed to the floor as Conner fell from behind it with Reggie on top of him. The big redhead was swinging and kicking wildly, attempting to dislodge Reggie, who'd locked his arms around the bigger man's neck and slammed his head into the floor. Conner was dazed long enough for Turner to set the SureFire on a box and handcuff him. As soon as the cuffs were secured, Conner twisted his body and kicked Turner, throwing him into a stack of old dresser drawers. The back of Turner's head hit hard against the top drawer, and what little he could see in the room went out of focus. The last thing Turner remembered was his flashlight dropping and rolling across the floor.

He was standing when he regained consciousness. Reggie told him he'd been talking and walking for several minutes, but not making much sense. One of the lanterns from downstairs was on a box in the middle of the attic now. Conner lay on the floor beside it. His hands were behind his back. His ankles were cordcuffed, and a second pair of handcuffs connected the two. He looked like a big, redheaded, beer-bellied, hogtied steer. Turner looked at him and was relieved; he was alive, bruised and bloodied, but breathing.

Conner had stopped thrashing, but groaned when he tried to move. Turner almost felt sorry for him. His position looked painfully uncomfortable.

"Think you can sit in a chair like a gentleman and let us take one of those cuffs off?" Turner asked, leaning to one side to look in Conner's face. He straightened up quickly as he felt a little dizzy. Conner nodded, and Reggie knelt down and removed the connecting pair of cuffs. Conner slowly, painfully stretched out his long legs and let Reggie help him stand and then sit on a large box. He kept his head down, but tried to shift his shoulders back.

"My ankle hurts," Conner whined. Reggie loosened those cuffs slightly. "Can't you take 'em off. I'm not going nowhere."

"No," Turner said.

Turner rubbed the back of his head. It was sore, and he could feel the beginnings of a good-sized lump. The cuffs would definitely stay on Conner's wrists and ankles.

"The bitch just couldn't keep her mouth shut, could she?" Conner asked, shaking his head. "I should've known."

"Nobody had to tell us anything; you did that," Turner lied. The guy was too cocky.

"Great, if you morons can find me, that means they can too."

"Why would they care about you? We've got all the money."

For the first time, Conner looked worried. He put his head back and stared at the rough wood beams decorated with layers of cobwebs. "You arrested her," he said and groaned. "I'm a dead man."

Turner was confused for a moment, and then he got it. "She doesn't want you making a deal and testifying."

"On my own, I'd live long enough to testify. With you, I haven't got a fucking chance." He closed his eyes for several seconds and then, "Call Winter. Get my lawyer," he ordered. "Maybe we can still work something out," he said.

"When you get to jail, you call your lawyer," Turner said. "Working it out isn't something we're gonna lose sleep over."

"You're an idiot. I know everything she's involved in . . . murder, drugs, robberies. I can give you fifty connections, clear a ton of crimes, but if I go to jail, they get me. I'm dead."

"What do you want?" Turner asked.

"First, my lawyer and then protection. Look, she's big time."

"If that's true, why would she waste her time with a punk like you?" Turner asked.

Conner sighed. They all knew he'd have to give up something before he got anything. Turner and Reggie exchanged a quick glance. This was easier than they thought it would be.

"Helen needed our uniforms. Her sister told her about Cullen's murder-for-hire deal in the hills. She finds us, offers to help and pretty soon she's running everything. Me, Cullen, Goodman we're bun boys, but making some heavy duty cash, so who cares."

"How'd Ramona end up dead?" Turner asked. That was the one thing that really bothered him. He couldn't see Helen killing her sister.

241

"Shithead Cullen panicked. Soon as he killed the little sister we're done. Some old bag lady saw him and told Helen. She took care of him and Goodman, then came after me. I hid most of the stuff. That's the only reason I'm still alive." His lip curled in an angry snarl. "Until that stupid cunt ripped me off," he said, cocking his head in the direction of Miriam's cabin. "If Helen's got it now, she found where Miriam had it stashed." He grunted. "Which is a shitload better than I could do."

"You can't really believe Miriam was clever enough to steal from you."

"How smart you gotta be to empty a storage locker . . . but she was too stupid to hide it from Helen."

Reggie stood behind him. "Running over your girlfriend with a two-ton truck probably wasn't the best way to get her cooperation." He took hold of the back of Conner's nylon jacket and lifted. "Stand up," he said. "We're leaving."

Conner got up slowly and groaned. It took a while for him to straighten his back. The fight had apparently left him with sore muscles and aching bones. The fact that he was overweight and grossly out of shape didn't help either.

"Do we have a deal?" Conner asked, looking around at Turner and then at Reggie.

"Don't know," Turner said. "Might have enough without your help, but it's worth a shot. We'll talk to the D.A."

Now, Conner became agitated again. "No, that's no good," he shouted. "Weren't you listening? You can't book me." Even in the darkened room, Turner could see the guy's face becoming nearly as red as his hair.

"Don't have a stroke," Turner said, curtly. "We'll book you at our jail and keep you isolated. I'll call Winter and have him meet us there."

That seemed to calm him. Turner wasn't looking forward to spending four or five hours on the road with this whiny jerk handcuffed in the backseat, but they had to get him back to L.A. He called Weaver, told him about the arrest and listened to a five-minute diatribe on the evils of ignoring the chain of command. Weaver's biggest concern was telling Lieutenant Metcalf. Turner convinced him not to say anything until Conner was sitting in the Parker Center jail. Even Metcalf would have a difficult time berating success.

Reggie jogged back to Miriam's cabin and drove his city car around to the road in front of the two-story cabin. Turner notified the local police and asked them to send an officer to secure the cabin. They offered to call the family and take a burglary report naming Conner as the suspect/arrestee, one more crime to tag onto Conner's growing list of offenses.

The storm had settled into a steady drizzle as they drove down the mountain away from Arnold and through the city of Murphy, passing a dozen familiar wineries off the main road. Any other time, Turner would've stopped at a few of them. He enjoyed finding new wines and was always searching for a better Cabernet. He liked to drive up north to Napa and wander through the wineries to supplement his small but expensive inventory.

The dreary weather and dark clouds made it seem later than it was. Reggie was driving cautiously on the wet, curvy mountain road, and it seemed to be taking forever to get back on the interstate. There was just enough room in the backseat for Conner's legs to wedge in behind the passenger seat. Normally, Turner would have sat beside him to keep him from kicking Reggie or trying to get his hands in front of him, but it was impossible for the big man to move, let alone get in another position. He complained almost immediately about his hands and feet going numb with the handcuffs. Turner reached over the seat and pulled him forward to check his hands. They were pink and warm, so he told Conner to shut up, and he'd let him get out and stretch in an hour.

As soon as he stopped grumbling about his handcuffs, Conner began nagging Turner about calling his attorney. Turner listened patiently for a few minutes, and then told Conner if he didn't sit back and stop talking no one would call Jack Winter, and he'd have to do it himself with his one phone call after he was booked. Finally, he slumped into the corner of the backseat and was quiet.

The landscape was blurred with the steady drops of rain on the window, but it was comforting to hear nothing but the rhythmic tapping of the windshield wipers. A break in the guard-rail caught Turner's eye as Reggie slowed for a hairpin turn; black rubber marks on the road pointed to the gnarled metal that had been scant protection from the sudden, dangerous drop. He caught a glimpse of something perched in a grove of pine trees below the railing and yelled at Reggie to stop the car.

Reggie pulled into a turnaround at the end of the guardrail well off the road.

"What's wrong?" Conner mumbled, opening his eyes.

"Go back to sleep," Reggie ordered.

Turner nearly slipped in the mud as he got out and walked to the back of the car where Reggie was waiting for him. He closed his jacket and flipped the hood over his head.

"I'm gonna take a look," Turner said. "Stay where you can see me and the asshole in the car."

"What'd you see?" Reggie asked, ignoring the rain that drenched his hair and face.

"Maybe nothing. Might be old damage, but these skid marks look pretty fresh and I thought I saw something down there."

"Hurry up, I don't wanna get caught up here in the dark in this rain."

Turner climbed over the railing and walked along the inside as close to the top as he could. When he reached the twisted, damaged end of the metal, he looked down and saw several of the trees had broken branches. The brush was flattened, but there was nothing there. The ground was muddy and slippery. He looked down at his ruined boots and figured they couldn't get much worse, but this must've been an old accident, and he was wasting time. He tried to pull himself up using the twisted end of the rail, but the ground gave way, and he slipped, sliding on his stomach a few feet until he landed on a narrow ledge below the road. The ledge was wide enough to walk on and it led back to the highway. His clothes were covered in mud, and he could feel that mud had gotten into his boots, but all he wanted to do was get back in the car and drive away from here. When he turned to start climbing toward the road, he saw it, something bulging out from under the thicket at a forty-five-degree angle from where he stood. It was about a hundred feet down and couldn't be seen from the road. It had to be a car. He had taken off his radio equipment, so he yelled up to Reggie that he was going to work his way down.

His leather soles couldn't get any traction on the muddy slope, and he slid and stumbled most of the way until he reached heavier ground cover. A few feet from the site, he stopped to catch his breath. When he glanced up, the tip of the rear fender was all he could see until he lifted away some of the branches. The Cadillac insignia on the trunk of the mangled car froze him before the confusion and then panic hit. He tore at the pine needle branches and thorn-covered undergrowth that had been dragged and tangled around the car as it crashed through the heavily wooded gorge.

"No, no, no," was all he could say over and over as he worked feverishly to reach the driver's door. He heard Reggie shouting at him, but he couldn't stop. At last, he reached the door. Her father was slumped over the steering wheel. The door was locked, but the window was broken. Everything was electronic. There was no way to open the door. He picked up a rock and cleared away the rest of the glass, reached in and felt for a pulse on the old man's neck. He was dead. The skin was cold; his eyes were open and cloudy. Miriam wasn't in the passenger seat and he felt a sense of relief, but then he saw her frail body curled up on the floor. He crawled over the hood to the other side of the car. That door was open. He reached inside and tried to find her pulse, but she was so cold, and lividity had started under her arms and legs where the skin had turned a slight pink-red. Miriam was dead. He shook his head. He didn't want to believe any of this. The impact had torn the bandage away from her nose. It was dangling from her cheek. He pulled it off, threw it on the ground. When he looked up, he noticed the passenger window for the first time. There were gunshot holes in the window, but they were from the inside.

He crawled back to the other side of the car, picked up the pieces of glass he had knocked out of the driver's window. It was difficult to be certain, but the rounds may have been fired through the driver's window and penetrated to the passenger side. He pulled more branches away from the car. There were holes in the front door, a lot of them.

Turner examined the old man's body, no bullet wounds. He didn't want to do it, but climbed back to the other side of the car, lifted Miriam's body from the floor and gently placed her on the seat. She'd lost weight in the hospital; too skinny, he thought and felt sad . . . foolish. He forced himself to look at her broken body, no bullet wounds. The crash had killed them, but somebody had obviously forced the Cadillac off the road.

His cell phone wasn't working, and Reggie wasn't anywhere in sight, so he found a place where there was enough brush to support his weight as he pulled himself up to the road. It was slow going, and he'd managed only a few yards when he heard the unmistakable report of a high-powered rifle. He flattened his body against the wall of the mountain and waited. More shots, a smaller caliber fired rapidly. They weren't shooting at him, but Reggie was alone. He dug his boots into the soft muddy dirt and scrambled to the ridge, ignoring the painful cuts, torn skin and his throbbing knee. Just beneath the damaged railing, he wiped his muddy hands on his shirt, unholstered his .45, and crawled along the road until he reached the Mustang. He heard the report two more times and fell face-first onto the ground. The bullets went through the door of the car and inches above his head.

"Conner," he shouted, and then "Reggie." There was no answer. He controlled his onset of panic and told himself to calm down and think.

He peeked around the tire. It was hopeless trying to locate anything in that wall of trees. There were two more quick shots, but not in his direction. He ducked back, then a third shot, and it was quiet. He waited, expecting he would die, but pissed off because he really wanted an opportunity to get a shot at this bastard. How could he shoot what he couldn't see? The only chance he had was to cross the road and that meant crawling along the edge for a quarter of a mile or so, then making a run for it, and coming back behind the shooter.

"Turner," Reggie shouted. "You alive?"

"So far," Turner answered.

"Come out. I got him."

Turner stood up slowly from behind the car and saw Reggie standing on the other side of the road. He leaned over and looked in the blown-out rear window. Conner was bleeding badly, his head, shoulder, legs. He'd been hit multiple times but was still breathing.

"My phone's dead," Turner said, as he took the first aid kit from the glove compartment and crawled into the backseat.

"I called. Is he dead?"

"No, but it's bad."

Reggie slung a rifle over his shoulder and reached down. For the first time, Turner noticed the body in a heap at his partner's feet. Reggie took hold of the collar of the dead man's parka and dragged him across the road. He dropped the body in front of the car and put the rifle on the hood. There's a bit of irony, Turner thought. It was a FN FAL .308 with high-powered scope, the same kind of rifle Conner had the first time they saw him. He wondered if it was the same assault rifle that had killed Cullen.

The dead man was Rigoberto Gomez, Alex's big brother. Turner recognized the heavily tattooed neck, memorializing a lifetime of crime and allegiance to the Mexican Mafia. Under the parka, Rigoberto's white t-shirt had two bullet holes in the center of his chest. A single bullet had penetrated his cheek below his left eye, and his right lower leg had a compound fracture.

Turner pointed at the protruding bone. "Try to run?"

Reggie took a blanket from the trunk and tossed it over the body. "Fell out of a tree. Damn hard climbing trees in this weather."

"I'll bet," Turner said, taking Conner's pulse. He'd bandaged the head wound and tied tight compresses on the other places where he was bleeding. Conner's pulse was weak, and he'd lost a lot of blood from the least dangerous of his wounds: a chunk of scalp had been sliced off when a bullet ricocheted off the car frame. His breathing was shallow and labored. Turner feared that the worst possible scenario was about to unfold. Beverly's son would be returned to her in a big black body bag.

It was less than thirty minutes, but seemed like hours before the ambulance and law enforcement officers arrived. The Calaveras County sheriffs and local police argued about jurisdiction, and not only summoned the town doctor as a paramedic for Conner, but the on-call medical examiner as well. He was a young pediatrician who dutifully confirmed Rigoberto's death, and declared that he would personally oversee the autopsy in the morning. He took several minutes examining the Cadillac and the bodies of Miriam and her father, concluding they had died from injuries incurred in the collision with the juniper pine; but he also agreed with Turner that it was a homicide. Gunfire had forced them off the road and caused the crash.

Conner had been loaded onto a helicopter and flown to the nearest trauma center in San Jose, where that city's police department would babysit him if he survived.

When reinforcements arrived, Turner brushed broken window glass off the police car's front seat and collapsed. He hadn't slept or eaten for several hours. Physically and mentally his body had shut down. His knee ached; his arms and legs were cut and bruised from clawing his way out of the gorge. His clothes were muddy, and he smelled like a compost pile. Reggie got in the driver's side and sat quietly. There wasn't anything to say. He just stayed with his friend.

It was past midnight when the sheriff's shooting team finished taking their final measurements and completed the initial interviews. Sergeant Weaver drove up to the yellow crime-scene tape minutes before the road was ready to be reopened to traffic. He found Turner and Reggie sitting beside each other in the front seat of Reggie's bullet-riddled city car. The young doctor had cleaned and bandaged most of Turner's injuries, and two of the younger deputies delivered food, coffee and blankets after hearing the details of the shooting. These baby cops looked at Reggie as if he were their spiritual leader. Turner didn't mind.

He knew cops admired any man who'd confronted the devil and walked away a winner. Reggie hadn't depended on some shaky DA or liberal judge or a jury with an average IQ lower than this night's temperature to do the right thing. He did what needed to be done. The good guy won and the locals were loving it.

Weaver seemed stunned by the extent of the damage and Turner's filthy condition. After a couple of sandwiches and several cups of coffee, Turner was actually feeling alive again. He'd called Beverly, and she was on her way to San Francisco. She didn't say anything, but he knew she was disappointed in him, and he wasn't too crazy about the way he'd handled everything either. He needed Conner alive to testify and should've been smarter about getting him back to L.A.

Turner watched from Reggie's car as the search and rescue team removed Miriam and her father from their car. A chain of men in yellow slickers pulled on ropes dragging the covered stretchers up and over the side of the mountain, before loading them into a coroner's van shared inappropriately with Rigoberto. Turner wondered why he felt worse about the old man than he did about Miriam, a woman he once thought he loved and might eventually marry. Her death bothered him, and he knew he'd most likely find the image of her mangled body added to his growing list of frequent nightmares, but Miriam had recklessly gambled and lost. Her father was a good and gentle man who did nothing except try to protect her and make her life tolerable.

The last bit of business was towing Reggie's car. They took all his gear out and loaded it in the trunk of Weaver's car. Turner noticed Reggie hadn't been writing in his notebook. He sat quietly while they waited for the crime scene to be cleared. He answered questions and helped investigators piece together the chronology of events. He took them back to the tree that Rigoberto had abandoned, and helped them find his spent casings. He'd stood twenty yards from the tree in a wide clearing and had taken four shots at Rigoberto, hitting him three times, twice in the chest and once through his cheek when he turned his head. According to Reggie, after Rigoberto fell out of the tree, he was balancing on his one good leg with the assault rifle in his hands trying to fire when he was shot. One of the slugs they'd recovered in the tree trunk would've been head high for the dead man, Reggie's fourth shot that had missed. The one question no one could answer was why the gunman fell out of the tree. Reggie said he didn't know, but Turner noticed a slight smirk when he said it. Reggie had been his partner for several years and that smirk usually meant he knew exactly how it happened, because he made it happen, but wasn't about to tell anyone.

Weaver had a few more details to work out with the local authorities, so Turner got into the backseat of the supervisor's car, intending to stretch out and probably sleep most of the way back to L.A. Reggie sat up front and finally pulled out his diary. He made a few quick notes and put it back in his jacket pocket.

"You're not writing much these days," Turner said.

"Nothing to say."

"Isn't that good?"

"Maybe . . . don't think so."

"You probably don't need it."

"I still think about the kid," Reggie admitted, but wouldn't look back at Turner.

"That's not gonna change."

"It's worse after something like this . . . when someone like her dies."

"You're always gonna think about him. Do it and move on." Turner didn't know what else to say. Bad memories, evil thoughts, they were part of this life. You have them; you can't ignore them, just don't act on them.

"I should get out of this business," Reggie said. He sounded as if he meant it.

"Don't kid yourself. This is what you do, who you are."

"What about you?" Reggie asked, and turned around to look at him.

Turner didn't answer. He smiled and closed his eyes. The one absolute certainty in his life was his love for this job. Just don't ask him to explain it.

TWENTY-FIVE

Turner slept through most of the next day thanks to Eddie, who lowered the ring on all the phones and refused to let anyone disturb him. The following two days weren't much different. He'd get up just long enough to eat, drink some water and go back to bed. By the end of the week, he wasn't sleeping as much but was enjoying the solitude. Eddie and Daryl were his only companions, but even they were just as content away from him in some other part of the house. Isolation was a salve for his mind and spirit. His cuts and bruises were superficial and healed quickly. The deaths of Miriam and her father were persistently in his thoughts. Could he have done anything differently and saved their lives? It was a stupid question . . . actions, reactions, moments in time with unforeseen consequences. How could anyone predict or change these things?

The one question he did need answered he was afraid to ask. Finally, after eight days, Reggie came to visit and told him. Conner was dead. He'd died before Turner had arrived back in L.A. Beverly got to see him briefly, but he'd never regained consciousness. The funeral was two days ago and his crimes essentially got buried with him. A lot of file numbers on a lot of crime reports got cleared, but as far as the news media was concerned Helen Sanchez, Rigoberto Gomez and their little band of desperados did it all. Ian Conner, his buddies and Miriam were unsuspecting pawns caught in a scheme they couldn't have understood. They were forgiven. Turner and Reggie on the other hand weren't, and they were looking at some serious discipline, maybe even termination. Their inappropriate and unapproved actions outside their jurisdiction had been the catalyst for a number of deaths, according to Lieutenant Metcalf who wanted both men sent to a board of rights. The BOR was the lieutenant's second choice after the district attorney turned him down on prosecuting the two officers. Weaver told Reggie, the DA's exact words were, "Are you out of your fucking mind? These guys are heroes." Metcalf didn't agree and wanted to make an example of them.

"So it looks like Tony and Earl will get another shot at us," Reggie said. He and Turner were sitting on the front porch of the Redondo Beach house with their feet resting on the railing. "I might just retire and save them the trouble."

"Why? If they're gonna fire you, make them work for it," Turner said. He was feeling better and ready for a fight.

"Got things to do."

"Like what?" Turner asked. He sat up a little. He'd heard guys threaten to quit all the time when things weren't going right, but Reggie wasn't one of them. He didn't make idle threats. If he said he was thinking of retiring, he'd probably already worked out the numbers and could do it. Turner knew he could face another round of discipline, but didn't like the idea of not having his partner if he survived.

"Travel."

"That's what old people do. You'd be bored in a week if you couldn't shoot somebody."

"Who says I couldn't shoot people," Reggie said, and smiled at Turner's concerned expression. "I'm kidding, Turner."

"So I get stuck working with Miller. That's not funny."

"I wouldn't worry about it, yet. They might fire you."

Turner knew it was a joke, but he wouldn't be the first guy who got punished in this department for doing something heroic that made the brass look foolish or inept, or worse— they couldn't take the credit for making the right decision. In a bureaucracy, initiative frequently got confused with anarchy.

They sat for a long time not talking, each man with his own thoughts. He was comfortable with Reggie and would miss his friend. Eddie came out in the late afternoon and held open the screen door for a few seconds.

"You two awake?" he asked, peeking around the door to see their faces.

"What do you need?" Turner asked. He was disappointed. The silence was nice.

"Wanna beer?"

"Yes," Reggie said quickly.

The old man brought out three cans of Budweiser and a folding canvass chair, and settled in beside them.

"Too bad they buried that little girl up north . . . woulda like to go," Eddie said between sips.

Turner really didn't want to talk about Miriam. He almost got up and went inside, but didn't want to hurt Eddie's feelings.

"Mind if I stay for dinner?" Reggie asked, trying to change the subject.

"Cooked for you," Eddie said, glancing over at Turner. He knew he'd made a mistake talking about Miriam and was disappointed in himself. "Sorry," he said, softly.

"Nothing for you to be sorry about," Turner said, and patted the old man on the arm.

When the sun had nearly disappeared below the horizon, they got up to go inside for dinner. At the same time, a new beige Audi made a U-turn in front of the house and parked. They stopped and stared at the car until Weaver got out, then waited while he came up onto the porch.

"That's your ride," Weaver said to Reggie. "But I'm borrowing it tonight. I'll pick you up tomorrow, and you can have it."

Reggie looked at Turner who suspected they were thinking the same thing. Why would you give a new car to someone you might fire.

"Where's mine?" Turner asked, thinking it was a joke.

"At the office, pick it up in the morning . . . new silver Honda."

Weaver laughed. "You two look confused. Don't be. Seems somebody up there likes you, and I don't mean up there," he said, pointing to the sky. "I mean the sixth floor."

"What the hell are you talking about?" Turner asked.

"Chief made a new deputy chief this afternoon and put him in the Professional Standards Bureau. First thing the guy does is tear up Metcalf's personnel complaint on the two of you." Weaver was grinning as if he'd done something.

"Why?" Reggie asked.

"I don't know. Who cares," Weaver said.

"Who's the new guy?" Turner asked. He couldn't think of anyone at that rank who'd care what happened to him.

"Black guy . . . Jones, I think . . . came from the chief's office. I don't know him. He practically spent his whole career inside. Chief promotes him every couple years, but he never leaves Parker Center. Smart guy doesn't know shit about police work." Weaver stopped and caught his breath. "Don't know why he gives a rat's ass about you two."

Turner and Reggie both looked at Eddie, who was sitting in his canvass chair grinning.

As soon as Weaver left, Turner cornered Eddie and made him explain why his son would save his and Reggie's careers.

"I didn't think he even liked me," Turner said.

"He don't," Eddie said. "But he owed me, an' I collected."

"You're really something, old man," Turner said.

"I owed you . . . he knows that too."

The three of them had dinner, and Reggie left as soon as they finished dessert, a Rémy Martin to celebrate. Reggie wouldn't say whether or not he'd show up at work the next morning. If he did, it wouldn't be the new car that enticed him to stay with the police department. Turner knew him like a twin brother. If Reggie didn't retire, it was because Eddie had made the effort to save his job. His moralist partner would never disrespect the old man by throwing away his gift.

TWENTY-SIX

Thanking Deputy Chief Dan Jones wasn't something Turner felt compelled to do. Danny didn't use his influence because he wanted to help. There must have been a speck of residual guilt he felt about selling his father's house. Of course, he'd never admit that. Turner figured Eddie had probably used up what little leverage he had with his son to help him. Somehow he'd make it up to the old man.

He'd intended to go to work the next morning, but instead found himself driving north in the direction of Beverly's place. It was clear and sunny, the kind of day that made him feel as if there were plenty of good options and opportunities available. Thinking about seeing her again made him happy, but a little apprehensive. He hadn't called.

Weaver had talked to her. She didn't blame Turner. She understood that he'd done everything he could to protect her son, so why was he so nervous about seeing her again? She was a good woman who had a screwed-up son. That wasn't all her fault.

His new boots hurt his feet. He hadn't had time to break them in properly, but the old ones were ruined from his day in the mountains. The long rest and recovery had made a big difference in his appearance. He'd lost some weight, but the right knee was healed and the limp gone. His new Levi's and black shirt made him look tall and trim. The new mustache was still filling in, but he thought if he had a cowboy hat he'd look like the Marlboro Man's father. He pulled down the rearview mirror and examined his new look, too much grey in the mustache. Maybe he should have shaved.

It was midday when he pulled onto the dirt driveway of Beverly's home. He didn't know why, but he stopped immediately after he made the turn and shut off the engine. She was outside, preoccupied with washing one of the horses under what looked like a small outdoor carwash, so she didn't seem to notice him. There'd been some changes to the property. New stalls had been constructed, and it looked as if she'd taken on a few more horses to board, at least a half dozen from what he could see.

The sleeves of her pink, underwear-like shirt were rolled up. Even from this distance, he could tell she had more water on her than on the horse. Still, she was such a beautiful woman. She wore sunglasses, a goofy-looking straw sombrero covered her head, rubber boots reached nearly to the knees of her bleached jeans, and rubber gloves up to her elbows. He was amused. It was quite a picture, not the dainty little barmaid any longer.

Why he was parked here was still a mystery to him. Watching her, he was more convinced than ever she would accept him and maybe even love him. There was no denying he had feelings for her, so what was his problem. He knew, but didn't want to admit the truth. She might be able to forgive and forget, but he realized he couldn't. In just the few minutes he'd been here, so many dead faces flashed through his mind like a broken film projector. She was shrouded by his ghosts. He couldn't see that lovely face without remembering Miriam, her father and so many of the others who'd touched her son's life.

He made a U-turn and drove back slowly for several miles the way he had come before heading toward downtown, his job and friends. It would feel good to work again, but he knew it was different. It wasn't enough.